Bolan threw back the storm door and scrambled into the darkness

A Black Hawk helicopter had touched down at the northeast corner of the house. The Executioner stroked the trigger of his Galil assault rifle, watching as a ragged line of holes punctured the chopper's windshield.

The UH-60's triggerman was waiting for Bolan to reach the other side of the aircraft. There had been no time for him to unbolt the big M-60, but he had a submachine gun, leading Bolan a yard or so with his initial burst.

As the shooter attempted to correct his aim, the Executioner hosed him with the Galil. The crewman toppled backward, his lifeless finger clenched around the trigger of his subgun. It kept firing as the guy went down, the bullets rattling around inside the twin T700 engines.

The massive engines detonated with a roar. Jagged pieces of rotors sliced through the air while the warrior hit the deck. Debris rained around him, smacking into the turf.

A moment later he was on his feet, feeling satisfied. Whatever happened with the White Wolves now, they would find themselves on foot in enemy territory, sixty miles from the South African border and safety.

The warrior set off at a jog in search of Kebby Seko, hoping to find his ally alive.

MACK BOLAN®
The Executioner

DON PENDLETON'S
THE EXECUTIONER®
FEATURING MACK BOLAN®
KILLING RANGE

A GOLD EAGLE BOOK FROM
WORLDWIDE.

TORONTO • NEW YORK • LONDON
AMSTERDAM • PARIS • SYDNEY • HAMBURG
STOCKHOLM • ATHENS • TOKYO • MILAN
MADRID • WARSAW • BUDAPEST • AUCKLAND

First edition October 1994

ISBN 0-373-61190-0

Special thanks and acknowledgment to
Mike Newton for his contribution to this work.

KILLING RANGE

No man is prejudiced in favor of a thing knowing it to be wrong. He is attached to it on the belief of its being right.

—Thomas Paine

The pleasure of hating, like a poisonous mineral, eats into the heart of religion, and turns it to rankling spleen and bigotry; it makes patriotism an excuse for carrying fire, pestilence, and famine into other lands; it leaves to virtue nothing but the spirit of censoriousness.

—William Hazlitt

Private pleasure is one thing, but public action is another. It's time the haters had a taste of their own medicine, and today the doctor is in. It's my turn to carry the fire. We'll see what's standing when the smoke clears.

—Mack Bolan

THE
MACK BOLAN®
LEGEND

Nothing less than a war could have fashioned the destiny of the man called Mack Bolan. Bolan earned the Executioner title in the jungle hell of Vietnam.

But this soldier also wore another name—Sergeant Mercy. He was so tagged because of the compassion he showed to wounded comrades-in-arms and Vietnamese civilians.

Mack Bolan's second tour of duty ended prematurely when he was given emergency leave to return home and bury his family, victims of the Mob. Then he declared a one-man war against the Mafia.

He confronted the Families head-on from coast to coast, and soon a hope of victory began to appear. But Bolan had broken society's every rule. That same society started gunning for this elusive warrior—to no avail.

So Bolan was offered amnesty to work within the system against terrorism. This time, as an employee of Uncle Sam, Bolan became Colonel John Phoenix. With a command center at Stony Man Farm in Virginia, he and his new allies—Able Team and Phoenix Force—waged relentless war on a new adversary: the KGB.

But when his one true love, April Rose, died at the hands of the Soviet terror machine, Bolan severed all ties with Establishment authority.

Now, after a lengthy lone-wolf struggle and much soul-searching, the Executioner has agreed to enter an ''arm's-length'' alliance with his government once more, reserving the right to pursue personal missions in his Everlasting War.

PROLOGUE

The twin Sikorsky UH-60 Black Hawk helicopters had been following the river for an hour, skimming low to frustrate any radar stations covering the borderline between South Africa and the Mozambique. The choppers had been painted black, without identifying marks, and they were flying without lights, their fifty-three-foot rotors whipping up a dust storm in their wake.

Each Black Hawk carried ten armed passengers in addition to the standard three-man crew. The troops were dressed in black, from Kevlar helmets to their combat boots. Black combat cosmetics disguised their hands and faces, but the features were Caucasian, fixed in grim resolve. They carried automatic rifles, submachine guns, semiautomatic pistols and grenades. Spare magazines were slotted into canvas pouches slung across their chests or strapped around their waists.

They had been following the Olifants River and guiding on it from their lift-off point in Kruger National Park, a slow loop east-southeast in the direction of their target. Overhead, a full moon provided all the light the pilots needed, and the troopers seated nearest to the open doors could pick out the occasional hyena, antelope or wildebeest that fled before the sound of their approach.

The blacks would hear them coming, too, Jon Koenig realized, but there was nothing to be done about the noise. Without their running lights, regardless of the moon, a sentry would be momentarily confused about directions... and it only took a moment, at their present speed, for the assault force to approach within a killing range. The rest was simple strategy, the way they had rehearsed it.

They would teach the worthless kafirs something this time. Warnings had been fruitless, threats the same. Attempts at reason never seemed to penetrate. The revolutionaries had been cautioned to refrain from giving aid and comfort to the white man's enemies inside South Africa, but they refused to listen. One hard-headed bastard in particular continued to defy his betters, sending money, men and arms across the border to the ANC and other black subversive groups.

Nacala.

It was time for him to pay. The order had come down through channels; the arrangements had been made. With his selection as the leader, it was Koenig's privilege to choose the shock troops for the raid and brief them on their target, poring over maps and photographs and floor plans, running through the drill with blanks a week before the lift-off, on a friendly ranch northeast of Pietersburg.

The training was behind them now, live ammunition in their weapons, grim determination in their hearts. Each man among the raiders understood the crucial nature of their mission. While Nacala lived, he would continue to fund raids across the border, killing white South Africans regardless of their age or gender. No man on the strike force needed a reminder of the cruel indignities inflicted when a band of black guerrillas razed the Stano farm, below Messina, two weeks earlier.

It was a shame, thought Koenig, that their schedule wouldn't give them time to pay the bastards back in kind, but time was of the essence. In and out, like clockwork, was the order of the day. A clash with regulars in Mozambique would be disastrous, feeding kafir propaganda mills the kind of information they adored.

"Two minutes." The pilot's disembodied voice sounded small and metallic in Koenig's earpiece. He disengaged the headset, raised a hand to capture the attention of his troops and showed them two stiff fingers. Several of them smiled in answer to the signal.

They were good, this lot. All blooded veterans, with not a virgin in the group. It was impossible for him to guess how many kafirs they had killed, altogether, through the years. At least a hundred, maybe twice that many, warring in the sacred cause of race and homeland.

In another minute and a half, they would be able to improve their scores.

Koenig sat with one hand on his submachine gun's pistol grip, the other on the quick-release latch of his safety belt. Behind him, close enough to touch, the crew chief had his forward window open, ready with the big M-60 that would cover their approach. Once Koenig's men were on the ground, the gunner would restrict himself to a selective cover fire, but it was all his, going in.

Another forty seconds.

Koenig found that he could hardly wait.

THE NIGHTS WERE always long for Julius Nacala. When his men were off across the border, punishing the racist Boers, he often waited up for word of their success or failure, even if the sunrise found him sitting in his study, hollow-eyed, a mug of lukewarm coffee in his hand. On other nights, like this one, sleep lost out to memories of friends and allies martyred in the cause.

It had controlled the best part of his life, this endless quest for justice and revenge. Nacala sometimes thought there should be some way to have one without the other, but the fine points of philosophy eluded him. Mandela was the thinker, mellowed—some said broken and emasculated—by his years in prison. Julius Nacala had been lucky when it came to staying out of jail, but when he started listing relatives and friends assassinated by the Boers—or the white Rhodesians, in their day—the list went on and on, each name another pebble splashing down into the stagnant cistern of his soul.

There came a point in time when justice and revenge were all the same to people raised on grief and bloodshed. It was possible for grievances to be forgiven, laid aside, but Nacala didn't expect his people to forget about the past until some effort had been made to pay the white man back for generations of brutality.

It was a savage business all around, but there was still a strong degree of white resistance in South Africa, committed to the notion that the subject race would never have the courage or intelligence to manage national affairs without direction from a pale-skinned master. Nacala was convinced that only punishing defeats in combat would eliminate the bigots or revise their skewed perception of the world, while men of goodwill struggled to negotiate a just and lasting peace.

Nelson Mandela, while he lived, was the negotiator. Nacala knew the words, but they didn't come from his heart. Perhaps, with all that he had lost in fifty-seven years, they never would.

A time was coming, he was certain, when the gun would have no part in race relations on the border, but that time had not arrived. Nacala hoped that he would live to see it, but a part of him suspected he would have no place in such a world.

Old warriors were a liability, once men decided they should live in peace. The soldier with his scars and lifelong bitterness was a reminder of the bad times, shunned by those who sought a brighter day.

So be it.

For all that Africa had cost him in his fifty-seven years, Nacala knew that he was blessed in having spent his life there. Fate could just as easily have dropped him in Manhattan, Rio de Janeiro, or New Guinea, and he would have missed the great adventure that had been his life. For all the pain and suffering, the blood and tears, there had been grand, triumphant moments, love and laughter... all the things that made a human life worthwhile.

His glass was almost empty when he heard the helicopters. Not that he was fully conscious of the distant sound at first, much less equipped to pinpoint its location, but the throbbing sound invaded his unconscious mind and filtered through in seconds flat.

Nacala froze, his eyelids dropped to screen out all distracting stimuli, and in another moment he had swiveled toward the west. He couldn't see the aircraft yet, but they were coming. There was danger in the wind.

He shouted to the sentries, one of them replying from the middle distance with a bark of affirmation, ordering Nacala back inside the house. He hesitated for another moment, staring into darkness, then retreated to his study, closed the tall French doors behind him and turned the latch.

He kept a rifle in the study, one of several weapons stashed around the house where he could reach them in emergencies. The weapon was a Spanish CETME Modelo 58, selective fire, feeding 7.62 mm NATO ammunition from a 20-round detachable box magazine. Nacala hadn't fired the rifle in a year or so, but it was clean, well oiled and loaded.

There was no doubt whatsoever in his mind that it was white men coming for him in the middle of the night. The people's government of Mozambique knew all about his border raids and didn't try to interfere, despite official statements from the capital denouncing terrorism and the like. No black regime in Africa would move against Nacala while the common enemy held power in Johannesburg, but that didn't prevent the whites from reaching out to bring him down.

Well, let them come. It had been tried before, and he was still alive, still fighting for the cause.

He cocked his rifle, killed the lights and settled in to wait.

KOENIG WAS READY when the crew chief opened fire with his M-60, the helicopter banking slightly to give the gunner a better angle of attack. Below them, lights were winking out around Nacala's compound, but the moon was bright enough to show him several sentries ducking and dodging, as machine-gun bullets kicked up dust around their feet. One man, and then another, went down.

Their helicopter settled on the north side of the house, as planned, while the companion airship landed on the south.

Divide and conquer. Koenig hit the ground running, shouting orders to his men and racing toward the house that was their final destination. They had studied floor plans, purchased from a traitor in Nacala's family, and Koenig knew exactly where to go.

A rifleman was waiting for him on the broad veranda out back. The man stood his ground as Koenig came in view, his backup team in black behind him, closing the gap. Instead of running for his life, the sentry raised his weapon, tried to aim, but his excitement got the best of him, and he began to squeeze off hasty rounds before he found his mark.

It was a fatal error.

Koenig had the range, and instinct did the rest. He stroked the trigger of his MP-5 A-3 and stitched a tidy line of holes across the man's chest. His target toppled over backward, triggering a last round toward the stairs before he hit the flagstones, twitching in his death throes. Sprinting past him, Koenig veered a short step to his right and kicked the dead man's rifle out of reach.

No point in taking chances, he recalled an old instructor telling him in boot camp, years ago. A wounded snake is the first one that will turn and bite you when your back is turned. The man who made sure of his kill would live to boast about them over whiskey when the battle has been won.

He recognized the tall French doors ahead and raked them with a burst of automatic fire, dodged left and hesitated long enough to palm a frag grenade and yank the safety pin. His men were ducking under cover as he lobbed the charge, a perfect pitch from thirty feet. A heavy wooden table, tilted on its side, protected him from flying glass and shrapnel as the hand grenade exploded, shattering the French doors and the room beyond.

He followed through immediately, ears still ringing from the blast. Nacala's study was a smoking shambles, but the devastation wasn't great enough to hide a corpse, and Koenig found himself alone.

He cursed and kept on going, hesitating for an instant at the closed connecting door, aware that danger could be waiting for him on the other side.

No options. He hadn't come all this way to cower in fear when the kafir revolutionary was within his grasp.

The door swung inward, a delay of two or three important seconds, but he made the corridor beyond and took no fire. In one direction, on his left, were several bedrooms. On the right, according to the floor plans Koenig had seen, would be the kitchen, dining room, the parlor, other rooms reserved for guests and meetings.

Koenig turned right and started pacing off the corridor, the MP-5 A-3 preceding him. He reached the parlor, peeked round the corner of the wall...and nearly lost his left ear to a rifle bullet snapping past his face.

Nacala!

He had glimpsed the man for an instant, there and gone, but it was all the time he needed for a positive ID.

They had him.

It was Koenig's play, and he was ready. Silent signals warned his troops to wait and join the skirmish only if he found himself pinned down, or if they saw him fall.

He went in low, a diving shoulder roll that took him underneath Nacala's line of fire. The man's weapon stuttered, half a dozen wasted rounds impacting on the wall where Koenig would have been if he had charged into the room erect. Instead he rolled behind a heavy couch and kept on going, wriggling around the far end and emerging on Nacala's blind side, staring at his human target down the barrel of his subgun.

The long burst ripped Nacala from his right knee to the armpit, punching him over sideways in an awkward sprawl. His rifle clattered on the floor and spun beyond his reach, assuming he had any will or strength remaining to defend himself.

A pool of blood was spreading from beneath Nacala's body as the raiders stood above him, but the man's eyes were open and alert. He seemed immune to pain, somehow, and Koenig felt a certain disappointment. He had hoped for tears and trembling, perhaps a futile plea for mercy, shattered by his own derisive laughter and a bullet from his gun.

He saw, now, that Nacala was determined not to give them any entertainment for their trouble, and they had no time to make him squeal. The disappointment was dissolving into anger, Koenig feeling cheated in a way that he could barely understand.

"It's shock," one of his troopers said. "You hit the spine or something. Stupid kafir doesn't even know we're here."

Nacala's voice surprised them, coming, as it seemed to, from the next thing to a corpse. Amazingly he spoke to them in Afrikaans.

"I see you, white man." He stared into Koenig's eyes, defiant in the face of mortal pain. "You all come down to this, one day. When I see you on the other side, we will play this game again. My rules, next time."

The rage took over then, and Koenig held the trigger on his submachine gun down until the magazine was empty. In the ringing stillness afterward, he knew that they were running out of time.

"We go."

They jogged back to the chopper unopposed, past scattered bodies stretched on the ground. All black. A glance back toward the other helicopter showed him two commandos lifting what appeared to be a wounded man in through the open loading bay.

No matter.

Casualties were part of warfare, and the victory had gone to Koenig's side tonight. He had removed Nacala and a number of his terrorists from action on the revolutionary side, and that had been his mission. It was unimportant how the kafir died, as long as he was dead.

Repeating that at intervals throughout the long flight home, Koenig started to believe that it was true.

They had a chance, if each man did his duty. There was still a chance to save the country and their race. The Communists and kafirs wanted war. So be it. But they wouldn't be allowed to write the rules.

Not this time.

Koenig closed his eyes against the moonlight and repeated to himself that he had done his best.

He was a hero, now.

1

The camp was dark and still at 2:30 a.m. Not everyone was sleeping, to be sure—the sentries pacing off the wire were proof of that, and lights still burned in the CP hut—but instinct and experience combined to tell the prowler there would never be a better time to make his strike.

Mack Bolan lay outside the camp, some fifty yards due west, and scanned the compound through a set of night-vision glasses that turned the landscape sickly green. In addition to their infrared capacity, the glasses also magnified, allowing him to give the sentries nicknames if he wished. The nearest to him, presently, was the Kid, a smooth-faced individual who toted an H&K G-3 A-3 assault rifle.

Away to the Kid's left was Baldy, slipping off his forage cap to run a handkerchief across his shiny scalp. On Bolan's right, roughly eighty yards away, was Scarface, sporting ugly keloid furrows on his jawline.

These men and their companions in the camp were seasoned killers, raised with hatred and fanaticism as a bitter supplement to mother's milk. The khaki uniforms they wore were nondescript, devoid of patches or insignia, but the men had been branded with the mark of Cain, for all the world to see.

If you grew up hating, lived for violence, it showed.

The men who stood before him now were Africans, although their skin was white. They were twelfth- and thirteenth-generation Afrikaners—still called Boers, by some—who traced their lineage back to pioneers from Holland. Their ancestors had fought the mighty Zulu war chiefs for the right to carve a homeland from the wilderness. A century before this night, their great-grandfathers had defied the British empire to protect that homeland, suffering political defeat but never losing hope. Somewhere along the way, like many others of that age, they had decided that a pale skin was a gift from God, the token of a master race.

The children's children of those Boers still believed the same. The men who stood before him now were totally prepared to kill—or die—for that discredited idea.

The Executioner wasn't specifically concerned with personal opinions, though, no matter how pernicious they might be. He was about to drop the hammer on these men because they had allowed their prejudice to take a giant step from feelings into terroristic action, wasting human lives and jeopardizing global peace as a result.

The camp was situated in a sparsely settled region of the Orange Free State, a hundred miles due north of Lesotho, roughly the same distance southeast of Johannesburg. The nearest neighbors were a family of cattle ranchers, twenty miles beyond the point where Bolan waited in darkness, staring through his glasses at the sleeping camp.

The men inside the compound called themselves Wit Wolwe—literally, "White Wolves." Their cut-and-paste philosophy had borrowed bits and pieces from the leading racists of the century, including the assassinated Dr. H. F. Verwoerd, B. J. Vorster, Adolf Hitler and the American Ku Klux Klan. They even took a page or two from Henry Ford, condemning Jews in ill-considered writings from the 1920s. Anyone and everyone was welcome, if their message added up to hate.

Above all else, the White Wolves pledged themselves to restoration of South African apartheid—total separation of the races, marked by ruthless subjugation of nonwhites—as practiced in their homeland prior to 1990. Given any chance at all, they would reverse the march of progress and obliterate the sacrifice of countless men and women, black and white, who lost their homes, their families, their lives in the pursuit of justice.

To that end, the White Wolves had adopted terrorism as their means, a racial bloodbath as their goal. Within the past twelve months, they had been linked to bombings and abductions, murders, drive-by shootings, the assassination of a civil-rights crusader whose demise had triggered weeks of bloody violence nationwide. Black spokesmen charged that white South African police were stubbornly reluctant to investigate and prosecute the Wolves, suggesting possible collusion in their crimes.

Of late, informants told the CIA and other Western agencies, the White Wolves had been raiding in Lesotho, in Botswana, in Zimbabwe, Mozambique—wherever targets lay within their reach. Aside from striking hated enemies and working to destabilize black governments, the raids distracted world attention from South Africa, while far-right politicians worked behind the scenes to reinstate some measure of apartheid's brutal code.

This much was known to Bolan when he entered the Republic of South Africa. He had been working quietly for days since then, collecting inside information on his own and drawing up a list of targets, looking forward to the time when he could move against his enemies.

Tonight.

It was a start, but only that. He meant to catch the White Wolves with their guard down, shake them up a bit, and see what followed after that. Unraveling their network would require some time—a scarce commodity in Bolan's world—but he was starting with a deadly sucker punch to speed things up.

From that point, it would be an all-or-nothing race to find out who survived.

The Executioner was dressed in midnight black, his close-fitting nightsuit under military webbing, handy pockets carrying survival gear and silent instruments of death. His face and hands were daubed with camouflage cosmetics to prevent an errant moonbeam giving him away.

Geography and politics had forced a compromise on military hardware. Bolan wore his Desert Eagle .44 Magnum pistol on his right hip, the Beretta 93-R underneath his arm, but the requirements of "deniability" had forced him to abandon any weapons manufactured in the United States.

His rifle, just beside him on the ground, was the Israeli Galil R-4 assault piece, chambered in 5.56 mm and produced under special contract for the South African military. Even his grenades were "clean," the British L2A1 model presently used by Her Majesty's troops around the world. If he was forced to ditch the weapons unexpectedly, none of them were traceable to Bolan or his contacts in the States.

He tucked the glasses safely in their pouch, picked up his rifle and began to creep toward the camp. A chain-link fence had been erected to keep scavengers at bay, with a snarl of concertina wire on top. He knew the fence wasn't electrified because Baldy's rifle had accidentally brushed against it during a turn.

It all came down to timing, now. His observation of the camp had shown him that the sentries didn't have a beat, per se. They worked at something close to hundred-yard intervals, each man completing one full circuit of the camp in twenty minutes, give or take. That gave him six or seven minutes to effect his entry without being seen.

He chose a section of the fence that lay in deeper shadow than the rest, and waited for the nearest guard to move away. His cutters made short work of the chain link, and Bolan wriggled underneath a flap that measured three feet wide and two feet high. Before continuing, he closed the flap behind him and secured it with a pair of plastic twist ties.

It should pass inspection if the roving sentries didn't look too closely, and he planned to offer them a loud distraction in the meantime.

Bolan's closest cover was the shadow of a prefab hut with aerials protruding from the roof—the camp's communication center. He was crouched beside it, merging with the night, when Scarface made his pass, oblivious to the warrior and the flap in the fence. The sentry's eyes were focused on the endless night beyond the wire, and only God knew where his thoughts were straying. To a woman's bed, perhaps, or to the first cold beer that he would purchase on his next trip into town.

The Executioner removed a fist-size block of plastique from his fanny pack, secured the blasting cap and switched

the silent timer on, five minutes, counting down to doomsday in his mind.

Another gap between the prowling guards, and Bolan
flitted like a shadow to the nearby mess tent, where a squat
propane tank stood on cinder blocks. The warrior's second
plastic charge went underneath the tank, the timer counting backward from 4:30 as he turned away.

Next up on Bolan's hit parade was the nearest barracks,
one of four that should accommodate some thirty men at
any given time, if it was full. He estimated about one hundred feet of open ground between the barracks and the mess
tent, then hesitated for a precious moment while he double-
checked the sentries. Baldy was well behind him, Scarface
passing on his left, while the Kid was across the compound
pacing off the wire perimeter.

He wound up sacrificing speed for safety, understanding
that a sprint, however quiet, was more likely to alert the
nearer guards. A late-night stroller might be overlooked,
dismissed as any other comrade bound for the latrine, while
furtive sprints were much more likely to produce a general
alarm.

He took his time, with precious little to spare. Crossing
the open space with shoulders squared, he braced himself
for the stunning impact of a bullet, wondering if he would
hear the shot that cut him down. It only took one glance,
from any of the sentries, and he could be dead before he hit
the ground.

He reached the barracks without incident, blessed by luck
or a skillful application of "role camouflage." Whichever,
Bolan didn't have the time to count his blessings. In another moment, he had fixed a plastic charge against the
short south wall of the building, situated to inflict the maximum possible damage on the barracks and its sleeping occupants.

The timer read 3:35 and counting as he scanned the camp
and headed for another barracks, separated from the first
by six or seven paces. No lights showed as he crouched in
midnight shadow to complete his deadly work. He set the

blasting cap, switched on the silent timer and checked the LED display against his watch.

So far, so good.

He had two charges left, the fanny pack a great deal lighter than it was when he had crept into the compound. Still three minutes remained, and if he played his cards right, met no opposition, he could plant the last two charges and withdraw before all hell broke loose.

It sounded good, in theory, but it didn't work that way.

From his position near the barracks, Bolan's unobstructed view of the roving sentries was restricted to the young man he had christened Scarface. Baldy should have been behind him somewhere, roughly parallel with the communications hut, while normal progress would have brought the third man to the southeast corner of the camp by now.

The last place Bolan should have met a sentry was emerging from the field latrine that stood between the second barracks and the third. It was an easy piece of ground to cover, call it fifteen seconds if he dawdled, decent cover while he made the shift.

No problem.

Not until he made his move, and there was the Kid, stepping out of the latrine, his rifle slung across one shoulder, zipping up the fly of his fatigues. It could have been a keeper, even so, if the Kid had been lighter on his feet or moved directly toward the point where he had broken off his tour....

Instead the gunner hesitated, then opted for a short-cut and turned to his right. He froze at the sight of Bolan in his battle dress and war paint, blinking twice as the astounding vision registered.

Recovering too late, he fumbled for his weapon, almost dropping it. He took a short step backward, started to bring his weapon into target acquisition and opened his mouth to warn the camp.

A single round cracked out of the Galil in Bolan's hands and struck his target in the throat. Explosive impact lifted the Kid off his feet and dumped him in the dust.

The warrior was out of time, with three full minutes remaining before the charges blew. Three minutes in a shooting gallery could be a lifetime, Bolan knew, and then some. He would have to find an exit from the camp, and soon, if he intended to survive.

His secret passage through the fence was out, an exit meant for stealth, not haste. The other sentries were approaching, shouting to the camp at large, and half-dressed soldiers were erupting from the barracks huts.

By the time his charges blew, the buildings might be empty, several dozen men pursuing him around the compound while his plastic charge demolished prefab walls and roasted empty bunks.

He swiveled toward the nearest barracks, where his final charge was counting down, and fired a short burst toward the doorway. One commando went down in a heap, his submachine gun spitting aimlessly, a deadly strobe light in the darkness. His companions beat a swift retreat, and in another moment several weapons had begun to snap at Bolan, firing through the open door and windows.

Fair enough.

It helped that most of his opponents had been sleeping when the feces hit the fan. Still groggy and disoriented, searching for a likely target, they were firing all around the compound, raising hell with no result except for scattered casualties from friendly fire. The chaos was a shield of sorts, and Bolan meant to use it well.

He had his sights fixed on the motor pool, but that meant navigating roughly one-third of the compound under fire. If the warrior made it that far, he'd have to snag himself a vehicle and crash the gate, with every gunner in the camp unloading as he passed.

No sweat.

The hardest part was getting there, with two more barracks in his way. Emerging from the cover of the field latrine, he had a frag grenade in one hand, with the pin already gone. He tried to take advantage of the night and the confusion, almost making it in a headlong rush between the buildings.

Almost.

One of the Afrikaners spotted him and shouted to another, cutting loose with automatic fire. The gunner's haste was all that saved Bolan's life. A line of bullets spit dust behind him, tracking him from left to right.

He fired a one-handed burst from the Galil, and his adversary staggered, going down on one knee, clutching at his side. It wasn't a mortal wound, but it was bad enough to spoil the gunner's aim while Bolan gained the sanctuary of the barracks and kept on going, right around in back.

When he had covered half the distance, he got rid of the grenade, with a looping toss that dropped the bomb through an open window as he passed. Bolan counted down the five seconds, reaching the corner before the lethal egg exploded. Windows shattered all around the barracks, shrapnel slicing through the walls. Someone started screaming on the inside, wordless, incoherent cries of agony.

He left them to it, sprinted around the corner with the Galil in hand and spitting death among his enemies. He made it fifty yards to reach the motor pool. The commandos milling on the doorstep of the final barracks could have stopped him with concerted action, if they had been ready to defend themselves.

Strike two.

He fell upon them like a Norse berserker, firing left and right, his automatic rifle opening a runway through the ranks, survivors lunging to escape the line of fire. He estimated twelve or thirteen men, and dropped perhaps a quarter of them where they stood, the others scattering in panic. Two or three dived underneath the barracks; others ran ahead of Bolan toward the motor pool, Grim Death on their heels.

He took them out and kept on going, dropping the empty magazine and snapping a fresh one into place without breaking stride. The covered motor pool was thirty feet ahead of him. Fifteen. He launched himself into a headlong dive that carried him behind a flatbed truck and out of view from snipers who had finally found the range.

Six vehicles had been assembled in a kind of open shed, the broad, flat roof supported by upright metal poles. Two trucks and four military-style jeeps lined up with their noses pointed toward the center of the camp.

He wriggled past the trucks and heard them taking hits. A windshield cracked, imploded, and he heard some kind of liquid dripping.

The plastic charges had been timed to detonate together, and they didn't let him down. From eighty yards or less, it sounded like the crack of doom, a thunderclap that deafened Bolan. The propane tank took off like a demented rocket, soaring better than a hundred feet straight up and riding on a tongue of fire. A shock wave rippled through the earth as the communications hut, the mess tent and the western barracks came apart.

He had no way of tabulating casualties in that inferno, and he didn't care to try. The warrior used his last two charges in the motor pool and punched in ninety seconds on the clock. One charge went beneath the first truck on the north end of the shed, its mate beneath the last jeep on the south.

And that left four.

He had decided that a jeep would give him better speed and mileage in the bush, although it sacrificed the flatbed's weight and ramming power in a crunch. A hasty glance showed Bolan that the jeeps were left with keys in the ignition. This wasn't Johannesburg, with thieves on every street. The vehicles were safe...unless some wild-assed warrior trashed the camp and borrowed one to make his getaway.

The gate was on his left, roughly thirty yards away. Unguarded at the moment, it was still within effective range for any gun in camp. That number had been pared by the explosions, but the Wolves still had some bite left in them yet.

And it would only take one bullet, stray or otherwise, to end the game.

With all the gunfire sputtering around the compound, Bolan almost missed the sound of helicopter rotors, drawing closer by the moment, closing from the south.

More hostile guns to deal with, Bolan thought. It could mean nothing else. And they would have mobility superior to his. Escaping with his skin intact had suddenly become a hundred times more difficult.

He chose the middle jeep in line and slid behind the wheel, his rifle on the seat beside him. He started to count down the seconds, gambling on the engine for a first-time start, aware that if he missed it there wouldn't be a second chance.

Ten seconds.

Bolan gave the key a twist and stepped on the accelerator, offering a silent prayer of hope. The engine fired and caught, a rush of pure adrenaline in Bolan's veins before he put the jeep in gear and lifted off the clutch.

His vehicle exploded from the motor pool and swerved hard left in the direction of the gates, his startled adversaries tracking with their weapons, missing with their first few rounds. Five seconds later, hell on earth consumed the motor pool, the plastic explosives ripping through the vehicles from either side, igniting gasoline and diesel fuel, the firestorm feeding on itself.

He glimpsed the helicopter's running lights before he hit the gate and powered through. The waning moon was bright enough to let him run without his headlights for a while, and Bolan would have left them off in any case.

The hunters had enough of an advantage as it was.

The Executioner was running for his life.

2

It was supposed to be a milk run, damn it. Aldis Sharp was bringing up supplies and three new men, a simple turn-around that should have put him back in Clarens shortly after two o'clock. They often made the runs at night for reasons of security, to stop the kafirs spying and forestall embarrassment of the authorities.

You had to walk a fine line in the modern world, not like the good old days when his father was a boy and every kafir knew his place. Today, the bloody bastards were armed and organized, prepared to set the world on fire.

But Sharp hadn't expected it to start tonight.

They were a good three miles from camp when the explosions started, brilliant fireballs springing up around the compound. Summoned forward by the pilot, Sharp was forced to make a swift decision. Should they forge ahead, or cut and run?

His gut was all for turning back, but that would mean he was a coward. They would go ahead, at least to have a look and find out what was happening.

As they approached the camp, his passengers were shifting nervously, young faces marked by various expressions of concern, disquiet, even fear. Sharp understood their feelings, shared them to a great extent, but he refused to let them show.

And that made him superior.

He felt the youngsters watching as he threw the forward window open, primed the big M-60 on its swivel mount. Ahead of them and so much closer now, the camp was burning fitfully, the larger darkness punctuated by erratic muzzle-flashes.

Gunfire.

Had the kafirs found the camp, somehow? Security was tight, but not invincible. Were they attacking, even now? Or had some other strange calamity engulfed his comrades on the ground?

There was only one way to find out.

No one answered their radioed inquiry as they approached, which meant that communications had either been knocked out, or else the operator had his hands full at the moment, fighting for his life. In either case, it made the situation that much more severe.

Sharp almost hoped it was the kafirs. He had grown up hating them, had killed his share before tonight, but it would never be enough while even one of them remained. They bred like rodents, threatening to overrun the world if they weren't restrained, but Western nations with the most to lose had closed their eyes in lieu of coping with the danger. It wasn't "politically correct" to kick the underdog these days, not even when he tried to rip your leg off at the hip.

Sharp caught himself considering the fact that an assault by blacks could only help the cause, regardless of its outcome. If his comrades beat the kafirs back, then they would have a victory to boast of, and the rebels would be taught a valuable lesson. If the blacks prevailed, there would be several dozen martyrs for the movement, worth their weight in gold when it came down to free publicity and new recruits.

Sharp only hoped that he wasn't among their number when the sun came up.

They were a hundred yards from the camp's southwestern perimeter when the motor pool went up. Sharp saw a jeep burst from the open shed a moment prior to detonation, racing toward the gate. At least one vehicle was saved, he thought, before the rest were blown apart and left in flaming ruins. Small comfort, in the circumstances, but at least it wouldn't be a total loss.

Sharp's pilot circled once around the camp and came in from the north to make his touchdown. Sharp was scanning with the big M-60, but he found no targets. There were bodies scattered here and there, some of them smoldering, but all of those he recognized were comrades, not a kafir in the bunch.

A sudden movement on his right flank startled Sharp. He swiveled the machine gun toward a jogging figure, lifting off the trigger as he recognized the sergeant, Rudd. He wore an undershirt and khaki trousers, caked with dust. A deep cut on his forehead bathed the left side of his face in blood.

"You must go after him!" Rudd shouted toward the compound's gate.

"Go after who?"

"The man who did all this. He stole a vehicle and wrecked the others."

"What man? Was he a kafir?"

"Just get after him for Christ's sake! We've got no way left of catching him."

Sharp didn't fully understand, but he remembered the escaping jeep and turned to bark an order at his pilot. Sergeant Rudd was backing away, a bare arm raised to shield his eyes, as they took off.

One man had done all this, and then he had escaped. Could that be true? The only way of finding out would be to run him down, and that should be no problem with the helicopter.

THREE-QUARTERS OF A MILE beyond the compound, Bolan left the bare dirt road and veered off to the west. His mental map of the terrain showed rocky hills in that direction, better for concealment than the open plain.

Ideally the warrior would have circled back to where his own Land Rover was concealed, a mile north of the White Wolves' compound, changing clothes along the way and slipping out of range while his surviving adversaries tried to salvage something from the ruins. Taking out the motor pool had been a telling blow...until the helicopter came along.

And that changed everything.

It was the kind of problem that a soldier stumbled into sometimes, unforeseen and unpredictable. No matter how you mapped out a mission, the wild cards still cropped up from time to time, demanding that a warrior play his hand as it was dealt. Nobody's fault, but that would be small consolation if the snafu got him killed.

He had no way of knowing if the helicopter would be armed. Regardless, there were men and guns enough around the camp to finish him, and it would only take one lucky strafing run to do the job.

Without a place to hide, the warrior knew, he was as good as dead.

The thought didn't prevent his mind from functioning, nor did it lead him to despair. Another man might easily have given up, but Bolan's nerves were stainless steel. He had confronted mortal danger frequently enough to recognize its every face, but none of them produced the kind of awe his enemies might wish. A threat to life or limb produced immediate defensive action, but no enemy had ever seen him cowed in fear.

He held the jeep's speed close to sixty-five klicks per hour on the open ground. It wasn't great, by any means, but he was more concerned about a broken axle or a flat, just now, than by his fear of being overtaken by the whirlybird.

His stolen vehicle couldn't outrun the chopper; there was no point trying. What he *could* do, with a fair head start and tons of luck, was reach the nearest line of stony hills before they found him and choose a place to make his stand.

He had a plan in mind, but it was still evolving, taking shape. The fine points would depend upon terrain and timing, factors he could grapple with, manipulate to some extent, but never totally control.

He spooked a pack of jackals and sent them dodging off to either side. A whiff of death reached Bolan's nostrils as he passed their killing ground. Good eating for the scavengers tonight, and there would soon be more fresh meat to share around.

How long before the chopper found his trail?

The pilot would require a briefing, with the emphasis on brief. Perhaps two minutes from the time he touched down in the compound to another lift-off, following the unpaved road awhile before it dawned on him that he was stalking wary prey. The chopper might be forced to circle back, waste precious time in searching for his tire tracks through the bush... or they might strike it rich the first time.

Bolan checked his rearview mirror, then swiveled in the driver's seat to glance across one shoulder. Nothing. Would he see the chopper coming, running lights and all?

The hunt would be a great deal easier with searchlights, but the moon was bright enough to serve. He listened for the sound of rotors, his own pulse throbbing in his ears.

Selecting the terrain was one thing, bringing down a helicopter would be something else. Surprise was critical, and he had to bring the chopper into range before he opened up with the Galil. He knew a helicopter's weak points, had exploited them to personal advantage more than once, but every time was different, fraught with peril of its own. The dark could hamper him, or his opponent's angle of attack.

He would require surprise, audacity, a steady hand.

And even then, it might not be enough.

In front of him, the craggy hills rose out of nowhere, like a line of blunted, broken teeth. He stood on the accelerator, driven by a sense of urgency that he couldn't deny. A pothole nearly jarred him from the driver's seat, but Bolan kept on going, clinging to the wheel with fierce determination.

It was all or nothing now, and he was playing for his life.

He reached the hills, turned north and traveled for another quarter of a mile before he found a spot that met his needs. The ground was relatively flat beneath a rugged cliff some thirty feet in height, with jumbled boulders at the top that might disguise a cave.

He parked the jeep, nose in against the cliff, and killed the engine, listening. He heard the helicopter now, still faint and far away, but it was coming. It had been too much to hope that they would miss his track completely in the dark.

How long before the whirlybird swept into view?

If it was audible, he guessed five minutes, maximum. A man could scale the cliff in that amount of time, if he was motivated, find himself a sniper's nest that overlooked the jeep and bring the chopper under fire when it was close enough to guarantee a hit.

Not bad.

He turned the headlights on and left them burning as he stepped out of the jeep.

THEY ALMOST MISSED the trail, but Aldis Sharp had been a hunter since his childhood, and he spotted tire tracks on the second pass. At that, a precious quarter hour had been wasted, following the road, then doubling back when it became apparent that their prey wasn't a total fool.

The rest was relatively simple, flying low enough to keep the trail in sight and slow enough to pick up any deviation in the runner's course. So far, the track had run directly westward, toward the line of nameless, rocky hills that Sharp had prowled on more than one occasion, stalking game.

It was a different kind of hunt, this time, but on familiar ground. It made him curious about the gunman they were stalking. Any local would have known about the hills, that there was no fair passage for a vehicle of any kind. To Sharp's mind, that betrayed his adversary as a stranger to the district, someone who was in for a surprise when he came up against the hills and found his route cut off.

Unless . . .

There might just be a method to the bastard's madness, after all. Suppose he was a local, white or kafir, and he knew exactly where the hills were situated. It was possible, Sharp thought, that others would be waiting for him. He could ditch the stolen jeep and cross the rough, low-lying hills on foot, to meet his allies waiting on the other side. More vehicles, perhaps, and wouldn't that be lovely?

Sharp was smiling at the picture in his mind, a veritable kafir convoy rolling underneath the moonlight, carrying their hero back to some elaborate heathen celebration in his village. Maybe they were even bound for Swaziland, 150 miles away, with passage on from there to Mozambique.

No matter.

Even in the swiftest vehicles, with four-wheel drive, Sharp's quarry didn't stand a chance against the helicopter. Even holding back a bit, the chopper made three times the speed of any vehicle on open ground, and obstacles meant nothing in the air. It would be over soon, and no mistake.

He hoped the gunman was a kafir. Granted, there were white men who betrayed their race by siding with the blacks, but Sharp believed that most of them were wimps who lacked the courage for a paramilitary operation. They preferred to donate money that would arm the kafirs, rubbing shoulders with Mandela and his ilk at cocktail parties. It would be snowing in the deepest pits of hell before those spineless sissies found the nerve to stand and fight like men.

The blacks, by contrast, had begun to show a fair amount of nerve in recent years, since everything began to go their way. It was the valor of a rogue hyena, Sharp would say if he was asked, the kind of scavenger that waited for his prey to weaken, growing old and soft and riddled with disease, before he ran in for a quick nip at the jugular. You saw it all the time in nature. Driver ants could overwhelm a man if they were numerous enough, the man too old and slow to run away.

Of late, with the concessions from Pretoria, the kafirs had begun to think that they were winning, and the white man was about to drop his banner in the dust. It might be true for some, but Sharp and his comrades were prepared to lay down their lives in defense of race and homeland. Some had made the sacrifice that very night.

Sharp meant to pay the killers back with interest, teach the lot of them a lesson any stray survivors would remember to their dying day and pass along to others of their kind.

Resistance to the rotten winds of change wasn't extinguished in South Africa. If anything, the Afrikaner spirit had been growing stronger, dedication reinforced by each atrocity the kafirs perpetrated, each new threat from the United Nations. When the fateful day of reckoning arrived, the White Wolves would be ready to repay their enemies for every insult, every drop of blood shed by the kafirs and their friends.

Tonight, Sharp had a chance to make a start.

He saw a speck of light on the horizon and leaned forward, squinting through his goggles as the pilot spoke into his mouthpiece.

"Headlights."

Stupid bastard, coming all this way without his lights, and now he turned them on. Perhaps he *was* a stranger to the territory, startled and chagrined to find his route cut off as far as he could see on either hand.

The lights were stationary. They had seemed to move at first, but that was an illusion, fostered by the helicopter's motion. It was worse than stupid, turning on the headlights for a start, then sitting still to let them draw his enemies. The man had to be insane.

Or crafty like a fox.

He spoke another order to the pilot, and the helicopter veered off course, to come in from the southern flank, downwind. It was impossible to take the runner by surprise, of course, with all the noise their engines made, but they could still defeat a simple ambush if they tried.

The jeep faced toward a rugged cliff, some thirty feet in height. Its summit was a tumbled mass of broken stone that came from higher up, another slope immediately to the west. The cliff and crowning rock pile overlooked the stranded jeep. It struck Sharp as a perfect shooter's stand, the sort of blind he might have chosen for himself, if he had been the hunted man.

They circled wide around the cliff top, probing with the searchlight, Sharp alert to any sign of movement below. The jeep was definitely empty, and the cliff was bare, but it would be a relatively easy climb.

It might require a foot patrol to root the bastard out, and that was fine, but Sharp decided he would do his bit to stir things up beforehand, while his men were getting ready for their hike. He chose the largest fissure he could see, leaned

into the M-60 and unleashed a hail of bullets from the open
window.

Any moment now, Sharp thought, and he would have a
running target, trapped beneath the searchlight and his
blazing weapon, cornered like a rat in a latrine.

If he was lucky, maybe he could teach the kafir how to
dance.

FROM HIS POSITION underneath the jeep, Mack Bolan heard
the first long burst of automatic fire. It sounded distant,
somewhat muffled by the helicopter's rotor wash and engine noise, but still he waited to be sure. If bullets started
ripping through the jeep and chewing up the earth around
him, he would know the odds had gone against him one last
time.

But they were firing at the cliff, no doubt about it now.
Shell casings pattered to the ground like hailstones, but the
lead was going elsewhere, chipping abstract patterns on the
jumbled stone, some thirty feet above his head.

That gave him time for one last bid to save himself, but he
would have to execute the move precisely. No mistakes, no
second chance.

He picked the driver's side and wriggled out from underneath the jeep, dragging the Galil R-4 behind him as he
scrambled to his feet. The helicopter hovered forty feet
above him, give or take, and slightly to his left as Bolan
faced the cliff. It wasn't bad, as sighting angles went, and
there was no time to improve his field of fire.

He brought the rifle to his shoulder, sighting quickly in
the moonlight. It was mostly grass where he had parked the
jeep, no swirling sand to sting his eyes, but still the windy
rotor wash was a distraction. It wouldn't divert a bullet, but
it made him squint a little, bringing tears to his eyes.

The rifle's magazine held thirty armor-piercing rounds. It
was enough. It had to be.

The tail rotor would be first, because it was the easy shot
to take and it would throw the whirlybird off-balance if he
got it right. Bolan fired an 8-round burst, not bothering to
wait to judge the impact of his rounds.

He swiveled slightly to his right and fired a dozen rounds into the chopper's starboard engine, letting one or two kick high enough to find the central rotor shaft. This time, he was rewarded with a puff of smoke and a bang.

Contact.

He was ready when the helicopter rolled to starboard, giving him a clear view of the forward gunner and a slice of profile for the second officer. He raked the cockpit with his last ten rounds and dropped the empty magazine, reloading smoothly as the chopper went berserk.

It seemed to flinch from Bolan with a conscious effort, a reaction of the pilot as his sidekick's head exploded and a burst of armor-piercing bullets ripped through his controls. Black smoke poured from the starboard engine as the chopper tried to climb, defeated by the pull of gravity.

The pilot did his best, with fresh brains in his lap, one engine gone and the tail rotor shot to hell. He fought the big Sikorsky through a left-hand turn, away from Bolan, but he lost it halfway there. The chopper kept on turning, made a full three-sixty, snarling back toward impact with the cliff.

The fuel tanks didn't blow immediately. Bolan watched the chopper crash, its cockpit crumpled like a soda can before it slithered down the cliff face, trailing sparks and shrieking like Godzilla raking claws across the biggest blackboard in the universe. It struck the earth with a resounding crash, back broken, and the giant rotors whipped themselves to pieces, jagged chunks the size of surf boards sailing overhead. He smelled the jet fuel spilling out before a spark caught from the dying engines, and the whole thing went up in flames.

A hundred feet from the inferno, Bolan felt the heat like summer sunshine on his face. He stared into the flames for several moments, waiting for a sign of life, aware that none would be forthcoming. Finally he reached inside the jeep and switched the headlights off, to spare the battery.

So much for hot pursuit.

He would be cautious, even so, on the return trip to his hidden vehicle, the more so driving back to Jo'burg through the early-morning darkness, when security police were on the prowl. His white skin ought to see him through all right, but you could never tell. The last thing Bolan needed at the moment was a confrontation with the law.

He had more targets waiting for him in the city.

And he didn't mean to keep them waiting long.

3

It was a thirty-minute drive through morning traffic from downtown Johannesburg to suburban Alexandra, on the Pretoria Main Road. Arnold Schuster hated city driving, but he did it well enough to pass for a professional. An hour with any street map printed in the English language, and his photographic memory would guide him like a native. He could rattle off the landmarks on demand, or give directions that would lead a total stranger to his destination every time.

It helped to know the territory, most especially when there might be enemies around, and need for hasty exits from an unfamiliar place. The Company had taught him to survive in strange surroundings, merging with the scenery and watching out for tails. Experience and Schuster's built-in instinct for survival did the rest.

But city driving was the pits. He could afford a driver these days, but he liked to keep things simple. One less person to rely on when the chips were down. One less potential traitor stepping up behind him with a dagger poised to strike.

If there was one thing Arnold Schuster understood with perfect clarity, it was the fine art of double cross. A mercenary known for transient loyalties, he trusted no one absolutely. Trust was a commodity like any other on the open market, subject to diversion if the price was right. To call a man disloyal, in Schuster's world, was simply to declare that no one had negotiated proper terms.

In the ten years since the CIA discovered it couldn't afford his service, Schuster had been "loyal" to Palestinians,

Biafrans, Turks, Bulgarians, Koreans and a certain Red Chinese who always paid his debts in gold. He trusted each of them to act on selfish interest, and he wasn't disappointed. Each of them, in turn, had trusted Schuster to perform a service in return for cash, and he had never let them down. If he was offered better wages at a later date to sell them out, well, that was business. Everybody knew and understood the rules.

And if a onetime ally got his feelings hurt, attempted to retaliate, the once and future spook was more than capable of fending for himself. The Red Chinese, for instance, had been sought by his superiors for all of thirteen months. Beijing had listed him as a defector, marked for execution on discovery, but they would never find him.

Not unless they started sifting shark shit in the China Sea.

Most recently, the once and future spook had sold his loyalty to a group of Afrikaner militants who called themselves White Wolves. If anyone had asked for Schuster's input, he could probably have given them a better handle, but he wasn't in the PR business. Rather, he was an "arranger," helping make connections where they mattered most.

In politics and business.

In the arms trade.

In the underworld.

A man like Schuster was of value to the Wolves because of his connections overseas. South Africa had been a leper nation for the past two decades, hemmed around by economic sanctions, social boycotts and the like to force a change in racial policies. Ironically the Zionist regime in Tel Aviv had gone ahead with arms sales to Pretoria, despite a worldwide protest, but a people under siege required more lethal goods and services than tiny Israel could supply.

It had been Schuster's job to make the deals, arrange for payments and deliveries, finesse the rough spots when philosophy began to interfere with business. Privately the fixer didn't give a damn about the Afrikaner "master race" or its survival in a changing world. The only color he was interested in was green.

And now, they had a problem.

Willem Grubb had rousted him from bed at some ungodly hour, yammering about a firefight in the bush. When Schuster tried to make it clear that he wasn't involved in the logistics of their little race war, Grubb reminded him that he was being paid—and very handsomely, at that—to cope with *any* problems that arose from interaction with the outside world. Grubb seemed to think the latest skirmish flowed from one of Schuster's deals, but he wasn't prepared to hash out details on the telephone.

The Alexandra office block was modern to the point of being hideous, all jags and angles, lots of burnished metal to reflect the sun and make pedestrians go cross-eyed on the street below. He parked in the employees' lot, below ground, rode the elevator up to nine, then turned left along the corridor to reach his destination halfway down.

Grubb's front was a security concern that dealt in bodyguards and high-tech gear for businessmen, celebrities and such. It helped that Grubb had put in thirteen years with the security police before he got the boot, accused of brutalizing suspects in the early days of the political reforms. Between Grubb's personal connections in Pretoria and Schuster's on the outside, they were well prepared to field a private army for the civil war that Grubb had been predicting since he lost his badge.

But it wasn't supposed to happen now, and not with someone else enjoying the initiative.

The secretary passed him through, and Grubb was waiting for him in the inner sanctum, smoking a cigar that smelled like gym socks gone to mold. The head wolf glared and grunted, waved him toward a waiting seat and sat in the high-backed swivel chair behind his glass-topped desk.

"You're late."

"I'd rather talk about our problem," Schuster said.

"Our problem? It's a fucking nightmare."

"So I gathered from your phone call. Try to take it easy, now, and tell me what's been happening."

THE EXECUTIONER COULDN'T read lips, but he felt safe in guessing at the topic of discussion. Willem Grubb was looking even worse than normal, scowling through a haze of smoke, while Arnold Schuster did his best to calm the portly fascist.

Two hundred yards downrange, and Bolan almost felt that he could reach out from his rooftop sniper's nest and flick the ash from Grubb's cigar. The set was perfect, and his vision through the telescopic sight was crystal clear.

No one had given him a second glance when he ascended to the roof, decked out in workman's coveralls and carrying a heavy metal toolbox. Bolan's order for a checkup on the air conditioner's compressor unit was a fake, but no one asked to see it, and he reached the rooftop unopposed. Once there, he used a simple rubber wedge to jam the door against surprise arrivals and unpacked his gear.

The toolbox measured twenty-seven inches, end to end. Inside, beneath a shallow tray of nuts and wrenches, lay a fieldstripped Walther WA-2000 sniper's rifle, fitted with a Schmid and Bender telescopic sight. In less than forty seconds, Bolan had the piece assembled, with its 6-round magazine in place, a live round up the spout.

The Walther was state of the art in terms of personal, long-distance killing machines. It measured just a fraction under three feet long, employing the bullpup design to minimize bulk. Its barrel was fluted longitudinally to forestall overheating and cut down on vibrations that spoiled a shooter's aim. The self-loading design eliminated awkward bolts, while retaining plenty of power with the standard .300 Winchester Magnum round it used.

Two hundred yards was child's play for the Walther and for Bolan, but geography dictated tactics. Any farther from the target, and he would have lost his view, with taller buildings in the way. A closer stand, by contrast, would have multiplied his risks of being seen or even captured when the hit went down.

The word on Grubb had come from Hal Brognola's contacts in the CIA and Interpol. Ex-cop, dismissed for racial violence—which implied a sort of flagrant terrorism in

South Africa, where torture and brutality toward blacks had always been a rule of thumb with the security police. These days, he worked "executive security" to pay the rent, devoting most of his attention to the White Wolves he had organized for die-hard paramilitary bigots like himself.

The visitor was Arnold Schuster, onetime covert operative for the CIA, relieved of his association with the Company when Langley learned that he was cashing in on private contacts in the field. At one time or another, he had smuggled arms, narcotics, fugitives from justice—even, it was said, a slave consignment on occasion, bound for harems in the Middle East. The Company had booted him in lieu of public prosecution, seized the bank accounts that it could find and left him to the tender mercies of the IRS. When Schuster disappeared, there was a general feeling of relief—until he surfaced as a free-lance fixer, traveling the world in style and reaping profits from the dark side of the street.

In the old days, before Watergate and congressional oversight, Langley would have measured Schuster for a body bag without a second thought. These days, they found it more productive to record his movements and associations, looking forward to the day when someone else could make the tag without a fuss.

Someone like Bolan.

He started running the ballistic calculations in his head—the .300 Winchester Magnum round loaded a 220-grain projectile with full-metal jacket, departing the Walther's muzzle at 2,680 feet per second. At two hundred yards, the velocity was still more than 2,200 feet per second, delivering better than 2,400 foot-pounds of destructive energy on impact. He adjusted for a standard 4.9-inch drop in the trajectory across two hundred yards and gauged the wind.

Dead calm.

The windows of Grubb's office would be thick enough for safety's sake, but there was nothing in the building plans—obtained for Bolan by a contract agent of the Company—to indicate that they were bulletproof.

Allowing for deflection on the first shot, Bolan picked his mark. He filled his lungs with air, released approximately half of it and held the rest. His index finger curled around the Walther's trigger, taking up the slack.

Downrange, his targets argued silently, Grubb sucking on his fat cigar and Schuster frowning, neither one of them aware that Grim Death was about to interrupt their spat.

"AND HOW WOULD I KNOW who trashed your camp?" asked Schuster, warming to the argument. "I haven't even seen the place, if you recall."

Grubb waved his stogie like a band conductor calling up more brass. "It is your job to know such things," he said. "Your contract is not limited to ordnance and supply. If anything, my first consideration in retaining you was the intelligence connection. You were advertised as an unrivaled expert in the field of terrorism and subversion."

Schuster nodded in agreement. "Expert, right. Not psychic. There's a difference, Willem. No one—not the Company, not Moscow, no one—can predict what each and every group of radicals is up to every minute of the day. I know at least four leftist groups inside South Africa that want your operation scrubbed, not counting tribesmen who would dearly love to boil your carcass down for soup. Beyond the border, you've got six or seven more guerrilla armies begging for a fight, plus every other government in Africa. I hate to break the news here, Willem, but you're not a man with lots of friends."

"You make a joke?" An angry flush was coloring Grubb's cheeks. "With seventeen men dead and still more wounded, you are giving me a comedy routine?"

"I'm trying to explain—"

"Enough for explanations! What I want now is results. You are supposed to have good contacts. Use them. Find out who has done this thing and bring me back a name. The man, the group—whatever you can find. We must retaliate at once, or run the risk of being made to look like fools and cowards."

There it was, Schuster thought. Coming back to ego in the end.

"I'll ask around," he said, "and see what I—"

The cracking sound was almost insignificant, like ice cubes settling in a glass of tea. Schuster's head was turning toward the window on his left when Grubb's big crystal ashtray suddenly disintegrated, flinging jagged shrapnel around the room.

No sound of gunfire, but experience told Schuster what was happening. He launched himself into a headlong dive for cover, shouting, "Sniper! Hit the deck, for Christ's sake!" as he vaulted from his chair.

The second shot was almost instantaneous, which meant the sniper had a semiautomatic rifle. This one sent Grubb's intercom flying in a dozen pieces, the White Wolves' leader cursing as a chunk of broken plastic caught him in the face.

"Get down!"

A third round drilled the chair where Schuster had been sitting just a heartbeat earlier. The chair fell over backward, struck his shin a solid blow and sent pain lancing up his leg.

Grubb hit the floor behind his desk on hands and knees, the reeking stogie still protruding from his mouth. The angry color had departed from his cheeks, and he looked a good deal whiter than he ever had before. He had begun to curse in fluent Afrikaans, but Schuster only caught the general tone of anger and amazement.

Number four was all it took to finish off the plate-glass window, jagged sheets cascading to the floor like crystal blades in some fantastic guillotine. They burst on impact, more like shattered ice than flying razors now, but each and every shard could still draw blood.

The outer door flew open, one of Grubb's commandos charging in to find out what the racket was. He had a pistol in his hand, for all the good that it would do him, matched against a sniper who was both proficient and invisible.

The fifth round struck Grubb's shooter in the forehead, lifting off his scalp and everything beneath it like a cheap toupee with brains attached. The dead man staggered backward, struck the nearest wall and slithered down until he was seated on the floor.

For perhaps a second, Schuster thought about the risk involved in reaching for the dead man's pistol. He was almost there, a simple lunge would do it, out and back. Except that any doubts he had about the sniper's marksmanship had vanished when Grubb's gunner bit the dust, and there was nothing he could possibly accomplish with a handgun, anyway.

Forget it.

Schuster lay facedown behind Grubb's desk and smelled the Afrikaner's rank cigar as it began to scorch the carpet. That was all he needed, coupled with the odor emanating from the dead man's bowels, a few feet to his right.

A final slug zipped through the window, kept on going through the open door to Grubb's waiting room beyond, and found the water cooler with a splash. The secretary had begun to scream hysterically. Another of his gunmen peeked through the open door for just an instant, ducking out of sight before the sniper had a chance to take him down.

And it was over, just like that.

The last shot had been audible, but only seconds after impact from the bullet. Schuster guessed their man had found himself a nest in one of the commanding office towers somewhere down the street. No silencer, which meant that he was more than likely on the move by now, retreating after squeezing off one magazine.

It came to Schuster in a flash that he was fortunate to be alive. The sniper could have killed him with his first shot, that was obvious. But something had deterred him.

What?

Forget it. Never look a gift horse in the mouth.

"Are you all right?" he asked the trembling Afrikaner.

"Yes." And then, as Grubb began to breathe again he added, "How could you let this happen, Schuster?"

God Almighty.

He had some questions of his own, just now, and Grubb's anger was the least of his problems at the moment. Someone very slick had come within an inch of killing him and pulled the shot, by all appearances, deliberately.

Before the sun went down again, he meant to find out who and why.

And having done that, he would take the bastard out.

No sweat.

IT TOOK LESS TIME to break down the Walther than to assemble it, and Bolan had it stashed inside the toolbox while the echo of his final shot was still reverberating in the street below. Pedestrians were gawking on the sidewalk, but they couldn't spot him from their worm's-eye viewpoint. Stooping to retrieve his rubber wedge, the Executioner descended swiftly, keeping to the service stairs and meeting no one on his way down to the street.

It was no accident that he had spared the two men in the office, taking out a button man to demonstrate that he could easily have dropped them, if he wanted to. The hit had been a conscious effort to unnerve his enemies, without inflicting mortal damage at the top.

Right now, he knew the White Wolves' leader and the rogue American who functioned as his go-between with foreign contacts. If the two of them were dead, it would have been like starting out from scratch. The wolf pack would have been disoriented for a time, but Willem Grubb was bound to have an heir apparent waiting in the wings.

This way, he shook up the opposition and kept them guessing, all without a major change in the equation. Every step he took from this point on would be designed to keep the shock waves spreading, stir up turmoil in the ranks, and frustrate any operational designs that Willem Grubb had on the drawing board.

And when he chose to bring their house down, it should be a relatively simple exercise. One final shove to do the job.

Except that nothing ever went that smoothly in the hellgrounds.

Never.

Bolan reached the ground floor of the office building and ducked out through the service entrance. He moved along the alley to a nearby garbage Dumpster, stepped behind it and removed his coveralls. They fit inside the toolbox, and he reemerged a different person, clad in lightweight slacks, a sport shirt and expensive running shoes.

His nondescript sedan was parked in a commercial lot that occupied the far end of the block. He came in from the alley, found the car and stowed his toolbox in the trunk before he slid behind the wheel. The cashier in the booth was busy with a nudie magazine. He glanced at Bolan's ticket, named a price and took his money, handing back the change without once looking at the driver's face.

Why should he?

It was white, this face, and in Johannesburg that spoke to some degree of common background and beliefs, a shared philosophy. In fact, as Bolan knew, the white minority that ruled South Africa wasn't unanimous in attitude, by any means...but black was still the color many Afrikaners looked for when they thought of trouble, crime or violence in the streets.

It had occurred to Bolan that his sniping mission would be blamed on left-wing blacks initially, but he was planning to correct that misconception very soon. Eliminating that presumption of a race war in the making was a crucial part of Bolan's strategy this time around.

The local hard-core bigots understood that many foreign whites regarded them with frank contempt, but it was easy to dismiss the world at large as a conglomerate of Communists and simpletons who couldn't understand South Africa's unique dilemma. Afrikaners who rejected the apartheid doctrine were denounced as traitors to their race, for giving aid and comfort to the enemy.

It all came down to racial hatred in the end, but it was prejudice with a political agenda. Whites had ruled South Africa by force since the seventeenth century, extracting fabulous wealth from the country's gold and diamond mines. The double impetus of wealth and power was enough to guarantee resistance when the winds of change began to huff and puff around Pretoria. Racism was the frosting on the cake, a crude philosophy of ethnic dominance passed down through twenty generations to the present day.

Times change, and people too, but change is seldom smooth and easy. Local politics wasn't the Executioner's concern, nor would he typically involve himself in a crusade for civil rights, but there was more at stake on this assignment than a simple clash of black and white.

The White Wolves were committed to a course of terrorism that transcended race and politics, expanding from their home base in South Africa to set the continent on fire. Though relatively short on numbers, they possessed a grim potential for destruction that could hardly be ignored.

He merged with midtown traffic, concentrating on the next stop on his grim itinerary.

Some attention for the wolf pack.

Before he finished with them, Willem Grubb and company would wish they had a nice, safe den in which to hide themselves away.

And Bolan wished them luck.

All bad.

4

The pigs were watching her again. She knew it first by intuition and confirmed it with her eyes. Their arrogance was such that the surveillance team made no attempt to hide or even to divert suspicion from themselves.

Smug bastards. Even now, with all the world against them and their time so obviously running out, they still behaved as if they were the very masters of creation. First, they passed the laws that governed daily life, then they ignored the ones that inconvenienced their pursuit of power. Anyone who crossed them was an enemy deserving of surveillance, social ostracism, maybe worse.

It had been worse for Bridget Linder and her husband, Jan. At one time, she had blamed her husband's chosen business for the troubles they endured, but time had pointed out her fundamental error. It wasn't Jan's business that offended those in power, but the fact that he refused to be manipulated like a puppet, coached on what to say and where he ought to stand on any issue at a given point in time.

Jan Linder had inherited the paper from his father. More important, he had also grown up with the classic newsman's curiosity, an urgent need to flip rocks over and expose the wiggling maggot-life beneath. Except in bed with Bridget, Jan was never more alive than when he smelled a story breaking and the state attempted to suppress some bit of information he desired.

One thing that Jan hadn't inherited from Dieter Linder was his father's prejudice against the native blacks. It was a constant thorn in Dieter's side, the fact that he had raised a liberal of sorts, though Jan would never qualify as anything but moderate in terms of the solutions he proposed to the apartheid question. He was never militant, much less a left-wing agitator, but he was tenacious when he got a story in his teeth and tasted blood.

Jan's father had been dead a year or more when Jan first ran a front-page story on police brutality against black workers in Johannesburg. The story grew into a series, and he started losing friends around the country club in Germiston. Detectives dropped in at the *Chronicle* to question, pretending to believe that Jan had information on the whereabouts of terrorists associated with the ANC. When he wasn't intimidated by their visits and insinuations, traffic officers began to tag his car for a prodigious number of imaginary violations. Late-night calls disturbed their sleep at home, continuing despite the shift to an unlisted number.

The security police at work.

Six months of personal harassment did the trick, and Jan decided to retaliate in print. His editorials grew more opinionated by the day, and he assigned his most tenacious news hawks to uncover dirt on the security police, expanding swiftly to include the cruel regime they kept in power with their truncheons, dogs and guns.

In time, he drove the pigs to desperation. They couldn't admit that they were wrong in treating blacks like animals, because the reigning government might tumble down around their ears, and with it the facade of white supremacy. Likewise, it was apparent to the men in charge that Jan would never let them rest.

Not while he lived.

Official records called Jan Linder's death an accident. He had been driving from Pretoria to Germiston one rainy night, alone, returning from a meeting with a confidential source, when his Mercedes-Benz had suffered "a mechanical malfunction," left the road and rolled three times before it finally exploded into flames. The medical examiner was confident that Jan had died on impact, feeling nothing when the fire broke out.

So much for the official story.

Bridget knew her husband had been murdered, probably by officers of the security police. She also knew that she could never prove it in a court of law. If she was ever to enjoy the cold dish of revenge, she had to decide upon some other means to make the bastards pay.

Her answer was the *Chronicle*.

It came to Bridget automatically, a part of her inheritance when Jan was killed. Of course, no one believed a woman would be equal to the task of managing a daily paper, much less keeping up her husband's penchant for crusades. Before the reading of Jan's will, she had a buy-out offer from a fat cat in Johannesburg, a name associated with the right-wing party that was working overtime to save apartheid from the march of progress. When she turned the offer down, the price was raised—eventually doubled, rising far beyond the paper's worth—and Bridget knew the pigs were frightened.

It was good to see them squirm.

And yet, it was an uphill fight to start with, stepping into Jan's shoes at the *Chronicle*. His people barely knew her, and they clearly doubted her ability to keep the operation solvent, much less publish quality material. It took the best part of a year for them to realize that she wouldn't be bullied, bought or frightened off. Reporters who believed that they could coast on gutless stories, writing fluff, were soon among the unemployed. A new man planted on her staff by the security police was found one evening, riffling Jan's private files, and Bridget filed the charge of burglary herself. Next day, his face and story filled the *Chronicle*'s front page, beside an editorial that blamed the state in no uncertain terms.

From that point on, the government harassment changed in tone and quality, if not in focus. Years ago, Bridget Linder might have simply been banished from her homeland, but the custom had been disallowed in court, a change effected by the crushing weight of world opinion. Censorship was dying in South Africa these days, except for certain libel rules that had been weighted heavily in favor of the state.

For all that, Bridget found a way to keep the heat on those in power, stepping out beyond the scope of Jan's attacks on brutal tyranny, producing more than one irate denial from the chief of the security police.

And always, she was searching for the crucial bit of evidence, the name or clue, that would allow her to expose her husband's murder for the heinous crime it was.

Someday, she vowed, the story would be told, regardless of the cost. Jan's killers might be dead themselves, by then, but it would make no difference. She would see their names in print, on record for the world to read, and she would leave their reputations on the rubbish heap, where they belonged.

But in the meantime, Bridget had to make a living, and she had to stay alive.

The *Chronicle* had started losing advertisers lately, several major clients dropping their subscriptions after Bridget failed to heed their "friendly" warnings on the hazards of a personal crusade. She had been worried for a time, until the money started flowing in from Indian and native businessmen—the very "coloreds" who were still regarded with disdain by other dailies in Johannesburg. They made the crucial difference, and she even turned a tidy profit in her second year as publisher and editor in chief.

Around that time, the pigs had started watching her in shifts. They tried to hide, but some of them were clumsy at it, and she often wondered whether she was meant to see them, one more trick designed to shake her up and put her nerves on edge. They still regarded her as "just a woman"—though, admittedly, a woman who could give them problems if she wasn't beaten into line.

They tailed her car sometimes, especially at night. It was impossible to miss the unmarked government sedans with one or two clean-cut Gestapo types inside. They hung two car lengths back in traffic, never coming any closer, switching cars and men before she really got to know their faces. Sometimes, they were parked across the street when Bridget left the office for home. On other days, she found them waiting down the block when she set off for work.

She took for granted that her telephones were tapped, and she encouraged her reporters to protect themselves by any means available when they were using confidential sources. Twice, her people had been lured into traps and attacked by hoodlums. One, a male reporter, had been beaten up and robbed, the theft of money to make the crime seem less political. Another, Bridget's best female reporter, had been dragged into a car, manhandled, threatened with a four-man rape if she continued working for "that bloody rag in Germiston."

Both stories made the *Chronicle*'s front page, complete with scathing editorials from Bridget's pen, and they were syndicated to the world at large. With that, eight months ago, the physical attacks had broken off. The personal surveillance even faltered for a time, as if the enemy were hanging back and taking stock.

But now, the pigs were watching her again.

One man, this time, and he wasn't concerned enough with anonymity to bother parking down the block. He sat across the street from Bridget's home: dark hair, dark suit, a dark sedan. The car wasn't exactly standard issue, but it fit the general mold. Whatever doubts she might have had about the stranger's purpose were immediately canceled by the way he sat and stared directly at her door.

She sat and watched him from her upstairs bedroom window. It would be amusing, Bridget thought, to call the Germiston police and tell them she had spotted a suspicious person in the neighborhood. Of course, the pig would only have to flash his badge to scare them off, but it would be another small annoyance added to the growing list.

She was about to leave the window seat and make the call, when something happened that amazed and frightened her. The dark man left his car, glanced up and down the block, then crossed the street. He hesitated for a moment at the curb, then moved along the walk toward Bridget's door.

Her heart was pounding hard against her ribs. She told herself that he hadn't come to arrest her—the security police would never send one man alone, when they could use a team of three or four—but that made Bridget's trepidation all the worse.

She didn't recognize this man from previous surveillance. Two or three of the detectives who had shadowed her since Jan was killed she could have picked out in a crowded room. This stranger had a grim set to his mouth, and unforgiving eyes.

He disappeared from view, directly underneath her now. The doorbell chimed, its normal cheery tone atypically discordant to her ears.

Suppose the pigs had finally run out of patience? Would they try to kill her here, at home in broad daylight? She was expected at the office in an hour. If she didn't show on time, they would expect a call, some explanation for the change in her routine. If she couldn't be reached at home or on her mobile telephone, her staff would put the wheels in motion for a search, alerting the police.

And, Bridget thought, by that time, it could be too late.

She left the window as her doorbell chimed again, retrieved the Walther PPK she kept beside her bed and went downstairs to meet the stranger on her doorstep. Jan had taught her how to use the gun, but she had never fired it at a living target.

Well, there was a first time for everything.

She didn't have to check the Walther. It was loaded, with a live round in the firing chamber, and she flicked the safety off with her thumb as she hurried downstairs.

Bridget reached the door just as her uninvited visitor rang the bell a third time. The chain was still in place as she unlocked the dead bolt, turned the knob with her left hand and eased the door open by roughly two inches. She held the Walther flat against her thigh, concealed from where the stranger stood, its muzzle pointed at the floor.

"What is it?"

"Bridget Linder?"

"Who are you?"

The stranger's voice was deep and mellow. He was handsome, in a rugged sort of way, not totally unlike her Jan. She caught herself before that train of thought went any further. This man was an enemy... or was he?

"Mike Belasko," he replied by way of introduction. "You don't know me—"

"No," she interrupted him. "I don't."

"I'm hoping you might have some time to talk."

"I'm late for work."

"It wouldn't take that long."

"If you have business to discuss, please call my secretary at the *Chronicle*. She'll set up an appointment for—"

This time, the stranger interrupted her. "It isn't business," he explained. "It's personal."

"There's nothing personal between us."

Bridget's palm was slick with perspiration where she clutched the Walther automatic, but she had her left hand braced against the door—insurance—and she couldn't let the weapon go.

"I hoped we might be able to discuss your husband's death."

A chill began to worm its way down Bridget's spine. It took another moment for her to discover that she wasn't breathing. With a conscious effort, she relaxed her death grip on the PPK, afraid it might go off by accident.

"You'd best explain that."

"Can we talk inside?" he asked.

She smelled a trick. How stupid did the bastards think she was?

"As you so aptly pointed out, I don't know you."

The stranger risked a smile. "If I intended any harm, do you suppose I'd ring your doorbell in the daylight, with your neighbors watching?"

It was time to put him off or take a chance. She brought the Walther out of hiding, let him see the business end.

"I'm armed," she said.

"I'm not." He spread his jacket open to reveal an empty shoulder holster on the left. As Bridget watched, he turned and raised the jacket's tail, to show her he had nothing tucked inside the waistband of his pants.

He was a large man, powerful, athletic-looking. If she let him in, she faced the risk of being overpowered in a physical attack. Her only means of self-defense would be the pistol, but at least she had eight chances in the clip.

"What do you know about my husband?" Bridget asked.

"Enough to make an educated guess that he was murdered. The security police are sitting on it, am I right?"

It struck her that the man had no Afrikaner accent. He wasn't a Briton, that much was obvious. American? She felt a new frown tugging down the corners of her mouth.

"Who are you, really?" she demanded.

"I'm a friend. At least, I'd like the chance to be."

She hesitated for another moment, making up her mind. "When I step back, you'll come inside and take a seat," she said at last. "You'll stay there while we talk. If you stand up or try to reach me, I won't hesitate to shoot you dead."

"Sounds fair to me."

She kept him covered with the Walther as she slipped the chain and took three paces backward. He stepped across the threshold, closed the door behind him, waiting.

"Where's that seat you mentioned?"

"Lock the dead bolt first," she ordered. Just in case he had a friend outside she hadn't seen. If someone tried to force the door, she would have time enough to put a bullet in his chest.

"This way," she said when he was finished, pointing with her left hand toward the living room.

He led the way and sat down in the middle of the sofa. Bridget took an easy chair directly opposite and fifteen feet away, a coffee table in between them. She could watch the street from where she sat, a window at the stranger's back.

"Okay?" He didn't sound sarcastic or amused.

"All right. What do you know about my husband's death?"

"It's more what I've been told about his life. He didn't like injustice, and he said so in the *Chronicle*. I think it got him killed."

"That's all?"

"Not quite. Are you familiar with a group of men who call themselves White Wolves?"

"I am. They're racist paramilitary thugs."

Bolan smiled. "The very same."

"What of it?"

"They were organized three months before your husband's so-called accident. I'm no believer in coincidence."

"Jan had his share of enemies before the Wolves were organized. Besides..."

She stopped herself before the words could pass her lips, afraid of giving too much away.

"They'd need official help to cover up the crime," he finished for her, never flinching from her gaze.

"Are you a telepath, as well?"

"Not necessary. It's the obvious conclusion."

"Not to everyone, it seems. Some call me paranoid."

"A little paranoia doesn't mean there's no one out to get you," he replied.

She almost laughed at that, surprised to find out she was smiling at this total stranger.

"Suppose you're right. What then?"

"They shouldn't be allowed to get away with murder."

"No." Her own voice sounded small and far away.

"I'd say it's payback time."

"And what is that supposed to mean?"

"There's only so much you can hope to get done through the paper, am I right?" He didn't wait for her to answer him this time. "The courts are unresponsive, since they still rely on the security police. Unless I miss my guess, you'll have to handle it yourself... or maybe leave it to a friend."

"Some kind of extralegal justice, I suppose."

"I'm not much interested in labels."

"What do you propose? A revolution?"

"Not my style," Bolan replied. "I work much better on my own."

"I see."

She didn't, really, but she had a hunch what he was getting at. Again, she smelled a trap. It would be child's play for the bastards who had killed her husband to arrange this visit, offer her a chance to see Jan's death avenged, and thereby build a case for treason that would have her spending life in prison.

"Have you heard the news this morning?"

"On the radio."

"Was there an item on the White Wolves?"

"Not that I recall."

"You'll need to check your sources at the office. Late last night, the Orange Free State, near Bethlehem."

"What happened?"

"Ask around. You should turn up enough to know I'm serious."

"And then?"

"Your call. I'll leave a number where I pick up messages around the clock."

"What reason would I have for calling you?"

The stranger shrugged. "We have some enemies in common. I intend to take them out. I thought you might be interested in helping."

"Helping how?"

"My work depends on information, up to date and accurate. The word is, you have special contacts all around South Africa. The kind of people who won't talk to anybody else. Good people in the ANC, for instance."

Bridget stiffened. "If I had that kind of information, it would be—"

"Restricted, sure. Let's try it this way. You go on to work and check that story on the Wolves. Decide on whether you should take a shot at trusting me. I won't make any trouble for you if you pass."

"That's big of you."

"And while you're making up your mind, I have a few more stops to make. Be sure to check that story, now. And while you're at it, find out what went down with Willem Grubb this morning at his office."

"Grubb?"

"I'm only getting started," Bolan said. "One way or another, I've got work to do."

For just an instant, Bridget thought she had been wrong about his eyes. They weren't unforgiving, after all, but rather weary. Almost sad, in fact. She would have bet this man had seen his share and more of suffering.

But had he been a simple witness, or the cause?

She played a hunch. "You come from the United States," she said, not making it a question.

"So?"

"You've come a long way to avenge a man you never knew."

"Your husband's only part of it," Bolan said, "and I'd be lying if I said he was the most important part, right now. You know the Wolves are making border raids?"

"I've heard that, yes. There's been no solid proof, so far."

"But you believe it, anyway."

"Perhaps."

"I plan to catch them at it," Bolan stated.

"You? Alone?"

"That all depends."

"On what?"

He shrugged. "On luck. On you."

"I'll take that number." She was anxious for the man to leave, so she could put her thoughts in order. Bridget held the Walther steady as he reached inside his jacket for a pen and spiral notebook, tore a single page out, wrote the number down and dropped it on the coffee table.

"I'll be going now," he told her, rising slowly from the couch. "I'd just as soon you didn't shoot me."

"No."

"Okay, I'll be in touch."

She trailed him to the door and watched as he unlocked the dead bolt, lingering a moment on the threshold.

"What?" she asked.

"Whichever way it goes, you ought to watch your back, the next few days. It could get hairy. When the heat comes down, I wouldn't want to see you burned."

"I'm not afraid of fire," she said.

"It hurts some, all the same."

He closed the door behind him as he left, and Bridget double-locked it, watching through the peephole as he walked back to his car, across the street. She had begun to tremble, and she waited for the tremors to subside. It got a little better as the American slid into his car and drove away.

She wasn't frightened of the man, and that surprised her. Neither was she ready to accept him as her friend, but he had given her some food for thought.

The obvious conclusion was a setup. The security police were fond of setting traps for their political opponents, prosecuting anyone who took the bait. Or, could it be...

She wished she were already at the office, so that she could check the tantalizing leads Belasko left behind. Depending on the news, she had a choice to make. But she was far from trusting the American yet. Perhaps she never would.

She took the Walther pistol with her when she left the house and drove to work.

5

The target was an old apartment house in Malvern, several miles due east of Johannesburg proper, which the White Wolves had coopted as their own preserve. Most of the flats were empty now, some of them trashed beyond repair, but there were always several Wolves in residence at any given time. A fugitive with nowhere else to hide could rest in Malvern long enough to get his bearings and proceed to someplace more secure. The latest weapons shipment could be hidden in the basement for a while. From time to time, interrogations—even executions—could be carried out in special rooms with mattresses suspended from the walls, to muffle screams.

The wolf's lair was an open secret in the all-white neighborhood, ignored by the police unless they got complaints from local residents, the latter being either sympathetic to the Wolves or frightened into silence by the proximity of automatic weapons. It was said that the security police dropped off their stubborn prisoners from time to time—all blacks, of course—and let the White Wolves "soften" them a bit. If fatal "accidents" resulted now and then, the booking sheets would indicate a prisoner's release some twelve or eighteen hours prior to time of death.

Case closed.

His lead had come from local spotters, processed through the CIA to Hal Brognola and the team at Stony Man. They came up with an address and a general description of the property, but he was flying blind in terms of floor plans and the average number of opponents quartered on the grounds. A drive-by showed him that the building occupied a corner lot, an alley in the back, with windows painted over and a rusty fire escape in back. Their closest neighbor, to the south, was an apartment building one floor taller than the wolf's den, and its overlook gave Bolan an idea for his approach.

He had exchanged his stylish business suit for workman's denim, and the two-door for an aging van with rust spots on the sides. He parked behind the second building down and climbed in back to choose his gear, slipped into military webbing with the Desert Eagle on his hip before he took the Uzi submachine gun from its place behind the driver's seat. The Uzi hung beneath his arm on an assault sling, and he covered his equipment with a lightweight plastic raincoat prior to exiting the van.

The fire escape was old and spotted with corrosion, but it held his weight. As Bolan passed each floor in turn, he glanced into the flats whose curtains were open, half expecting to find a startled tenant staring at him through the glass. In fact, he made the passage unobserved and reached the building's roof without a challenge. Moving past the television aerials, he reached the northern edge and stared down at the wolf's lair, twelve or thirteen feet below him.

It wasn't the leap that worried Bolan. Rather, he was troubled by the thought that someone on the top floor of the old apartment house would hear the sound of impact when he landed, maybe come to find out what was going on. In that case, Bolan knew, he would be forced to kill before he made his way inside the house.

He minimized the risk by climbing over, dangling by his fingertips, and dropping less than five feet to the roof below. At that, he still expected trouble, crouching with the sleek Beretta 93-R in his fist, prepared to greet the first arrival on the roof with silent death. When no one came, he kept the piece in hand and moved on tiptoe toward the door that lay downstairs.

And found it locked.

The lock was old and cheap, no challenge for his pick. He felt the tumblers drop in seconds, turned the knob and gave the door a gentle shove.

Inside, a four-inch chain held fast.

He used the cutters next, a calculated risk considering the noise, but it was either that or find another way inside the house. Like kicking in a blacked-out window, with no idea of who or what was waiting on the other side. The warrior took his chances, waited for an answer to the sound of chain links being snipped in half and stepped across the threshold when the new sound brought no challenge from inside.

A flight of stairs led steeply downward, dim light showing from the left, a dingy corridor below. He dropped the raincoat, slipped his cutters back into their belt pouch and removed the Uzi from its shoulder sling. A chubby eight-inch silencer was threaded to the muzzle, adding three pounds to the weapon's total weight and giving him at least some margin of surprise if he was forced to drop his targets one by one.

He picked up voices coming from the far end of the corridor and moved in that direction, toward an open door. The others, six of them on either side, were closed and silent, no light showing underneath. Two men were heatedly debating something in the room ahead, both speaking Afrikaans, their tone completely typical of men who pride themselves on biceps measurements and the amount of whiskey they can guzzle in a finite length of time.

The warrior risked a glance around the doorjamb and found them facing each other over cards, with money on the table. He cleared his throat and let them see the Uzi, their startled faces drained of color in the moment when they realized that neither one of them would take the jackpot. They were scrambling for side arms when he held down the Uzi's trigger and canceled all their bets.

Two down, and the Executioner went hunting for another target in the maze.

IT WAS HIS THIRD DAY in the chair, and Kebby Seko had decided it was time for him to die. He didn't relish the decision, but it struck him as entirely logical. His enemies would never let him go, and if the torture didn't kill him, he would surely die of thirst and hunger in a few more days.

Why drag it out for the amusement of these men who took their names from animals?

They hadn't broken him so far, and Seko's only consolation was that he would probably expire before he gave them any information they could use to good effect. There would be no confession they could flaunt in public, though his tape-recorded screams might offer some amusement to them in the days ahead.

If nothing else, when they returned from swilling coffee and resumed the beating, Seko hoped he might provoke his captors into sudden, lethal rage. An observation on the love life of the fat one's mother could be useful. Possibly a word or two about the redhead's pregnant wife.

He knew the redhead's wife was big with child because the bastards talked in front of him like he was nothing, just another kafir, on a par with sticks of furniture. They registered the fact that he was breathing, but they couldn't think of him as human, since his skin was black. Above all else, captivity had rendered Seko harmless in their eyes. It didn't matter what he heard or what he knew, because they never meant to let him leave the house alive.

It had been risky, coming for the devils on their own home ground, but there had been no other way. Their border raids had grown more frequent in the past six months, and Seko was assigned to see what he could learn about the group firsthand. It was impossible to infiltrate the movement, since they had no trusty whites at their disposal, but he did his best. It was a fluke that he had been betrayed by one of those misguided blacks who view the white man as their lord and master, their salvation from a wasted life.

And here he was, trussed up, bleeding, groggy from a lack of sleep and the repeated pummeling he had endured for the past three days. His throat was parched, his empty stomach growling, but the thirst and hunger didn't occupy his mind to any great degree.

He was concerned with death, now, and the quickest way to bring it on.

The ropes that bound him to the straight-backed wooden chair were tight, the knots professional. Without assis-

tance, there could be no hope of breaking free. The one release that he could hope for had to be coaxed from his
tormentors, and he knew that failure would prolong his
suffering.

The thought of death didn't intimidate him. Every native African was raised with knowledge of his own mortality, his relative unimportance in the universal scheme of
things. He didn't grow up with the white man's notion that
the world revolves around his every whim and all creation
was designed for him to plunder as he liked. He knew that
he would surely die, and having witnessed countless deaths
by violence, starvation or disease, he didn't fear the end.

The point, at least in Kebby Seko's case, would be to
make the crossing with a minimum of extra hardship on
himself. The past three days had finished off his education
on the subject of man's inhumanity to man. He was prepared to graduate, with honors, but he had to goad his captors to their breaking point before he reached his own.

He guessed that it was all of twenty minutes since the pigs
had left him, chuckling to themselves and rubbing knuckles that were raw from hammering his face. His head felt
huge, misshapen, and he was a bit surprised that he could
form coherent thoughts, but there it was. More evidence
that blacks would ultimately outlast whites because of their
endurance, the ability to soak up pain and keep on with their
daily lives.

When they returned, the fat man and the sneering redhead, Seko planned to take control immediately. He would
start the moment they came in, convince them he had
changed his mind, decided to spill everything he knew. The
moment that he had their full attention, he would start ha-
ranguing them with insults, always striking at the racial
pride that was their central creed and reason for existence,
keeping after them until they snapped and beat him sense-
less in a screaming rage.

If there was time, and he was able, Seko thought that he
could turn his head just so and make the most of every blow
they landed. It would take a few to render him uncon-

scious, and with any luck at all, they would respond to his attack with savage force, enough to finish it.

His buzzing ears picked up the sound of footsteps in the hallway, voices drawing closer by the moment. Fat Boy was the louder of the two, his sidekick hissing when he laughed—a wet, reptilian sound. It would have been a pleasure, Seko thought, to swing a fist or boot against that smirking face and see it shatter, but the opportunity wouldn't be his.

Next time, perhaps. Another life.

They came in through the door, with Fat Boy leading, finishing a joke that made the redhead hiss as if he were about to suffocate. They spoke in Afrikaans, as plain as Greek to Kebby Seko, but he smiled through cracked and swollen lips as if he understood the punch line perfectly.

"What's so funny, kafir?" Fat Boy asked him, switching back to English as the common language.

"Nothing," Seko answered.

Fat Boy slapped him, just a love tap really, but it sparked a painful throbbing in his skull. "Don't lie to me, you bastard. You were smiling. What in hell's so entertaining?"

"Just a story," Seko answered.

"Story?" Fat Boy grinned and glanced back at his comrade. "Share it with us, won't you?"

"If you're sure..."

"By all means. I insist."

"All right. It's about the fat man who was sleeping with his mother. He finds out she was also bedding two Zulu warriors on the side—"

"You bloody bastard!"

Seko saw the big fist rushing at him, and he turned his head to take it square between the eyes. A burst of colored lights exploded in his skull, and he was taking other hits now, fast and furious, too many of them for his reeling mind to put the simple strategy of self-destruction in effect. He tried to keep his face up, take the worst of it head-on, but he was fading fast, the darkness flooding in behind his eyes.

He only hoped it was the last time he would have to make that journey on his own.

THE HUNTER BAGGED his third wolf on the stairs between the fifth and sixth floors, coming up to join the poker players with a six-pack and a plastic tray of sandwiches in hand. He gaped at Bolan for a heartbeat, knowing he was dead, then turned to bolt downstairs. The Uzi stuttered briefly, three rounds punching home between the runner's shoulder blades, and he was airborne, vaulting headlong into a collision with the nearest wall.

He struck the landing in a heap, with Bolan coming down on top of him, prepared to cover any stragglers on the next flight down, but they were all alone.

On five, he followed tinny sounds of music to the bedroom where a solitary wolf was stretched out on his bunk, a small transistor radio beside him, thumbing through a tabloid paper sporting swastikas above the banner headline. It was all in Afrikaans, but Bolan got the message loud and clear.

"Sieg heil."

The gunner bolted upright, dropped his paper and twisted sideways, lunging toward a shotgun propped against the wall. He almost made it, but the Uzi got there first, a stream of parabellum manglers opening his rib cage from the armpit to the hip and dropping him facedown beside the bunk.

And that made four.

He scanned the other rooms, retreating toward the stairs, and came up empty. There was space enough for several dozen tenants, if they pushed the limits of togetherness, but it appeared that most of Willem Grubb's commandos had their lodgings elsewhere.

Fair enough. The Executioner would take what he could get.

No sign of life on four. He descended to the third floor, ticking off the numbers in his head. He had no concrete deadline for the mission, but it went against the grain for him to linger overlong on hostile ground. The sudden in-and-out was Bolan's style, without a lot of dawdling on the way.

It fell apart on three, the sound of angry voices drawing him along the corridor until he reached the source, an open doorway on his left. Inside, the walls were hung with mattresses, some of them bloodstained, but the makeshift insulation didn't do much good when they forgot to close the door.

Two sweating thugs were working out their anger on a naked black man, seated in a wooden chair, with ropes securing his arms and legs. The taller, fatter of the two was getting into it with special zeal, as if he had a private score to settle with the prisoner. His khaki shirt was flecked with blood, and he was panting from exertion as he swung his meaty fists against the captive's unprotected face.

"Hey, Slugger."

Bolan didn't raise his voice, but both men froze, their faces swiveling in his direction, taking in the Uzi at a glance. The fat man wore a shiny automatic on his hip, but his companion seemed to be unarmed. That made it easy when they bolted, Porky clutching at his weapon, soaking up a 4-round burst from Bolan's subgun before he had a chance to draw. He hit the floor with a resounding thud and drummed the floorboards with his boot heels for a moment, finally going limp.

By that time, his companion had decided it was best to hide behind their prisoner and try to make himself invisible. It worked about as well as catching water in a sieve.

"Stand up."

The redhead did as he was told, hands loose against his sides, bewildered anger written on his face. He glanced from Bolan to the dead man on the floor and back again.

"Speak English?" Bolan asked him.

"Yes."

"Would you prefer to live or die?"

"I have a choice?"

"You might. I have a message for your leader. Can you handle that?"

The redhead nodded, starting to appear relieved.

"I didn't hear you."

"Yes. I'll take your message."

"Fine. You tell Grubb I'm borrowing your prisoner, to start with. Tell him that I could have given him a nose job at the office, when I dropped his button man. And while you're at it, let him know he's out of business, will you? Done. Kaput. I'm closing out his show."

"Who are you?"

"Names don't matter," Bolan told him. "Willy needs to think about his chickens coming home to roost. He's running out of time, and he's got debts to pay. I'm coming to collect."

"I'll tell him."

"Marvelous. You have a pocket knife?"

The redhead nodded once more, apprehensively. His right hand disappeared inside the pocket of his khaki pants and came out with a switchblade.

"Cut him loose," Bolan said, "and be careful while you're at it. Any slipups, and I'll have to decorate this playroom with your brains."

Another moment, and the prisoner was free, but it was all that he could do to hold his head up, much less stand. His clothes were lying in the corner, where they had been tossed aside, and Bolan pointed to them with the muzzle of his subgun.

"You're doing fine," he told the slender bigot. "Now, why don't you get him dressed."

It was the first time that the redhead showed an inclination to resist, but he thought better of it, stepping lively as the Uzi followed him across the room and back. While Bolan watched the corridor, his hostage helped the black man dress, delayed by pain that kept his movements slow and awkward.

Bolan took a chance and asked him, "Can you make it out of here?"

"I'll do my best," the black man answered him in perfect English.

"Fine. Let's do it."

"What about this pig? There might be others of his kind downstairs."

"We made a deal," Bolan replied. "But it looks like he could use a nap."

The black man flashed a grin and swung on his tormentor, driving a powerful fist into the redhead's face. It took only one punch, and he was down, sprawled on the floor beside his late and unlamented friend.

The recent prisoner reached out to claim the dead man's pistol, glancing back at Bolan for approval as he made the move. When Bolan nodded, he retrieved the automatic from its holster, drew the slide back and confirmed a live round up the spout.

The last two Wolves they met were lounging on the ground floor, in a kind of parlor gone to seed, both swilling beer and watching soccer on a twelve-inch black-and-white TV. The black man braced his liberated pistol in a firm two-handed grip, but Bolan nudged him with an elbow, showing him the Uzi's silencer as a reminder.

"It's my treat," he said.

They went downstairs together, Bolan in the lead, and they had almost reached the parlor when the nearer of his adversaries glanced around and saw them coming. Blurting out a curse in Afrikaans, the young man tried to reach the automatic rifle he had laid across a nearby coffee table, but he didn't have a hope in hell of getting there alive.

The Uzi caught him rising from his chair and dumped him back again, bright crimson spouting from a line of holes across his chest. The second wolf responded with a jerky little dance that brought him to his feet and facing his assailants, reaching for the pistol tucked inside his belt.

Too late.

The punk was dead before he hit the threadbare carpet, Bolan stepping over him to snag a jacket from the wall hook, draping it across his shoulders, with the Uzi hidden underneath.

"We're parked next door," he said, "around back."

"I'll make it," the man said, smiling through his pain.

"I bet you will."

6

His name was Kebby Seko. He spoke English like a native, and the first thing he communicated to the Executioner was a refusal to seek medical attention in Johannesburg.

"I'll be all right," he said, reclining in the back of Bolan's van, invisible to prying eyes.

"I've got a first-aid kit back there, for what it's worth," the warrior said, glancing in the rearview mirror at his unexpected passenger. "It's in the flight bag."

There were sounds of rummaging, and Seko said, "I have it. Thank you."

"You should really see a doctor. There must be someone you can trust. A native doctor in Soweto, maybe?"

"They would not trust you," the black man told him, working on a painful smile. "Besides, I would bring trouble to their doorstep that they do not need."

"You have to think about internal injuries."

The recent captive shook his head. "My hosts were careful not to cause me mortal damage while they still had hopes of getting information they desired."

"It looked like they were losing it when I got there," the Executioner replied.

He was surprised to hear a rueful laugh from Kebby Seko. "That, I fear, was my idea. The best laid plans of mice and men, you know? Of course, I did not know a white knight would be coming to my rescue."

"Well, we're even there."

The face in Bolan's mirror registered surprise. "You did not come to find me, then?"

"Not quite."

"The gods are smiling on me, then." A cautious frown replaced the look of disbelief. "But tell me, sir, why were you even there?"

"The name's Mike Belasko," Bolan told him. "I was dropping in to pay a little visit on the Wolves."

"With automatic weapons?"

Bolan shrugged and smiled at Seko in the rearview mirror. "You could say we aren't the best of friends."

"But you are not South African."

"That's right."

"Nor British. You do not have the accent."

"Right again."

"In fact, I think you are not European."

"No."

"I see."

"They must have wanted you for something serious," Bolan said, "if they took you home for supper."

Seko hesitated for a moment, studying his savior with a curious expression, finally deciding it was safe to go ahead. "They learned that I was asking questions, making inquiries," he said. "The past three days, they have been trying to persuade me that I ought to tell them my employer's name."

"I take it they were disappointed."

"More so now, I think."

"So, you're official," Bolan said. "They didn't grab you off the street because they came up short on punching bags around the gym."

"That is not their style," the African replied. "The White Wolves hate all blacks, of course, but they do not waste time on random acts of violence in the streets. South Africa has many hoodlums who will do that kind of thing for sport, you understand?"

"I do."

"The White Wolves see themselves as an elite contingent. They are fighting to preserve the Afrikaner way of life—that is, apartheid. Politics and race cannot be separated in their way of thinking. Every target has political significance."

"And you?"

"I was a nuisance and potential threat. They would have killed me soon. Perhaps tomorrow, or the next day."

Bolan played a hunch. "You're not South African."

Seko sidestepped and cautiously returned the serve. "I think you are an agent of the CIA," he said. "Clandestine ops, perhaps?"

"You might say that." It was a useful fiction, and he didn't plan to brief his momentary ally on the secret team at Stony Man.

"I knew it." Seko beamed. "But we are told your agency does not engage in such displays of force."

"Let's say I'm with a branch that never got the word."

"For that, I'm grateful," Seko said, and added, "Mozambique."

"Excuse me?"

"I was sent from Mozambique. In my country, I am like an agent for your FBI."

"The FBI's restricted to internal matters," Bolan said.

"As are we," Seko replied. "Except that lately..."

When he hesitated, Bolan said, "I know about the border raids. It's part of why I'm here."

"There have been six raids into Mozambique that we're aware of," Seko told him, "in a period of eighteen months. Two weeks ago, the Wolves killed Julius Nacala and a number of his men."

"You have hard evidence?"

"It would not stand in court," his passenger replied, "but we are not concerned about a trial. My government has filed complaints on previous occasions, with Pretoria and the United Nations. The South Africans insist their country is too large, their problems too diverse, for them to monitor civilian groups for a potential violation of the law."

"That's rich."

"And they point out that we have turned a blind eye to the ANC, where border crossings are concerned. Nacala was himself involved in the guerrilla war from time to time."

"They're right."

"Of course, but it is not the same. Our government does not oppress the whites, or any other group. We have our faults, like any nation, but we have not built our whole society on death and torture."

"Granted there's a difference," Bolan said. "You still got caught on foreign soil, conducting some illegal business. They could just as easily have handed you to the security police."

"It did not suit their purpose. I am not here to undermine the government, you see, although I hope to see it fall one day. The White Wolves hoped to find out what I know, identify my sources, and eliminate the danger to themselves. You spoiled their plan, I think."

"That's what I had in mind, though I'll admit I wasn't counting on a passenger."

"You saved my life. I am forever in your debt."

"Next time I'm in Maputo," Bolan told him, "you can buy me dinner."

"I look forward to it," Seko answered, "but I won't be going home just yet."

"Why not?"

"My mission is to find out all I can about these men and damage them, if possible."

"I'd say you've done your job."

"With all respect, my job was done by you. The only thing I might have damaged is the fat man's knuckles, with my skull."

"Don't press your luck. I've got a hunch your boss would rather have you back alive than know you took a couple of retarded neo-Nazis with you to the grave."

"Perhaps, but there is honor to be thought of. I could not respect myself if I allowed the job to go unfinished."

"Is it worth your life?"

"I might ask you the same."

They had been driving for close to fifteen minutes. Bolan saw a takeout restaurant approaching on his left and pulled into the parking lot. He parked some distance from the building, turned the engine off and swiveled in his seat to face the man from Mozambique.

"I don't suppose you're hungry?"

"Starving. I could eat a buffalo."

"Okay. I'll get us something in a minute. First, I need to know about your plans."

"I have none at the moment," Seko told him. "I have sources in the city, but their lives are now in jeopardy. If I approach them, it could be the end."

"So, you intend to do the rest of it alone?"

His passenger had stopped the bleeding from his nose and had begun to wipe the dried blood from his face. "It would be easier with help, but I will not be put off, in any case."

"I understand we're talking three, four hundred men," the Executioner reminded him.

"They only have one leader," Seko answered, meeting Bolan's gaze.

"Assassination? That's a risky business, all around. The best scenario, you make the tag and get away somehow, it's just another white man murdered by a black extremist. Worst case, you get caught or killed, they trace you back to Mozambique and lay it on your government. The Afrikaners come out looking sympathetic for a change, and they retaliate against the ANC or anybody else they feel like blaming for the hit. I wouldn't be surprised to see the border raids increase as a result."

"You have a better plan?"

"I do."

Seko looked skeptical, but he replied, "I'm listening."

"The first step," Bolan said, "is to eliminate the usual perspective of a black-white confrontation. Keep the Wolves from claiming they're the target of attacks from someone in the ANC or any other native group."

"And how would you accomplish that?"

"I've already started," Bolan said. "There's one survivor in the house where they were holding you. He took some lumps, but he's alive. I left a message with him, and he saw my face."

"But, why?"

"To throw their game off stride. They've always hunted blacks and armed themselves against retaliation from the natives. Now, they're being hunted by a white man, and they don't know who or why. With any luck, it just might shake them up and lead to a mistake or two. I'll take whatever I can get.''

''You would not kill their leader, this man Grubb?''

''If it's the only way to take him out, I wouldn't mind, but I'd rather try a different method, first. The Wolves are organized on military lines. In theory, that means no man is essential to the cause. Grubb dies, his second in command steps up to fill his shoes. It might slow down their operations for a while, but I'd prefer to bring them down across the board.''

''How would you do this?''

''Through exposure,'' Bolan said. ''You catch them with their pants down, turn the spotlights on and watch them crumble. Kill them if you have to, but make sure you wind up looking justified, for all the world to see.''

''A trap?''

The Executioner smiled. ''Here's what I had in mind.''

ROLF JANEK HAD BEEN dreading the American's arrival since he got the call that morning, but there seemed to be no way around the meeting. He would have much preferred to speak with Willem Grubb, but it appeared his oldest friend was running scared and didn't trust the telephone these days.

It was a pity, Janek thought. In sixteen years with the security police, he hadn't met another officer with Grubb's commitment to the state, his zeal for handling the blacks. When the reformers turned him out, South Africa had lost a valiant hero and, in Janek's view, had taken several long strides backward to the days of savagery.

He trusted Grubb implicitly, but the American was something else. He was a mercenary, loyal to no one but himself, no cause beyond the balance in his bank account. He worked for Grubb, just now, because the job paid well enough to keep him satisfied, but he had no investment in the land or people of South Africa. If they were beaten, overrun by Stone Age cannibals, it only meant that he would have to find himself another job.

And yet, he got results. The deal he struck for Czech munitions and explosives had been excellent, a decent price for items that were necessary to the cause. His friends in the intelligence community were greedy, for the most part, but they opened doors for trade in everything from arms to information, helping keep the White Wolves fit and ready for the holocaust that lay ahead.

Today, they had a problem to discuss. Janek already knew about the incidents from the previous night and the morning. Someone had attacked Grubb's training compound in the Orange Free State and massacred a number of his troops, survivors indicating that their adversary was a single man. Some hours later, Grubb and the American were sitting down to hash the problem out, when a proficient sniper wrecked the office and eliminated one of Grubb's bodyguards. Most recently, the housing block in Malvern had been raided, seven troopers killed.

Again, one man was seen. His comments linked him to the sniping incident and left no doubt that he was targeting the Wolves specifically.

Worse yet, the gunman had been white.

It troubled Janek, that part. He was used to dealing with guerrilla fighters from the ANC and other leftist groups made up of blacks, with scattered Asians here and there among the ranks. There had been rumors of a Soviet involvement, once, but it was never proved—and besides, the Russians were a different breed, these days. They had abandoned communism and the revolutionary creed, bogged down with problems of their own that ranged from Balkan civil wars to shortages of food.

What kind of white man would align himself with rebel blacks to scourge his own race in South Africa? And in Johannesburg, no less?

The world was filled with fuzzy-thinking traitors, Janek knew, but most confined themselves to "liberal" debating groups, the sort of armchair revolutionaries who were always crying for reform...until it reached their neighborhoods. In general, they weren't the kind to take up arms unless they heard a burglar prowling through the house at night, and armed, they posed a greater danger to themselves than to their enemies.

This man was something else again. Assuming he was on his own—a leap of faith that Janek wouldn't make without hard proof— he must be truly extraordinary.

Someone like the superman Grubb always hoped to find for his troops.

Pretoria was worried by the sudden rash of violence, Janek using all his diplomatic skill to reassure his boss that he could handle the emergency without imported help. The last thing Janek needed, at the moment, was a watchdog from the capital to follow him around and make bad matters worse.

His secretary buzzed him on the intercom. "Sir, Captain Schuster has arrived."

The military title brought a smile to Janek's lips. He knew a bit of Schuster's background, most specifically that he had never held a military rank of any kind before he joined the CIA, straight out of college, and began to look for easy money in the cloak-and-dagger world at large. It was an affectation Willem Grubb encouraged to give Schuster more respect among the troops, but Janek hoped he didn't take the captain's rank too seriously.

For himself, a frontline soldier in the war against black terrorists before he traded uniforms and found another mission, Janek harbored a disdain for officers that bordered on contempt. The fact that he was now a major hadn't changed his point of view.

And bogus officers, he thought, were less than nothing.

"Send him in."

He stood behind his desk as Schuster entered, letting the American do all the work. They shook hands briefly, and he pointed the man to a waiting chair. The broad desk stood between them like a playing field.

"I understand you've had some difficulties since last night," Janek said.

"Yes. You know the details?"

"More or less. We're waiting for a final list of casualties from the engagement in the Orange Free State. As for the rest—"

"We have a major problem," Schuster blurted, interrupting him.

The frown on Janek's face spoke volumes. "Can you be specific, *Captain* Schuster?"

If the American noted Janek's mocking tone, he covered his reaction well. "There was a prisoner in Malvern," he explained. "A black man."

"So?"

"He got away. That is, whoever crashed the party took him out of there."

"A black, you said."

"But not a native," Schuster added. "I gather they were pretty sure of that."

"How sure?"

"Enough to hold him three days while they tried to make him talk."

A worm of apprehension had begun to wriggle in the pit of Janek's stomach. "Did he talk?"

"According to the one survivor," Schuster said, "they hadn't cracked him when the roof fell in."

"So, they believe he was an infiltrator, but they haven't got the first idea of where he came from?"

Schuster nodded. "That's about the size of it."

"That's marvelous. And what am I supposed to do about it, now they've let him get away?"

"My guess would be he's in from Mozambique," said the American. "That business with Nacala has them pissed off in Maputo. They'll be looking for a chance to pay your people back."

"My people? What a wonderfully selective memory you have."

"I only meant—"

"Nacala's liquidation was a private operation, I believe."

"Which never would have gotten off the ground without intelligence from your division, Major."

"Granted . . . off the record. You will never find a single document to prove that charge."

"Who needs it? We're not suing anybody. All I'm asking for—all Willem's asking for—is some assistance in a time of need."

"If you had given me this black, he would be safely under lock and key today."

"Agreed. That would have been my first suggestion, if I'd known about him. As it is, I get the bad news just like you do, and they have me pass it on."

"This black from nowhere, does he have a name?"

"He called himself Waziri Koto. I assume it's bogus."

"We can check our lists, of course, but it's a safe assumption." Janek stared at Schuster for another moment, letting him begin to squirm. "And how am I supposed to find a nameless black man in Johannesburg, much less Soweto? It's like searching for a speck of coal dust at the bottom of a mine."

"You're saying they all look alike?"

"By no means. Only idiots believe that, in their hearts. I'm saying that the blacks have ways of covering their own when trouble comes. It doesn't matter if a black is wanted for the foulest crime, they take him in and help him hide from the police. With photographs and fingerprints, we might get lucky, searching house-to-house, but that would mean publicity, perhaps more rioting."

"We don't want that."

"So, now it's 'we.' I don't suppose a photograph was taken of this man, before the sluggers went to work?"

"No point. They didn't plan to let him go."

"Of course not. But he *is* gone, as you see. And I don't have a hint of who I'm looking for."

"It's tricky, I'll admit."

"It's a damn sight more than tricky," Janek told him, sneering as he spoke.

In fact, it could be catastrophic. If the missing black man was a spy of some sort, in from Mozambique to dig up dirt on the Nacala raid, his presence might be linked to the elusive gunman who was badgering the Wolves. But how? Since when had the Maputo government enlisted whites to raid across the border in South Africa?

And more to the point, how was Rolf Janek supposed to find either one of those nameless men, black or white, without raising a flap that would draw attention all the way to Pretoria?

"You must have contacts in the black community," Schuster said, "eyes and ears, that kind of thing."

"We do. They keep us briefed on native matters, agitators and the like. Their value in regard to spies from Mozambique is limited, at best."

"He can't just vanish," Schuster said, belaboring the obvious. "He didn't get this far without some kind of contacts in the country, right?"

"I'll make inquiries," Janek replied, incensed by Schuster's tone. He didn't need some washed-up spook to tell him how to do his job. "Of course, I can't be obvious about it, and we may get no results."

"I've been there," Schuster stated. "Just do the best you can."

"How generous." This time, he made no effort to disguise his pent-up animosity.

"It's nothing personal," the slim American assured him. "I take orders, just like everybody else. The man says 'Go and talk to Rolf.' Here I am."

"Next time," Janek answered, "if there *is* a next time, Willem should remember who his friends are. Three days wasted on a black who will not talk, and then they let him get away." He clucked his tongue and made a disapproving face.

"We've got embarrassment enough to go around," Schuster said. "At the moment, Willem's more concerned with making sure he doesn't get his ass shot off. You follow me? I'd be a liar if I didn't say the bad news from the last twelve hours has his nerves on edge. He would have come to see you on his own, but with the sniping things and all..."

He left the comment hanging there, unfinished, putting on a sympathetic air that didn't seem to fit. The last time this one sympathized with anybody, Janek thought, he had been looking out for Arnold Schuster's interest, first and foremost.

Taking care of number one.

He was a man to watch, and Janek made a mental note to do exactly that, from this day forward. The private resolution didn't stop him from shaking hands with Schuster as the visitor stood to leave.

"You'll be in touch, then?"

"Certainly. When I have something to report."

"Terrific."

That made three men to investigate, but two of them were ciphers, known by race and nothing more. The black man might have come from Mozambique. The white man who had rescued him was possibly associated with the black...or maybe not.

If they were strangers going into it, at least one thing was clear: they knew each other now. And something told Janek that they were many times more dangerous than two men acting on their own.

Of course, they hadn't dealt with Rolf Janek, yet.

They were about to learn how dangerous a man could be.

7

The Afrikaner People's Party had its central office in downtown Johannesburg, between a bookstore and a pastry shop. The bookstore was, in fact, an adjunct of the party office, stocking right-wing books and pamphlets that presumed to trace the white race back to Adam through a line of Norse and German offspring, while the other races came about by means of bestiality or Satan's curse upon mankind. It was a school of thought the Afrikaner People's Party took as gospel in its drive to bring apartheid back as the prevailing rule of law.

The party was another means for Willem Grubb to dominate white politics—by which he meant *all* politics—throughout South Africa. It was the lure he displayed for would-be followers, seducing them with visions of an Aryan Utopia where men were judged by pigment and the pale were always privileged to rule.

It was the carrot, and his White Wolves were the stick.

Mack Bolan knew the party's background from his briefing in the States. It had been operating for the past three years, achieving minor victories around Johannesburg and in the several provinces. Grubb had remained behind the scenes, so far, but no one seriously doubted he would be the party's candidate for president the first time he imagined there was any realistic hope of carrying the vote.

In recent months, the Afrikaner People's Party had been gaining strength, a beneficiary of fear and paranoia that had taken root among the nation's Boer population. Blacks had been released from total subjugation by dramatic changes in the law, the doctrine of apartheid was revoked—at least on paper—and for some the changes came too swiftly, where they came at all. Some whites were fearful of retaliation for their past mistreatment of the native population; others saw a bloody revolution coming, spawned by socialist ideals and flaming oratory. Gun stores had no dearth of customers these days, and public firing ranges crackled with the sound of a belated preparation for apocalypse.

Bolan hit the bookstore first, relieved to find himself the only customer at that time of the day. He wandered up and down the narrow aisles at will, uninterrupted, while the clerk sat behind his register and read a magazine. At several points around the shop, he left incendiary sticks wedged under books or tabloid papers, spreading them for maximum effect. When they went up, there would be no way for a single man to cover half a dozen fires.

The clerk ignored him as he left the shop and went next door. The hard part would be working up a realistic accent, German with a hint of British thrown in, from the years of occupation in the nineteenth century. No impersonator by profession, Bolan had a fair degree of field experience at taking on diverse identities, and he imagined he could pull it off.

The opposition wouldn't have much time to think, in any case.

He stepped into the office with the sun behind him, lighting up the secretary's smile. "Good day, sir. May I be of help?"

"Joseph Larsen, please." He knew the office manager by name from having telephoned an hour earlier.

"Are you expected, sir?"

"I am. Herr Grubb assured me he would call ahead."

The secretary looked confused and slightly troubled, but she stabbed a finger at the intercom and hailed the manager. Larsen was a portly man with thinning hair and a mustache that failed to compensate for what he lost on top. His suit was rumpled from the high-backed swivel chair behind his desk. He studied Bolan's face with something more than simple curiosity.

"You wish to see me?"

"Are the papers ready?"

Larsen frowned, without a clue to Bolan's meaning. "Papers? I'm afraid I don't understand."

"The papers, man! Didn't Willem call you?"

"There has been no call."

"My God, I don't believe it." Bolan made a show of glancing at his watch. "And we are almost out of time!"

"Perhaps if you explained—"

"The kafirs, man! They've hired a team of mercenaries to destroy the party and the White Wolves, too. Don't tell me Willem failed to warn you!"

"As I said—"

"Well, never mind. There's no time now. I need the files on membership, finances, everything. The money, too. Whatever's in the safe and confidential files, before they get here. Quickly, man!"

The office manager was changing colors, like a fat chameleon, pink flushing into agitated crimson. "I'm afraid I still don't understand," he said. "Who *are* you, sir?"

"I work for Willem Grubb, the same as you do, friend. Except you won't be working for him anymore, if you allow the enemy to have those documents. In fact, I'd say you won't be working anywhere."

The perky blonde had lost her smile and she was staring at them now, eyes flicking back and forth from one man to the other, following the swift exchange. Joseph Larsen thought about it for another ten or fifteen seconds, trying not to fold.

"I really ought to telephone..."

It was the cry of "Fire!" that changed his mind, a squeal that didn't seem to fit the bookstore's clerk. A glance in the direction of the windows showed them dark smoke pouring from the shop next door and drifting off across the parking lot.

"It's started, damn it!" Bolan drew the sleek Beretta from its armpit holster. "Are you satisfied?"

Larsen blinked at Bolan, the color draining from his face. "This way," he said, and turned back toward his inner sanctum. Almost as an afterthought, he barked, "Get out, Marie!"

Inside his private office, Larsen went directly to a closet and removed a metal briefcase that was large enough to pass for luggage on an airline. He deposited the briefcase on his desk and opened it, then walked back to a filing cabinet in the nearest corner of the room. He knew exactly what to look for, combing through the files and lifting out selected folders, setting them aside until he had enough to nearly fill the briefcase.

The man's eyes were frightened as he glanced from Bolan's pistol to the office door, expecting gunmen to burst in at any moment, spraying death around the room. As far as Bolan was concerned, the fire department and police would pose a greater threat, and he was running out of time.

"Come on, then! Hurry up!"

Larsen got the briefcase loaded, circling around behind his desk and kneeling on the floor. It took a heartbeat for the Executioner to realize that he was opening a floor safe, planted underneath his desk to keep it hidden from prying eyes.

"We really haven't got much cash on hand today," he stated. "I make it six or seven thousand."

"Give me what you have," Bolan said, "and be quick about it."

"Yes, of course."

The bills were neatly separated into bundles, ringed by rubber bands. Eight bundles wedged into the briefcase, filling out the space not taken up by fat manila folders.

"There, you have it all." He latched the briefcase and handed it to Bolan, clearly anxious to be gone.

"There's one more thing," Bolan told him.

"Yes? What is it?"

"When you speak to Grubb the next time, thank him for me, will you?"

"Thank him?"

"For the contribution. I'll be sure to spend it where it hurts the most."

"The contri—" Sudden understanding flooded Larsen's face, the angry color coming back. Without a thought for personal endangerment, he lunged at Bolan, groping for the metal case. "You bastard!"

Bolan caught him with a solid forearm to the throat, no killing force behind the blow, and finished with a tap from the Beretta. Larsen staggered backward, slumped against the desk and wound up panting on his hands and knees.

"Just tell him," Bolan said. "You're not the hero type."

Marie was nowhere to be seen as the warrior left the office for the short walk to his car. He heard the sirens coming as he slid behind the wheel and drove away, already thinking of the next stop on his list.

SOWETO TOWNSHIP LIES southwest of Johannesburg, separated from the white man's city by a stretch of open country and the giant mines where many of Soweto's black inhabitants worked sixty hours in a given week. In fact, the sprawling ghetto includes more than a dozen separate towns, most of them occupied by laborers and their dependents. Housing ranges from the relatively well-kept homes of black professionals, through flimsy clapboard houses, to the shantytowns where everything from corrugated tin to cardboard finds a place in the construction of pathetic shacks.

The town where Kebby Seko's contact lived was christened Meadowlands. There was no meadow to be seen, and blacks had been prohibited from owning land for many years, until the late reforms, but names meant little in the final scheme of things.

Just now, it was enough to have a place where he could rest and get his strength back, try to put out feelers for the plan that he had hatched with the American. It was basically the white man's plan, of course, and that could be a problem. Still, there was a sense of trust between them, Seko felt it in his bones.

"You are a lucky man," Jamal Tukuyo said. "You should go home. Be done with this."

"I cannot," Seko told him. "We've agreed upon a plan."

"The white man's plan." His contact made no effort to conceal the skepticism he was feeling.

"Not just his."

"Three days the white men beat you, and you find another one to be your friend before the wounds are even healed."

"He saved my life. Why would he do that, if his heart was bad?"

"A trick, perhaps. This way, he tells you where to go and what to do. You are his puppet, Kebby."

"No." The man from Mozambique felt sudden anger, whether at himself or at Tukuyo's words, he couldn't say. "He killed the men who beat me."

"So you said."

"I saw three of them die, Jamal. A White Wolf would not kill his own to fool a simple kafir."

"I suppose not." Even that admission from Tukuyo was reluctant, grudging.

"There is more."

"Eat first, talk later."

Seko ate another spoonful of the spicy lentil soup. It stung the inside of his mouth, where he had several lacerations.

"In the paper," Kebby said. "A sniper shot at Willem Grubb today."

"A sniper *missed*. Perhaps on purpose, Kebby."

"Yes! That's what I'm telling you. He spared Grubb's life to keep from handing them another martyr. If our plan succeeds, the world will see the Wolves and Willem Grubb for what they truly are."

"The world already knows," Jamal reminded him. "They pile on economic sanctions, putting black men out of work before the whites feel any kind of hardship... and the raids go on. It calls for blood."

"It calls for timing," Seko told his friend. "Grubb murdered in his office by an unknown hand, becomes a hero. Catch him with his soldiers, in commission of a crime, and you destroy the reputation with the man."

"This stranger comes from the United States?"

"Another reason to believe him," Kebby said. "He has no reason to support the terrorists."

"I do not trust the CIA. They killed Lumumba, you remember."

"More than thirty years ago, Jamal."

"They killed him, all the same."

"It was another time, with different men. I think this man will help us."

"Your superiors must still approve the plan."

"Of course."

Soweto's telephones were few and far between, with most of them installed in public buildings, virtually none in private dwellings. Seko didn't trust the local lines, in any case, suspecting they were monitored by the security police around the clock. A call to Mozambique would set alarm bells ringing, sure enough, and give the enemy a starting place.

That he was being hunted, Kebby Seko had no doubt. The White Wolves would be looking for him, and unless he missed his guess, they would recruit more eyes and ears from the police. Soweto harbored numerous informers, but Jamal Tukuyo was a trusted friend. As for his neighbors, they had seen a friend come calling; they knew nothing more.

"This plan will not be well received," Tukuyo said.

"It is my task to make them understand. We have a chance to crush the raiders, finally. It would be criminal to settle for a single man, when we can stop them all."

"But drawing them to Mozambique, another raid..." Tukuyo frowned and shook his head. "Suppose it leads to war?"

"It won't. Pretoria cannot afford to claim Grubb's private army as an adjunct to the lawful government. They seek improved relations with the West, not total isolation. If the Wolves are caught in Mozambique, their fate is sealed."

"Unless they slip away. You've had no great luck catching them on other raids."

"Because they always took us by surprise," Kebby replied. "This time, we'll be waiting for them. We select the killing ground, the date and time. With troops in place they will not stand a chance of getting out.''

"You hope.''

"I'll bet my life on it.''

"My friend,'' Jamal Tukuyo told him, "you already have.''

THE WEAPONS DEPOT was a small house on the western outskirts of Johannesburg. It rented by the year, the lease made out to one of Willem Grubb's lieutenants, under a fictitious name. The tenant was a young man, thirty-something, and a foreman at a local diamond mine. His neighbors didn't have a clue that he was also a committed terrorist, but several, if they had known, would have lined up on the porch to shake his hand.

The house was ordinary in appearance, two small bedrooms and a scruffy yard. It could have used fresh paint. If the police turned up with warrants, they would search the rooms in vain for any contraband. It would require a specialist to find the trapdoor, hidden underneath the master bedroom's faded carpeting, that opened on the only basement in the neighborhood.

Downstairs, secure against the damp in airtight lockers, Grubb's commandos kept a stash of automatic weapons, ammunition and explosives. It was relatively small, compared to other stockpiles, but the hardware would have sold for several hundred thousand dollars on the open market. There were killing tools enough to stage a minor coup or spread death far and wide in isolated raids.

This arsenal was going out of business, though, if Bolan had his way.

He half expected guards, but saw none on his drive-by, scouting out the neighborhood. At that, he played it safe and drove around the block, to park outside a vacant house that showed a realtor's sign in front. If anyone was watching, Bolan hoped his van and workman's coveralls would lead them to believe the house was undergoing some repairs.

He took the toolbox with his hardware stashed inside and walked around in back. The yard had gone to weeds behind its faded wooden fence, except where tethered dogs had left a bare strip on the northeast corner. Bolan stood beside the fence and faced diagonally toward his target, one house down.

Not bad.

He set down the toolbox and opened it, removed the Uzi submachine gun, extra magazines and silencer, grenades, the satchel charge. He might not use it all, but there was safe, and there was sorry. Given any choice at all, the Executioner would always bet on safe.

He took a moment to prepare himself, attached the Uzi's threaded silencer, fed surplus magazines and frag grenades into the spacious pockets of his coveralls. No war paint, this time; nothing to disguise his face.

The fence had never been designed to frustrate a determined climber. Bolan checked the house directly opposite his vantage point, saw curtains drawn across the windows and made his move. Another moment put him on the back steps of his target dwelling, one hand on the doorknob, peering through a window that hadn't been washed in months.

The kitchen was deserted. Bolan tried the knob and felt it turn. He stepped across the threshold, barely breathing, nostrils flaring at the scent of unwashed dishes in the sink. He left the door ajar and crossed the kitchen, following the sound of voices from another room beyond.

His information on the hidden arsenal had come from Kebby Seko, picked up on the street from God knew where. It would have been impossible for Seko to approach the house, a black man in the all-white neighborhood, but he had stored the information for future use. The target was ideal for Bolan, but before he pulled out all the stops, he had to reassure himself that Seko hadn't been misled.

Doubts vanished as he reached the open doorway to the living room. Two men were seated on the couch, three feet of empty space between them, watching news on television. Bolan didn't understand the newsman's monologue in Afrikaans, but even shaky video couldn't disguise the old apartment house in Malvern, photographed with shrouded bodies coming out the door on stretchers.

On the coffee table, arm's length from the nearer man, an automatic pistol lay beside an open can of lager. Number two was working on his beer, no gun in evidence, but he was almost certain to be armed.

The Executioner retreated silently to check the bath and bedrooms. All the doors stood open, and he scanned each empty room in turn. The larger of the bedrooms was his final target, but he had to take the watchdogs first, before he fouled their den.

Returning to the parlor, Bolan stood beside the open door, half-covered by the wall, both targets still within his line of fire. They were engrossed with beer and bad news on the tube, occasionally muttering what might have been a curse, exchanging sidelong glances, shaking heads.

He knew the feeling: they were soldiers of a sort, remembering their fallen comrades. Each new loss confronted them with grim reminders of their own mortality, made them realize that even members of the so-called master race were only human, after all.

The newscast switched to a commercial, and he made his move.

"Hello, there."

Both men jumped, the nearer swiveling to face his adversary at an awkward angle, while his sidekick choked on beer and let the can slip from his fingers.

Number one was first to make a move, and when it came, he did it wrong. His left hand stabbed out toward the pistol on the coffee table, groping blindly, while he never took his eyes off Bolan's face. He made it, but the piece was backward for his left, inverted like a bludgeon, when he brought it back around.

The Uzi stuttered, half a dozen parabellum manglers ripping through the gunner's chest and dumping him beside the sofa. His companion didn't try to hide. Instead he rose to face the enemy, one hand already slipping back to find the pistol tucked inside his waistband, on the right.

Another muffled burst, and it was over. Number two went down and took the coffee table with him, crushing it beneath his deadweight.

Retreating to the master bedroom, Bolan left his satchel charge and Uzi in the hallway, found the loose edge of the carpet on the threshold, and began to drag it back. He found the trapdoor with its recessed ring and flipped it open. Darkness waited at the bottom of a ladder, just below his feet.

He used a pencil flash to sweep the basement, leaning through the open trapdoor, lighting metal ammo boxes, longer crates for weapons, counting three times over.

The warrior had seen enough. He went back for the satchel charge and set five minutes on the timer, leaned in through the hatch and let it dangle by the canvas strap. It was a simple toss, no skill required. The charge dropped squarely on a pile of ammunition crates.

Retreating past the parlor, through the kitchen, Bolan heard the doomsday numbers falling in his head. He crossed the yard and scaled the wooden fence, used precious time to stow his weapons in the toolbox once again before returning to his van.

He was a full block out and rolling when it blew, a muffled blast at first, and black smoke rising in his rearview mirror. When the buried ammo started going off, it sounded like a down-home Independence Day.

Not yet, the warrior told himself, but someday. Someday soon.

His latest strike wouldn't defeat the Wolves; it wasn't designed to, but he trusted it would keep the heat on Willem Grubb and company. In time, when they were offered an escape hatch, he was betting they would take it. Anything to get the biting, scratching monkey off their backs.

And by the time they found out they had walked into a slaughterhouse, it just might be too late.

8

"You still don't have to do this."

"So I understand," Richard Modu answered.

It was almost comic, lying on the floor behind the driver's seat, while Bridget Linder drove him through Johannesburg, but they had taken pains to keep their meetings secret, and he didn't want to jeopardize her safety now.

"You trust this man."

It hadn't been a question, but she answered all the same. "I do. I can't say why I do, exactly. There's a quality about him, almost like..."

"Your husband?"

"No." She sounded sure about that part, at least. "Jan never would have tried the things this man has done. He had a different kind of courage, Richard."

"Yes. He was a good man, Bridget."

"Even so."

He waited for the rest of it, but nothing came. Modu shifted, rolling over on his side, and wondered how much farther they would have to go before they reached the meeting place.

He was accustomed to clandestine meetings, from his years as the Soweto secretary of the African National Congress. A lifelong moderate, he had been forced to spend the best part of his life in hiding, even though he didn't advocate armed violence, leaving talk of revolution to groups like the Azanian People's Liberation Army or the ANC's own militant wing, Umkhonto we Sizwe. Any blacks who didn't bow and scrape before the master race were "Communists" in those days—some in fact, as well as in the censored press—but atheism held no great appeal for Richard Modu. He still believed, in spite of all that he had seen and suffered in his thirty years, that there must be some grand design for life, a greater peace than he had so far known on earth.

Modu hoped he wouldn't have to die before he found that peace, but he was ready when the time came. He had lived with Death so long, now, he was certain it could never take him wholly by surprise.

He had agreed to meet the stranger with reluctance, giving in when Bridget asked because he loved her like a sister, owed her much, and knew that he could always walk away if there was too much risk involved. In ordinary circumstances, he wouldn't have played the white man's game, but things were far from ordinary in South Africa these days.

The natives hadn't triumphed yet, but it was coming. Modu felt it in his bones, and die-hard bigots in the white camp felt it, too. They were prepared for war, a last-ditch stand to save their dying system and the privileges accumulated over generations of oppression.

Moderate that Modu was, he realized that it wouldn't be possible to win the final victory without blood being spilled.

The stranger, this Belasko person from America, professed to have a plan that would insure the White Wolves got the worst of any confrontation that erupted. If it worked, Modu told himself, South Africa might be a slightly better place.

But if it failed...

Modu feared for Bridget Linder, if the plan went wrong. She was exposed, a member of the white community already marked as having "doubtful" loyalty to the state. No matter that the state was changing, shedding its repressive skin in favor of a touted fling at human rights. Old prejudice and patterns of behavior didn't vanish with a presidential proclamation or the passage of a law.

"I hope you're right about this man," he said.

"No obligations, Richard. If you have the slightest reservation, all you have to do is tell me. I appreciate your willingness to listen."

He had listened to the radio and read the daily tabloids, all about the recent violence in Johannesburg and elsewhere. The security police were holding certain information under wraps, he knew, and the reporters made up certain "facts" to suit themselves. But Modu had a fair idea of what had happened in the past twelve hours, give or take.

Someone, perhaps this Belasko, had begun to hit the White Wolves where they lived. The body count was rising rapidly, and they were all white bodies for a change. How long before the bigots started hitting back at random? Would they blame the ANC and try to make Mandela's people pay? Would the Pretoria regime declare a national emergency, imposing martial law?

"I hope it's not much farther, Bridget."

"Three miles, maybe four," she answered, checking out the rearview mirror for potential followers. "It won't be long."

He knew where they were going, but without the visuals he lost track of direction and the passing time. It stood to reason Bridget had to have added several extra turns, to see if they were being tailed. She knew the drill from dozens of clandestine meetings with Modu and his friends. He only hoped the stranger knew as much and took precautions of his own.

They slowed dramatically, turned left and crept forward. This would be the parking lot, he reasoned, Bridget looking for her contact, ready to depart at speed if there were any indications of a trap. Modu wasn't armed, but he would fight before he let the white men take him, even if it cost his life.

"They're here," she said.

That had to mean the stranger and his new companion, someone even Bridget hadn't seen. In retrospect, Modu wondered if he had been wise or foolish to accompany her this far.

Too late for second thoughts, in any case. Whatever lay in store for them, it was about to bridge the gap between anticipation and established fact.

"I see him," Bridget announced. "He's brought a van."

Another moment, and they pulled into a parking space. From his position on the floor, Modu glimpsed a gray van close beside them, on the driver's side. He stayed exactly where he was, while Bridget left the car and spent a moment talking to her contact, checking out the parking lot for spies. The instant that the back door opened, Modu made his move, a flying lunge between the Volvo and the open side door of the van.

Inside, when they were buttoned down, he huddled on a jump seat next to Bridget, facing two men he had never seen before: one white, one black. He wore a solemn face as Bridget made the introductions.

"Richard Modu, from the ANC, meet Mike Belasko from America and Kebby Seko, just arrived from Mozambique."

THEY COULDN'T MEET at Bridget Linder's home a second time, and Bolan had invited her to pick the spot. She named a shopping mall in Auckland Park and specified the west-side parking lot. For reasons of security, he didn't furnish a description of his vehicle, nor did he mention Kebby Seko on the telephone. They kept it short and cryptic, breaking off as soon as possible, the Executioner to make his pickup on the outskirts of Soweto and return to keep the rendezvous on time.

He thought that Kebby Seko looked a little better, after cleaning up and resting for a bit, but it was obvious that he was still in pain. They made the drive in silence, for the most part, Seko riding in the back and out of sight. The fact that he was carrying a pistol now, beneath his baggy shirt, didn't faze Bolan in the least.

In Auckland Park, he found the mall and circled west to reach the parking lot selected for the meet. Beyond the lot itself, no certain place was specified. He lingered in the driver's seat—a husband waiting for his wife, perhaps—and scrutinized each passing vehicle with care, alert for any glimpse of Bridget Linder—or a trap.

He didn't think that she would sell him out, but there was still a chance she might be followed. They had used a cut-

out when they spoke, his call to Bridget's home disguised as
a wrong number, slipping in directions to a pay phone near
her house. Ten minutes later, he had dialed the pay phone's
number and she picked up, right on time.

The only problem, now, would be a tail.

He made the Volvo from a distance, recognizing Bridget
at the wheel. He raised a hand; she saw him, pulling in beside the van. A hurried consultation, Bridget checking out
the lot herself, and then they made the transfer, her companion bolting from the Volvo's back seat to the van. If
anyone was watching, they were far away and hidden well
enough that Bolan couldn't spot them.

Bridget made the introductions, and they shook hands all
around. Modu was a slender man with close-cropped hair,
and he stood at least three inches shorter than the Executioner. He didn't fit the image of a wild-eyed terrorist, de-
scribed by Afrikaners when they spoke about the ANC.
Still, there were different factions in the movement, Bolan
knew, as in the civil rights campaign back home. Some went
for civil disobedience, while others staked their hopes on
power politics...and there were always some who favored
picking up the gun.

Modu broke the ice when they had finished shaking
hands. "What brings my brother here from Mozambique?" he asked.

"The men who call themselves White Wolves have several times crossed over to my country," Seko told him. "You
must know this. Very recently they murdered Julius Nacala
in his home."

"A faithful friend," Modu said. "He will be missed."

"The best way to remember him," said Kebby Seko, "is
by punishing the men who took his life."

Modu frowned at that. "We have already too much
bloodshed in South Africa," he said. "It seems a shame for
you to bring us more."

"I come for information only," Seko answered. "See my
wounds, and tell me who is violent."

"I would not have you suffer so," Modu said. "But there has been much killing since last night. Perhaps if you went home..."

His shifting glance included Bolan in the statement, and the warrior took that as his cue. "I'm responsible for the events you speak of. Kebby Seko had no part in any of the incidents, except as victim."

"I will accept your word on that. But you are an American, correct?"

"I am."

"What brings you here to kill South Africans of either race?"

"The Wolves are branching out," Bolan answered, "and the government has shown itself unable or unwilling to control them. They're raiding into Mozambique, Lesotho and Botswana, that we know of."

"African concerns, my friend. I'm sure you mean well, but— "

"Would you prefer to see them trample every native in the southern half of Africa? And what about apartheid? They're gaining power by the day, in politics. Between the bullet and the ballot box, they stand a chance of coming out on top, next time the presidential seat is up for grabs."

"A slim chance, possibly," Modu stated, "but the election of another bigot will not change the course of destiny."

"You may be right," Bolan said, "but a racist with a private army *and* the state behind him could erase the progress you've achieved these past few years."

"The people won't allow it."

"Meaning revolution?" Bolan asked. "That's not what I'd call an alternative to violence."

"History decides such matters."

"And the winners write the textbooks," Kebby Seko added, frowning as he spoke. "Sometimes it helps to give the course of destiny a nudge along the way."

"I've heard that argument before," Modu said.

"But did you listen?"

"Violence solves nothing in the long run."

"I respect your feelings," Bolan told him, "but technically, you're wrong. Eliminate a bully absolutely, and he can't harass you anymore."

"Until another bully takes his place."

"A different bully, possibly. We guard against that process by discrediting the apparatus, showing up the system for exactly what it is. Night crawlers hate the light of day."

"I will not urge my brothers to participate in acts of terrorism," Modu stated.

"No one asked you to," the Executioner replied. "We're hoping you may have the opposite effect."

"This plan of yours sounds most complex," the ANC official said.

"Your role, if you decide to help us, would be relatively simple."

"Simple?"

"All you have to do is go to jail."

"Pardon?"

"Let us start from the beginning," Kebby Seko said. "We share your wish that any major drive against the White Wolves should take place outside South Africa. Ideally we should hope to catch them in another country—Mozambique, for instance—where their criminal designs may be exposed for all to see."

"And what has that to do with me in prison?" Modu asked.

"Not prison," Bolan answered. "Jail. Specifically, detainment for interrogation by the state security police."

Modu stared at Bolan for a moment. "I have been their guest before," he said at last. "Twice I survived interrogation and was freed, no charges filed."

"That's what I understand. You know the ropes."

"What I *don't* understand is how my being jailed and beaten helps your cause . . . much less my own."

"We think Grubb's people work with the security police," Bridget said, laying one hand on Modu's arm. "You've said the same yourself."

"Of course." Modu kept his eyes on Bolan. "It is like the Ku Klux Klan in your United States. When bigots carry badges, they cooperate and scheme with others of their kind. I would expect no less."

"Exactly," Seko interjected. "That is why we need a man inside."

"Inside a cell?"

"Where better to supply the enemy with false directions, brother?"

"Twice they have interrogated me for six or seven days, nonstop. Four times I've been assaulted on the street by men who might have been plainclothes police. I never cried for mercy, never told them anything about the movement."

"Here's your chance," Bolan said. "And we haven't got six days."

Modu hesitated, weighing options in his mind. At last, he said, "Explain the plan."

"Tomorrow's *Chronicle* will carry advertisements for a brand-new series," Bridget told him, "documenting links between white terrorism and the state police. They will attempt to stop me first, I think."

"You take this risk for strangers?" Modu asked.

"No, for friends. For Jan. And for myself."

"We'll have her covered," Bolan said.

"I disappear," the lady publisher explained. "For safety's sake."

"I see." Modu sounded skeptical. "And where do I come in?"

"With your permission," Bridget said, "I'd like to name you as a source in the announcement of the series. It should be enough for the security police to pick you up."

"I daresay. And assuming I agree to play this game, what should I tell our friends? You have a message all prepared?"

"You tell them where she's hiding," Bolan answered.

"Mozambique?"

"We have precise coordinates, if you decide to play along. They'll find a farmhouse waiting for them . . . and a bit of a surprise."

"That still leaves me in jail," Modu pointed out.

"With nothing they can charge you on," the Executioner replied. "Admission of involvement with the Wolves would leave them open to at least a dozen different felony indictments. Anyway, by that time we should have the evidence we need to sink the officers involved. Whichever way it goes, you walk."

"Assuming I still can."

"Nobody's asking you to run a marathon. As it is, the sooner you break down, the better. We should have the wheels in motion by tonight, tomorrow morning at the latest."

"But the morning paper—"

"One of Grubb's good buddies is about to get a tip he can't ignore," Bolan said. "We'll be rolling by tonight, unless I miss my guess."

"The only question," Kebby Seko said, "is whether you will help us strike this blow."

Modu thought about it for another moment, finally nodding. "I will," he said. "But start from the beginning one more time."

THE DRIVE BACK to Soweto seemed to take forever, lying on the Volvo's floor, behind the driver's seat. Modu was embarrassed to discover that his hands were trembling.

"This plan is dangerous for you," he said to Bridget Linder, hoping she would change her mind, dead certain she wouldn't.

"I'm not afraid," she told him.

"Even knowing what they did to Jan?"

"Because of what they did. The bastards have already done their worst to me. I'm not afraid."

"You should be," he advised her. "You are still alive, still young."

"I'll be alive tomorrow, Richard."

"Maybe. Maybe not."

"I trust these men."

"You hardly know them. They are strangers."

"No more strangers than you were when we met, five years ago."

"That's different," he insisted.

"How?"

"I knew your husband."

"You and Jan were strangers once, I think."

"It is impossible to argue with a woman."

"Only when you're wrong," she told him, laughing at his chauvinist remark.

"I hope your estimation is correct."

Another silent mile slid by, and then she asked, "Are you afraid of the security police?"

"Of course," he told her honestly. "I know firsthand what they can do. But I will keep my word."

"Perhaps you shouldn't," Bridget said. "I mean, if anything goes wrong—"

"You trust these men enough for both of us. And I trust you."

"Don't make them hurt you, Richard. When they start to question you, just tell them what they want to know. It should be easy."

Modu had to smile at that. For all her knowledge of South Africa and human rights in general, Bridget hadn't grasped the central truth of a police state. Truth was never simple. It would never be enough. Interrogators came to every confrontation counting on their subjects to evade, deceive, prevaricate. The easy answers were rejected automatically as false, until coercion verified the "facts." In that way, truth was sometimes lost, the state persuaded to accept elaborate lies, concocted simply to prevent more pain.

No, it wouldn't be easy. He could vouch for that from personal experience.

But he would keep his word.

"You think eliminating Willem Grubb will change the country?"

Bridget shrugged. "It can't do any harm. Exposing his connection to the state is bound to raise some eyebrows, maybe even lead to an investigation of his crimes."

"The White Wolves are a symptom, not the problem."

"Agreed. But sometimes you can treat the symptoms and the illness, all at once."

"It would be nice to think so."

"Why do you keep on, if you believe it's hopeless, Richard?"

"Hopeless? Not at all." He frowned at the suggestion. "There is always hope. Without it, we are nothing."

"Hope and action," she corrected him. "We don't gain anything by standing on the sidelines, watching the parade go past."

"This isn't a parade," he told her. "It's an army, marching off to war."

"Sometimes," she said, "things don't get done without a fight."

"Is that what Jan believed?" He regretted the words, almost before they had left his lips.

"He died believing men could be persuaded by the printed word," she said. "It's true of some, but not for others. I don't plan to make the same mistake."

"I never saw you as a warrior, Bridget."

"Maybe we were both wrong, Richard."

"There are people in Johannesburg who would be glad to kill us both for riding down the street together," Modu said.

"I don't care what they'd like to do. Grubb's men are doing it right now."

"Two men against an army. I don't like the odds."

"But there are four of us," she pointedly reminded him.

"With one in hiding and another one in jail, that still makes two."

"They might find help in Mozambique."

"The government won't take a white man on to help them. No, they'll find themselves alone."

"Then, two will have to be enough."

"You still believe in magic, do you?"

"No," she said. "In hope."

Ten minutes brought them to a market on the outskirts of Soweto. Bridget parked the car and spent a moment rummaging inside her handbag.

"Please be careful, Richard." And with that, she left him on his own.

Modu raised his head to scan the parking lot, making certain there was no one to observe him as he left the Volvo. Even though he planned to be arrested in a few more hours, it wouldn't serve anyone's design if he was picked up as a car thief.

He began the short walk to Soweto proper. Moments later, when he stopped and looked back toward the market, Bridget's car was gone.

9

Although he wasn't fool enough to blame the telephone for bad news, Arnold Schuster had begun to hate it, all the same. Each time the damned thing rang, it seemed he had another problem on his hands, demanding full attention on the spot. Not one of them could wait, it seemed, until he caught a breather from the rest.

It had begun that morning with the call from Willem Grubb, which put him on the line for some demented bastard with a sniper's rifle. Bad enough that Grubb's commandos had been taking hits since midnight, now their faceless enemy was stalking Schuster with the rest.

No, that was wrong.

If anything, the shooter had been going after Grubb. It was a miracle he didn't nail them both, the way he dusted Willem's bodyguard... or, was it?

Could the whole bizarre event have been a warning, somehow? Was the sniper really that good?

Schuster knew that it was possible, of course. Too young for Vietnam, he had participated in a couple of the covert Reagan wars, when he was working for the Company, and he was perfectly aware that there were shooters out there who could clip your foreskin at a thousand yards, if they were so inclined.

And that was with your pants on.

Still, it was hard to figure. The attacks on Grubb's command hadn't been any kind of warnings. Men were killed, equipment blown away—and not just in the boonies, either. In addition to the sniping, there had also been a series of attacks around Johannesburg. At least eight men were dead, an arms stash blown to hell, a hostage liberated—not to mention some guy torching Willem's bookstore, waltzing out with cash and information on the movement that should never have been put on paper in the first place.

Stupid bastards!

Grubb was paying Schuster handsomely for his professional advice, but that advice was only followed half the time. Grubb needed contacts in the outside world, for arms and other things, so he had hired himself a fixer. On the flip side, though, when Schuster spotted problems with the way Grubb's troop was organized, maintained—whatever—it was argued that he "did not understand South Africa."

Terrific.

It was one thing when the action all took place across the border, in Botswana or some other godforsaken spot. In that case, Schuster could sit back and draw his paycheck, shrug it off if things went badly for the White Wolves in the field. He "did not understand South Africa"—their leader told him so—and how could anyone expect him to produce the satisfactory results?

But it was something else, you bet, when bullets started striking close to home. When Schuster's life was riding on the line, he didn't give a tinker's damn for Willem Grubb's opinion of the local politics or any other goddamned thing. Survival was the top priority, and he was looking out for number one with all the skill at his disposal. If it came to bailing out and leaving Grubb to sink or swim, well, Schuster was prepared to do that, too.

It wouldn't be the first time he had left a client in the lurch. That kind of thing could hurt your reputation in the long run, but it helped to know that none of those who might complain were still alive.

Of course, if Schuster had a choice, he would prefer to hang around and let the snow-white goose turn out a few more golden eggs before he hit the road. In times like these, the more cash you could lay your hands on in emergencies, the better. There was no such thing as having "too much" money in reserve.

The blinds were closed across his office windows, shutting out the sun. The plastic slats wouldn't stop a bullet—much less a rocket or rifle grenade—but Schuster still wasn't convinced the gunmen had him marked for death.

It might be wishful thinking, but he had enough experience with killers and with killing situations to believe that he could tell the difference.

The telephone was ringing, and his secretary was at lunch. He thought of just ignoring it, this once, but then decided that it might turn out to be important, something he could use to help himself and put the rocky ground behind him for a while. Reluctantly he lifted the receiver and punched a flashing button to connect the line.

"Hello?"

"How are you, Arnold?"

"Who is this?" Suspicion tickled the short hairs on his nape.

"We've never met. You wouldn't know my name."

"So, try me."

"Armstrong," the stranger said. "You can call me Jack."

For just a heartbeat, Schuster felt as if he had been punched directly in the solar plexus. "Jack Armstrong" was the recognition tag they used to introduce a fellow operative when he was working for the Company. It came from a cartoon strip, well before his time, but it had staying power, handed down from members of the old guard to the new guys coming in.

Jack Armstrong, the All-American Boy.

What better label for a spook who was prepared to lie, steal, sabotage and murder in the service of his country?

"Jack, of course. What brings you to Johannesburg?"

"I'm in between engagements, running errands for the Company," his caller said. "Thing is, I've stumbled onto something you should know about."

"Such as?"

"I'd rather talk about it face-to-face."

"Well, that's a problem, Jack."

"It could be worse, if someone's listening."

"I see."

In fact, he didn't see a goddamned thing, except that "Armstrong" was afraid of taps on Schuster's line. He could have told the guy that it was clear, he had connections to the state security police...but when he thought about it, Schuster wondered just how much protection he could count on from those friends of Grubb's. They hadn't done a thing to help the Wolves, so far. In fact, for all he knew, the sneaky bastards might be listening on Grubb's behalf, to double-check on Schuster's loyalty perhaps, or monitor the line for threats.

"We really ought to have this talk," the spook said, prodding him.

"What kind of schedule are you on?"

"My time is your time, Arnold, but I wouldn't wait too long."

"You *are* in Jo'burg?"

"More or less."

"Let's split the difference. There's a sidewalk restaurant in Selby, La Parisienne." He gave directions, naming streets. "I'll meet you there."

"No problem, Arnold."

It was getting on his nerves, this first-name crap, but Schuster let it slide. "Shall we say forty minutes?"

"Forty minutes suits me fine."

"How will I know you?"

"I'll know you."

The line went dead. Schuster muttered a curse as he cradled the receiver. That was all he needed at the moment, stupid cloak-and-dagger games, when he was busy trying to protect himself from unknown enemies. The more he thought about it now, the less he liked the whole idea.

It would be no great trick, he knew, for someone from the Company to track him down, but why would anybody make the effort? If the team at Langley wanted Schuster dead, they would have taken him by now. Of course, they had to stop and think about the information packets he had stashed in safe-deposit boxes on three continents, addressed to major newspapers and magazines, with postage paid for instant shipment if he failed to get in touch for any length of time.

He turned the problem upside down and thought about it from another angle. If the Company found out that someone else was trying for a tag on Schuster, would they help him out? He had no friends among the Langley brass, that much he knew beyond the shadow of a doubt. But would they make a token effort to assist him, out of selfish interest? Would an agent in the field break ranks to pass a warning on his own?

And if he did, that left the question of location. Granted, Schuster had been using his own name around Johannesburg, but he wasn't in any telephone directory, nor had he any reason to believe his presence in South Africa was common knowledge.

The meet could be a setup, granted, but his basic curiosity was kicking in. Besides, in Schuster's experience, the Company didn't announce itself like that before its operatives took you out. If someone out of Langley had a hit in mind, against their own best interest, Schuster would expect a more creative ambush from the old home team.

The racetrack was an easy five miles from his office, slow in city traffic, better once you left the downtown sprawl behind you, running south toward Selby. Schuster thought about alerting Grubb before he left the office, and decided not to bother. Willem had enough to think about, the way things were, and Schuster didn't care to bother with the kind of escorts Grubb would send, assuming he had any men to spare.

He took a pistol with him, though, the Ruger KF-91 he had been carrying since his arrival in Johannesburg. The piece was stainless steel, mat finish, double-action, chambered for the Smith & Wesson .40-caliber now standard with the FBI back home. The magazine contained eleven rounds, and Schuster kept a live one in the chamber, with the hammer down. Two extra magazines were slotted into special pockets in the lining of his sport coat, just in case.

An outing with a fellow spook, for God's sake. It was hardly what he had expected, but it just might do him good.

He rode the elevator down to the garage and kept his right hand near the Ruger as he walked back to his car. Another moment put him at the wheel. Three minutes later he was on the street.

Going to meet Jack Armstrong, the All-American Boy.

EMERGING FROM the phone booth, Bolan walked back to the van where Kebby Seko waited in the driver's seat. The man from Mozambique was nervous, but he did a decent job of hiding it.

"A sidewalk restaurant in Selby," Bolan told him. "La Parisienne. He gave us forty minutes."

"We'll have time to check the neighborhood?"

"It should be plenty." Bolan hesitated. "Due south, ten minutes, give or take."

"All right." He sat bolt upright in the driver's seat and clenched the steering wheel as if to hold himself erect.

"If there's a problem—"

"No, I'm ready," Seko answered. "I just want to do it properly."

"Just pick your stand and keep it simple," Bolan said. "You know the signal."

Seko lifted one hand off the steering wheel and scratched his earlobe. "Yes, I have it."

"Good. Let's roll."

Bolan's car was parked beside the van, the key in the ignition. The warrior swung out of the service station's parking lot and checked his rearview mirror as he merged with traffic. Two cars back, the van nosed into line behind him, keeping pace.

No problem, right. Except that any one of several hundred things could still go wrong and spoil the setup. Schuster could be paranoid enough to call for reinforcements, try to lay some kind of ambush at the restaurant. The prospect was unlikely, granted, but it couldn't be ruled out.

If there were shooters at the meeting, Bolan would be forced to scrub the plan and do his best with what he had...and it wouldn't be much. A foul-up now would jeopardize the whole play. Without the Schuster contact, Bolan ran a risk of losing the initiative, however briefly.

And that, he decided, couldn't be allowed.

For Kebby's part to work, it was essential that his meet with Schuster be conducted in the open air. If the man had suggested talking at his office, Bolan was prepared to counter with a nearby park, but the former agent's CIA conditioning was obviously still in force. For meetings with a stranger, he liked public places, ample visibility and multiple escape routes if the game went sour.

Excellent.

He planned to shake the man's confidence, not crush it. Giving Schuster room to run, ensuring that he got away to tell the tale, was part of Bolan's plan. It did no good to set him up and go through all the motions, if he kept the vital information to himself.

But he couldn't forget that they were gambling with Bridget Linder's life.

The lady had her share of guts, and then some, but her blithe acceptance of the risks involved didn't put Bolan's mind at ease. No matter how he tried to cover her, there was a chance of error, something that would allow the enemy to reach her while his back was turned, his consciousness absorbed with other things.

The hiding place had been her own selection, with collaboration from Modu and the ANC. At that, the certain knowledge of her whereabouts would be entrusted only to a chosen handful, men and women she had known for years, and whom she counted as her friends. If anything went wrong on that end, Bolan was assured that Modu knew exactly who to blame and what reprisals should be taken.

Not that payback would do Bridget any good, if she was dead.

The warrior told himself that possibility was still remote, perhaps one in a thousand if her friends were loyal and covered all the bases on security. It would be Bolan's job to keep the White Wolves occupied, so busy chasing shadows that they had no time for substance.

If it worked, he meant to waltz them through a series of disasters that could doom the movement and expose its covert allies in the ruling government. The warrior had no guarantee that it would all go smoothly, but he trusted Kebby Seko, and the rest would have to take care of itself.

Behind him, Seko was invisible, a glare of sunlight on the windshield hiding him, the gray van drifting in and out of view. As long as he kept pace and spotted the café where Bolan was supposed to meet his contact, they were fine.

The traffic wasn't bad, all things concerned. In Los Angeles or New York City, for example, traveling the same half mile could take three-quarters of an hour, and the locals wouldn't bat an eye. Johannesburg, a sprawling city in its own right, still had room to grow and breathe, as if its layout was symbolic of South Africa at large.

The winds of change were blowing through Johannesburg these days, and through the countryside at large. When Bolan sniffed that wind, it brought the smell of death to nostrils long familiar with the dark aroma. Nor was carnage in South Africa restricted to the long-term clash of white and black, which the removal of apartheid had done little—some said nothing—to alleviate. The native tribes were also at each other's throats, with Zulus in the thick of things, and Bantu warriors giving back as good as they received.

It was a recipe for chaos and disaster. Bolan couldn't help but wonder what his own grim contribution to the mix would mean, in terms of ultimate solutions to the many problems facing black and white South Africans each day. If nothing else, he thought, at least one vehicle for mayhem would have been eliminated, some corrupt officials purged from office, making way for others who—if it wasn't naive to think so—might attempt to do a better job than those who went before.

A white-on-blue metallic sign told Bolan he had entered Selby proper. His mind ticked off the spook's directions, turning left, then right, then right again, the gray van sticking with him all the way. He tried to put himself in Seko's place, a black man driving through the heart of white South

Africa and concentrating on the traffic laws with a fanatic's zeal, afraid of what might happen if police found any cause at all to stop the van.

It didn't happen, though, and Seko was a short half block behind him when he spotted La Parisienne. It was a fair-sized restaurant, with half its tables fronting on the sidewalk empty as he passed.

At least, the warrior thought, they shouldn't have a problem finding seats.

He motored past, examining the restaurant itself, the shops on either side, and those across the street. Unless the place was normally reserved for Schuster's meetings, watched routinely by a stationary team of gunners, Bolan reckoned it was safe. A phone call could work miracles, sometimes, but there was no way it could zap a shooting team across Johannesburg, from Schuster's office or another point of origin, to La Parisienne.

If there were gunners coming, they would be behind him, and his instinct told him Schuster would be traveling alone.

He drove around the block, and by the time he made his second pass, Seko's van had disappeared. It was supposed to work that way, of course, but there was still a fleeting moment of uneasiness, and Bolan double-checked his mirror, searching for signs of a patrol car's flashing lights.

All clear.

The rest of it was up to him.

A block up from the restaurant, he found a high-rise public parking garage and took a ticket at the entrance, following the painted arrows upward until he found an empty space three floors about ground level. The garage wouldn't have been his first choice, but it hardly mattered. It was situated well beyond the meeting place, and shouldn't be included in a cordon if, against all odds, police arrived before the Executioner could slip away.

He stood beside the car and scanned the floor of the garage to either side, in search of chance arrivals or departures. Finally convinced that he was alone, he slipped his jacket off, removed the shoulder holster, slipped it underneath the driver's seat and locked the car. That done, he shrugged the jacket on and struck off toward the numbered door that opened on a stairway to the street below.

It was a calculated risk, abandoning his side arm for the meeting, but he knew that agents of the CIA were typically prohibited from packing weapons while in transit. Any hardware they required could be provided by a local station chief, once they had demonstrated need and cleared the proper channels. Getting caught with firearms or explosives in the third world left an agent open to arrest and prosecution, facing prison time in nations where the Company had little influence.

The arms restriction would be known to Arnold Schuster from personal experience. If Bolan showed up packing, Schuster might decide to run or produce a weapon of his own, and that would blow the game before they even had a chance to play.

The goal, at this point, went far beyond removing Arnold Schuster. Bolan could have easily accomplished that when he was studying the former agent through his sniper scope that morning, or at any time since then. In fact, while Schuster was a part of the dilemma in Johannesburg, he also offered part of the solution.

Killing him just now, before he had a chance to help clean up his mess, would be a waste of time and energy.

Alive, he might redeem himself, albeit in a state of total ignorance. And when his time was up, when Schuster had outlived his usefulness . . .

No problem. He could smoke a turncoat anytime.

The Executioner was whistling softly as he closed the door behind him, paused and listened on the landing, making sure he had the stairwell to himself. When he was satisfied, he started down to meet the man.

10

Across the street from La Parisienne, the plate-glass window of a pharmacy served Bolan as a huge reflecting mirror, giving him a fair view of the restaurant and shops on either side. He stood and browsed, examining the pharmacy's display of items that appeared to have no link at all to medicine or illness. There were beauty products, cameras and watches, snorkels and a set of swim fins. Everything the downcast convalescent needed to recuperate.

No Arnold Schuster, though. Not yet.

Ten minutes remained before their scheduled meeting. He pictured Schuster sitting in his office for a moment, after hanging up the telephone, deciding whether he should keep the date or blow it off. The man would hesitate while he considered calling out a bodyguard, but that would probably consume more time than Schuster had allowed himself for meeting "Armstrong" at the restaurant. From what the warrior could determine, checking out pedestrians around him, Schuster hadn't phoned ahead to lay a trap.

His curiosity would pull him in, the Executioner decided. Where it went from there would all depend on Bolan's skill at selling Schuster on the script he had prepared with his impromptu allies. That, and Kebby Seko's clincher. If the former spook believed him, they were halfway home.

He checked his watch again, glanced back and saw his mark approaching from the north, on foot. The spook seemed perfectly at ease, a half smile on his face, as if enjoying some time away from the office. He paid no attention to the strangers passing him on either side...or so it would appear to any casual observer. Bolan caught the shifting, searching movement of his eyes and saw that Schuster wore a pistol underneath his arm.

No rude surprises so far.

Bolan let his contact choose a table, then he crossed the street and approached on Schuster's blind side, settling in the empty chair.

"I'm glad you made it."

Schuster covered his reaction with a smile for anyone who might be watching, looking Bolan up and down. "Jack Armstrong?"

"In the flesh."

"Nice shirt."

The warrior spread his jacket wide, to show he wasn't packing. "Just some old thing off the rack."

"I would have thought they'd try another name, by now."

"You know the Company," Bolan replied. "If it works, don't fix it."

The waitress brought another menu. Bolan ordered beer, to keep himself in character, and sipped it when it came. The afternoon was warm, despite the shade of an umbrella covering their table. Schuster kept his voice low-pitched, to frustrate any would-be eavesdroppers.

"Before we start, I'm interested in how you found me, Jack."

"You aren't exactly hiding, Arnold."

"All the same."

"Your name came up in conversation," Bolan told him. "I've been working out of Langley long enough for it to ring a bell. The fact is, strictly off the record, I'm a fan."

"Say what?"

He was afraid of pushing it too far, but Bolan had to give himself an air of credibility. In Schuster's world, that meant confessing to a fair amount of greed, duplicity and guile. If he came off like Mr. Clean, the former spook would automatically assume that he was lying through his teeth.

"I'm serious," he said. "You found a way to have your cake and eat it too. Word gets around, in spite of 'need-to-know.' The brass would like to have your balls for lunch someday, but that just tells the agents in the field you've got a pair."

"You want to start a fan club?"

Bolan shrugged. "I've always heard that imitation is the truest kind of flattery. When my time comes to pull the pin, I'd like to have a little something else besides the pension waiting for me, if you get my drift."

"You're looking for a sponsor?"

"Not at all. I've lined up projects on my own, no sweat. I'm just acknowledging an inspiration, Arnold."

Schuster frowned. "So, tell me, what's the rumble, Jack?"

"It may be nothing," Bolan said, "but, then again, you know how things come up from time to time."

"It happens," Schuster granted.

"Right. So, I was finishing an odd job on Mauritius last week, political, some give and take. I wrapped it up a couple days ahead of schedule, and I thought I'd have a look at Jo'burg. It's been six or seven years since I was here. Things change."

"I'd say."

There was a note of skepticism in the former agent's voice, and that was fine. If Schuster got the notion that his contact had been handling official business in Johannesburg, so much the better. It would help to smooth out any rough spots in the story Bolan had to sell.

"So, here I'm talking to a friend of ours, in the disinformation line, and he starts running down the latest on some local boys who call themselves White Wolves. That ring a bell?"

"It might."

"I thought it would. Your name came up, in fact, but later. Off the top, he started telling me some crazy lady runs a newspaper. The *Chronicle*, I'm pretty sure it was."

"Go on."

"Well, what I hear, she's got a hard-on for this wolf pack, right? Some kind of grudge that goes way back. Her husband used to run the paper and they messed him up, that

kind of thing. She's looking for a way to pay them back—
for years, I guess—and now she gets a break."

"What kind of break?" The sharpening of interest almost made him smile as Schuster took the bait.

"My contact didn't have the full specifics, but I understand it's documentary. Some kind of link between these
wolfmen and the state security police. For all I know, it's
something lifted out of the official files."

"She's printing this?"

"Some kind of front-page series, what I hear. It starts
tomorrow or the next day. Hell, it's probably too late already, but I thought it couldn't hurt to tip you off."

"It might not be."

"How's that?"

"Too late," Schuster said, almost talking to himself.

"You know the lady, then?"

"By reputation," Schuster said.

"Well, there you go." Bolan raised a hand to scratch his
ear. "Somebody calls her up and says, 'Hey, bitch—'"

The waitress was running, with a notepad in her hand,
when Bolan's beer mug suddenly exploded, flinging suds
and shards of glass in all directions, stinging Bolan's cheek.
He twisted in his chair and made a flat dive toward the
sidewalk, leaving Schuster to protect himself.

If anyone had seen his face just then, they would have
been confused by Bolan's smile.

IRONICALLY IT WAS the big municipal garage that Kebby
Seko chose to be his sniper's nest. While Bolan drove
around the block to make his second pass at La Parisienne,
the man from Mozambique saw golden opportunity in front
of him and grabbed for it with both hands, going for the
gusto.

The garage was one of those with an attendant on the exit,
to collect your money, but the entrance was controlled by a
machine, dispensing tickets while a wooden arm went up
and down. The van breezed through, its driver unobserved,
and Seko wound his way around the zigzag course until he
reached the penultimate level. Above him, there was open

parking on the roof, but he required a measure of concealment now.

Each floor of the garage was open on the sides, between
the ceiling and a waist-high concrete wall that kept incoming vehicles from plunging to the earth below. To the west,
in front of him, he had a clear view of La Parisienne. The
diners looked like pygmies, except that all of them were
white, and he couldn't make out their features from a distance.

Still, he had a cure for that.

The American's rifle was a marvel of the weapon build-
er's craft—ideally balanced, powerful and accurate, yet
small enough to be concealed beneath a trench coat. Seko
reached behind the driver's seat and took the weapon with
him as he left the van.

The shooting stand was Seko's choice, of course, but time
was limited, and there were other factors to consider. Selby
was an all-white suburb of Johannesburg, which meant that
blacks were limited in number and restricted to a narrow
range of occupations—cleaning up and serving on occasion, mostly sweeping and dumping trash cans on the night
shift. A black man strolling into any shop or office building on the street would be immediately suspect. If police
were summoned, and they found him carrying a firearm . . .

Seko didn't want to think about what followed after that.
He had assumed the risk when he agreed to work inside
South Africa, but that had been a relatively simple mission, gathering intelligence. Since joining forces with Belasko, he had graduated to a new plateau of danger. One slip
now, and Seko knew that he wouldn't survive the fall.

He chose his spot, believing that the overhang and its re-
sultant shadow would conceal him from observers on the
street below. That left foot traffic on the floor of the garage itself, and at the moment he was totally alone. There
was a staircase on his left, some twenty paces distant, and
he kept an ear cocked toward the door, alert to any sound
of footsteps on the stairs.

There was a risk of traffic, too, but he would hear a car
approaching well before it reached his floor. The whole ga-

rage was like an echo chamber, built specifically to reproduce and amplify the slightest sound.

He took the Walther WA-2000 from underneath his coat and snapped the bipod into place. The broad lip of the low retaining wall was perfect for a gun rest, and he sat down on the bumper of a two-year-old sedan before he started scanning through the rifle's telescopic sight.

Below him, details of the street leapt out in startling intensity and detail. Carefully he tracked along the sidewalk, seeking La Parisienne and picking out the tables ranged along the sidewalk. He was ready, waiting, when a trim, athletic-looking man sat down and took a menu from the waitress, obviously killing time. A moment later, Mike Belasko joined him at the table, ordered beer and they began to talk.

He had no skill at reading lips, but Seko knew what they were saying, more or less. The script had been worked out beforehand, pointing this man Schuster and the White Wolves toward a human target they couldn't resist. To guarantee the bigots went for Bridget Linder, though, Belasko had suggested they provide a measure of incentive.

Something called "the kicker."

Kebby Seko was prepared to kick.

He watched and waited, sweating underneath the collar of his shirt. The trench coat was an instrument of torture in the hot garage, but he couldn't remove his gaze from the American long enough to take it off. The signal would be coming any moment now, and if he missed it...

There!

Belasko scratched his ear, a gesture that would pass unnoticed in the course of normal interaction. Seko cranked the muzzle of his borrowed weapon slightly to his right and sighted on the beer mug standing in between the American and his contact. His attention focused to the point that Seko almost felt his stare alone could leave a scratch on stainless steel.

He stroked the Walther's trigger, felt the rifle jolt against his shoulder. The target was a hundred yards away, but he could almost taste the ice-cold beer. And when the mug exploded, Seko felt a rush as if the alcohol had gone directly to his head.

A hit!

The rifle was a semiautomatic model, no confusion with a bolt. He fired a second time as the American and his companion hit the pavement, scrambling for cover. The second shot ripped through the table, well away from any human flesh.

The trick, as Seko understood it, was to make the hit look real without inflicting any casualties. He was a decent shot, with military service in his native land, but he had never been required to miss such easy targets in his life.

Round three punched through a chair that had been occupied, a moment earlier, by Belasko's contact. Number four bit into concrete, spraying brittle shards. He lifted off the scope with two live rounds remaining, switched on the safety and sprinted for the van with gun in hand.

He wondered if the lone garage attendant sitting in the booth downstairs had heard the gunfire. Even if he had, distortion was the sniper's friend in urban settings, echoes battered back and forth between the ranks of buildings, sometimes louder in the street than at the point of origin.

In any case, he had no time to waste.

The van responded instantly to Seko's touch. He started down the ramp, not speeding yet, prepared to take his time and give a fair performance as a dim, distracted kafir if he got the chance.

If the garage attendant tried to stop him, it would be a different story. Seko didn't plan to spend another night in custody, with White Wolves or the state security police. If necessary, he would kill to keep himself at liberty.

Beginning now.

He stopped in front of the attendant's sliding window, noted the expression of surprise and vague amusement as his ticket was accepted.

"Has your van got engine trouble?"

"No, sir."

"No, sir? What was all that noise, do you suppose, that sounded like a string of backfires?"

"I don't know, sir. Possibly it was an echo from the street."

"The street?" He thought about it, blinked and shrugged. "Three rand to see you on your way."

The cash changed hands, and Seko pulled out into traffic, glancing at the mirror on his door to see if the attendant made a study of his license plate. From all appearances, the man had already forgotten one more kafir passing through his life.

And that was fine.

The man from Mozambique had yet another rendezvous to keep, and he didn't intend to be one minute late.

THE ROLLING ECHO of the final shot had died away, and angry shouts were rising in its place as Arnold Schuster scrambled out from underneath the table that had saved his life. It was a close shave, even so, but coming out alive was all that mattered.

Twice in one day. He was getting too damned old to play this game.

But not too old to win.

He looked around and spotted big "Jack Armstrong" on his feet, a semidazed expression on his face. For all his evident confusion, though, he kept his wits about him, lowering his voice to something like a whisper when he spoke.

"That's too damned close for me," he said. "I'm out of here."

"Somebody must have followed you," Schuster said.

"Followed me? You picked the spot, remember, Arnold? You're the one whose name keeps coming up in other people's conversations. What I see, somebody's out to make it past tense."

Schuster stiffened, half expecting the explosive impact of a rifle slug between his shoulder blades. It never came, and the former CIA agent's voice was fairly steady as he answered Armstrong.

"Either way," he said, "I can't afford to hang around. Somebody's calling the police right now."

"Same here." Armstrong was moving even as he spoke. "Good luck, you know? My treat, next time."

Except there wouldn't be a next time, Schuster told himself. He put the stranger out of mind and turned back toward his car. It struck him that there seemed to be no casualties, but that had no great relevance to Arnold Schuster at the moment.

He had *almost* been a casualty, goddamn it! And it was the second time in seven hours that an unseen rifleman had nearly blown his head off. Schuster didn't need a house to fall on him before he understood that some enormous pile of shit had hit the fan, and most of it was blowing his way at the moment.

Schuster dodged the manager of La Parisienne, a waspish, balding man who tailed him for a quarter block before he finally gave it up and stalked back to his restaurant. Afraid of lawsuits, more than likely, thinking anyone who stubbed his toe—much less caught bullets in his onion soup—was bound to file a case in court.

Forget about it.

Any day you walked away from gunplay was a good day. In other circumstances, Schuster might have taken time to count his blessings, maybe have a drink or three to calm his nerves, but this was different. He hadn't been caught up in some random act of terrorism by the ANC, a drive-by aimed at anyone with white skin covering his bones.

This shooting, like the one before it, had been personal.

Someone was gunning for Arnold Schuster. No more excuses, thinking maybe it was Willem Grubb the sniper meant to surprise. Grubb had himself securely tucked away, and this time they had come for Schuster, tracking him directly from his office to the restaurant.

He thought about the stranger, wondering if "Armstrong" was involved, dismissing it as too far-fetched. Why go to all the trouble of a setup just to miss the target one more time? If Schuster's contact was a part of it, it would have been much easier for him to drag a pistol out and blaze away at point-blank range.

But he had been unarmed, like any other gofer for the Company. No heat, and no intent to face the music when police arrived. Too many questions, all around.

The pieces hadn't come together for him yet, but Schuster saw the outline of a picture forming. "Armstrong's" tip about the *Chronicle* was priceless, if it turned out to be true. He knew the publisher only by reputation, hearing Willem curse her name whenever it was mentioned, but a major exposé on Grubb's connections with the state security police could ruin everything.

The last thing Schuster wanted at the moment was a full investigation of his paying clients. Grubb still owed him money on the last installment, and he had it in his mind to do more business in South Africa before he had to fold his tent and find another happy hunting ground. With any luck at all, if Grubb fulfilled what he referred to as his "destiny," then Schuster would be holding contracts with a brand-new government—and that meant easy money up the old wazoo.

Someone had twice tried to kill him.

No, scratch that. They had missed him twice, while coming close enough to blow his face off. Was it pure dumb luck, or something else that saved his life each time?

Not luck. He didn't buy it. That would mean his life was dominated by coincidence, beyond his ultimate control. If Schuster started seeing things that way, he knew the strain would drive him crazy.

That left "something else," and he would have to think about it, when he had the time. Right now, his mind was fully occupied with "Armstrong's" story and the need to head off any exposé of links between the White Wolves and the government. It stood to reason Grubb would have a few ideas on that score, none of them particularly healthy for the lady publisher.

So be it.

Her survival and success meant failure and disgrace for Schuster's clients. More important, it would mean a major source of income was eliminated overnight, and that could put a crimp in Arnold Schuster's life-style. Given that choice, well, there really wasn't any choice at all.

The woman would have to go.

The best part, Schuster thought, was that he barely had to lift a finger. All he had to do was make a phone call, and his colleagues would proceed from there.

It was a heady feeling, when he thought about it, having that much power at his fingertips. The power of life and death.

Before he reached his car, though, Schuster's mind was drawn back to the sidewalk restaurant and the crash of rifle fire.

There was power, he supposed, and there was Power.

He intended to repay the man or men who made him feel so small, as soon as he could find out who they were. They would discover Arnold Schuster was an unrelenting, unforgiving enemy.

A little something they could ponder, while they fried in hell.

11

The van was there ahead of him, as planned, but Bolan took it slow and easy. He'd turned the vehicle into a public parking lot adjacent to an auction yard. Both blacks and whites were in evidence, but no real interaction was visible between the two distinct and separate groups.

In the United States, he would have called the place a swap meet or a flea market. Here, on the outskirts of Johannesburg, he didn't have a clue to proper terminology, nor did he care. It mattered only that the man from Mozambique had done his job at La Parisienne and managed to escape without pursuers on his tail.

There was no empty space beside the van. Bolan parked a few yards down, got out and locked his car, then walked back to Seko's vehicle. The comfortable weight of his Beretta in the shoulder rig was reassuring as he scanned the parking lot for any hint of danger, finally deciding it was clear.

The van looked empty when he walked around in front, but Seko saw him coming, and he had the side door open as the Executioner prepared to knock. The Walther sniping piece was beside him on the floor, a semiautomatic pistol tucked inside his belt.

"No trouble?" Bolan asked.

Seko shook his head. "A man at the garage heard noises. I convinced him that a car had backfired in the street."

The fat garage attendant. Bolan had rolled past his window moments after Seko left the garage, with no idea the shots had emanated from the same garage. "He saw you, then."

The African smiled. "All kafirs look alike."

"Okay. You did a good job rattling the mark. I think we sold him."

"That means danger for the others."

"It means danger all around. We have to stay on top of it, that's all."

"I understand."

"About that contact for the video equipment . . ."

Seko checked his wristwatch. "I can pick it up within the hour, if you have the money."

Bolan reached inside his jacket, taking out a hefty roll of bills that he had picked up on his recent visit to the Afrikaner Party. "Courtesy of Willem Grubb," he said, and passed the cash to Seko with a smile.

"It's more than I require."

"A little something extra, just in case you hit a snag."

"I trust this man. He has done work for us before."

"Suits me, as long as we have visuals and audio."

"I don't anticipate a problem," Seko told him.

"Fair enough."

"You are convinced that Schuster and his friends will meet?"

"Not publicly," Bolan replied. "Grubb's already gone to ground, as I expected. If we play our cards right, we can flush him out of cover with our little scam and nail him in a box."

"The risk falls more on others than on us."

"To start with, anyway," the Executioner agreed. "That's why they had to volunteer. I don't draft anybody for the trenches."

"Have you thought about what happens if we fail?"

"I thought about it right up front," the warrior told him, "then I put it out of mind. Defeatist thinking slows reaction time. Too much of it becomes a self-fulfilling prophecy."

"I understand."

"I hope so. Bridget's fully covered at the moment, better than she has been since her husband died. As for Modu, he's been questioned by the state police before. He knows how far to stretch his luck before it snaps back in his face.''

"You can't be lucky always."

Bolan frowned. It would have taken too much precious time to tell his newest friend about the ghosts he slept with every night, the men and women who had joined his never-ending war as allies through the years. A fair percentage of them had been martyrs for the cause, and it was little consolation that the Executioner had managed to avenge their deaths a hundredfold.

He knew the old clichés by heart, from eggs and omelets to the bloody mathematics of "acceptable losses," and none of them seemed to fit at the moment. It would be a simple thing to minimize the danger, trivialize the sacrifice of others, but Bolan refused to play that game.

"We make our own luck," the warrior said. "Sometimes it works, sometimes it doesn't. Either way, you keep on fighting, or you haven't got a chance."

"Agreed. I only wish that my superiors could see that logic."

"Still no go for the reception?" Bolan asked.

"They are concerned that provocation of a border crossing may be deemed an act of war."

"With outlaws?"

"With South Africa. If military units are deployed, there is concern about reprisals from Pretoria. Of course, if the invaders should be killed or captured by civilians while a crime is physically in progress..."

"That's a different story," Bolan finished for him.

"Yes, indeed."

"You're telling me we don't get any backup, right?"

"My government agrees to help evacuate a village six miles inland from the border. If it happens that a group of foreigners should stop there, Mozambique police and troops will not protect them. If the foreigners survive and manage to commit a crime of any sort—"

"Like killing us," the Executioner put in.

"Official protests will be filed with the United Nations."

"That's a comfort," Bolan said. "And if the Wolves knock off a Yank, so much the better, right?"

Seko shrugged. "I can only speculate on this. If the United States should join the protest, it would carry greater weight."

"My hat's off to your supervisor," Bolan said. "He's managed to create a no-lose situation out of total shit."

"You are not worried," Seko said. It didn't come out sounding like a question. "You believe we have a chance."

"Against the Wolves? Damn right."

"And the South African police?"

"They make it tricky," Bolan said. "I don't shoot cops, regardless of the provocation."

"No?"

"Long story. If our plan works out, the press and public should be helpful on that end."

"I hope you're right."

"We'll find out soon enough. About the village..."

"It is fairly isolated," Seko told him. "Twenty-five or thirty families reside there. If their homes are damaged in the raid, I have received assurances from my superiors that they will be repaired."

"We'll need more hardware than I have on hand," Bolan said.

"That can be arranged."

He felt himself relax a bit. The odds were growing longer, but at least he wouldn't have to deal with foreign soldiers, in addition to his enemies.

"I guess the only thing we have to do now," Bolan said, "is bide our time and see who takes the bait."

ARNOLD SCHUSTER didn't return to his office after the shooting at La Parisienne. Instead he spent a quarter of an hour driving aimlessly around Johannesburg, eyes focused on his rearview mirror, watching for a tail. At length, when he had satisfied himself that he hadn't been followed from the restaurant, he started looking for a public telephone.

There were at least three ways the shooter could have found him, Schuster realized. Surveillance by a spotter was the obvious, and while he had been on alert since the attack at Grubb's that morning, it was possible that he had missed a tail. Not probable, he told himself, but possible.

A second possibility involved a phone tap or a bug inside his office. Both were swept at weekly intervals, the last time four days earlier, and he would have them checked again before the day was out. A sweep wouldn't reveal eavesdroppers at the central switchboard, but with Willem Grubb's connections to the state police, it seemed unlikely they would be on Schuster's case.

Unless...

He shrugged it off and thought about the final possibility: "Jack Armstrong." Granted, the attack had seemed to spook him, but his visible reaction could have been a sham. As for the stranger's motive, what he might have hoped to gain from putting Schuster on the spot, it was a total mystery.

His first task, at the moment, was to spread the word of Bridget Linder's plan to blow the whistle on Grubb's friendly give-and-take with the security police. Of course, if "Armstrong" was a ringer, then there might be no such plan, but Schuster wouldn't make that call. He was required, by common sense and mercenary ethics, to advise Grubb of the threat that he might be exposed. Wherever Willem took the game from there, it would be out of Schuster's hands.

Which left him more time for protecting number one.

Two misses didn't mean the shooter would deflect his aim a third time, and the former CIA agent didn't mean to give his unseen enemy another chance. If he couldn't shoot back, the next best thing would be for him to hide, deprive the marksman of his target for a while, and find out where he stood when everything was settled, two or three days down the road.

But first, he had to make that call.

Grubb's private number rang three times before one of his soldiers picked it up. "Hello?"

He recognized the raspy voice and didn't bother to identify himself. No point in taking chances. "Can you put him on?"

"He just sat down to lunch."

"So, keep it warm. He'll want to hear this right away."

The bodyguard muttered something unintelligible to himself in Afrikaans and set the phone down with a thud. The best part of a minute passed before another voice came on the line.

"What is it?" No preliminaries from the master of the White Wolves, hiding in his private lair.

"We need to talk," Schuster said.

"Go ahead. I'm listening."

"This line's secure?"

"Of course."

Well, what the hell. If Willem wasn't worried . . .

Schuster spent the next two minutes pouring out his tale— "Jack Armstrong," Bridget Linder, the attack at La Parisienne. When he was finished, there was brooding silence on the other end. Another thirty seconds wasted, give or take.

"Where are you now?"

"A public phone." Never mind the address. He had wheels, and he wasn't about to give himself away that easily.

"Do you believe this man?" Grubb asked.

"It could go either way. Thing is, it fits with what I've heard about the lady and her grudge against your side. She may have something, maybe not. But if she has it, you can bet she'll put the whole thing into print."

Grubb cursed and made a little sucking sound, as if attempting to dislodge a piece of food stuck in between his teeth. "I should have killed the bitch myself," he said, "instead of listening to Janek all this time."

"You'd better call him, anyway. It's his neck on the block, along with yours, if she starts naming names."

"And yours, perhaps?"

"Could be." The thought had crossed his mind, of course. "My contact didn't have specifics on the evidence.

Some kind of front-page series starting up tomorrow or the next day in the *Chronicle.*"

"There will not be a series," Grubb replied. "This kafir-loving cow is going out of business. Now. Today."

"You'd better talk to Janek, first," he cautioned. "He may have a way to shut her up without exposing your command to any heat."

"He has not managed very well, so far."

"He's still the law. You piss him off too much, and he can make things rough."

"I'll call him," Grubb conceded grudgingly.

"Good. I'll call you back this evening, find out what he had to say."

"Where are you going, Arnold?"

Schuster frowned at that. "I'm not sure, yet. Somewhere I can relax, without this feeling like I've got a bull's-eye painted on my back."

"You should come here."

"I'll think about it."

"You've done too much thinking, Arnold. Come and join me."

"Why?"

"Because I tell you, and because I pay your salary. Is that not good enough?"

It was an ultimatum, but he didn't take it as a threat. Not yet.

"Okay."

"I'll have a room ready."

The line went dead on that note, leaving Schuster with a dial tone humming in his ear. He cradled the receiver, stalked back to his car and got behind the wheel.

It might be safer, after all, with Willem's guns around him. Even so, he couldn't shake a sudden urge to empty his safe-deposit box and put South Africa behind him. Rest awhile and catch some sun before he found another trouble spot in which to ply his trade.

The world was full of strong men looking for connections. Schuster knew that he would never wind up on the unemployment line.

But he would have to watch himself the next few days, or he could wind up dead.

And dying was no kind of living at all.

HIS LUNCH WAS getting cold, but Willem Grubb had long since lost his appetite. The news of Bridget Linder's plan had put a tight crimp in his stomach, killing any urge for food.

It wasn't bad enough that the woman betrayed her own race for a tribe of animals as far removed from humans as the baboon or the chimpanzee. If she had simply gone off to Soweto with her dusky friends and stayed there, Grubb wouldn't have given her a second thought. But she was bound to force her views on others, through the pages of the *Chronicle*. Her husband's death had taught her nothing, and the state police had coddled her too long. If Janek had removed her from the scene in timely fashion, they wouldn't be faced with such a problem now.

Schuster was right about one thing, though. It wouldn't do for Grubb to have the woman killed without consulting Janek first. The murder of a public figure in Johannesburg was bound to draw attention, and the media connection would ensure some kind of coverage outside South Africa. Grubb personally didn't give a damn about publicity, but Janek held a somewhat different view.

And Schuster had been right, as well, when he remarked that it wouldn't be wise for Grubb to burn his bridges with the state police. He had a friend in Janek, at the moment, but it might be very different if the apparatus of the state was turned against his private army.

Never mind.

When Janek found out what the woman was planning, he would likely volunteer to do the job himself. If nothing else, he would most certainly agree that it was time to silence their most vocal critic in the media, before she ruined everything.

And it would help, Grubb thought, that Janek's reputation and pension were at stake.

He tapped out Rolf Janek's private number, known to only ten or fifteen persons in the city. It was picked up on the second ring, and he could picture Janek glancing at the readout on his answering device that automatically displayed a caller's number.

"Willem. I'm surprised to hear from you again, so soon."

"I have disturbing news."

"There seems to be no other kind, this morning. Very well, what is it now?"

"The Linder woman is planning to discuss our private business in the *Chronicle*. She may have documents. I thought you'd like to know."

The momentary silence pleased him. It was good to have that kind of power, dealing with the third or fourth most-feared policeman in South Africa.

"What do you mean, she 'may have' documents. She either has them, or she doesn't."

"That's the problem, Rolf. I don't know. The information came in secondhand, and now the source is unavailable."

"What source? Why unavailable?" The strain was showing now in Janek's voice.

"I don't have all the details," Grubb informed him. "Someone came to Schuster, possibly an agent with the CIA. He still has contacts there, you know, although they disavow him."

"Yes, go on about the *Chronicle*."

"A series starting sometime in the next few days, I'm told, with details on the link between your people and my Wolves. If true, it could be quite embarrassing."

"Embarrassing? Is that all you can say?"

Grubb smiled to think of Janek's always-ruddy face, its color shifting now from pink to crimson, fading into purple.

"Naturally," Grubb said, "I'd like to help, if possible."

"She must be silenced!" Janek blurted out. "Destroyed!"

"We're in agreement, then?"

"What are your plans?"

"I like to keep things simple and direct," Grubb said. "She won't expect my men to call on her at home."

"That leaves the paper and her staff. They can still put out the story, even if she disappears."

"But not if your department is conducting an investigation," Grubb replied. "With human life and national security at stake, you have authority to confiscate her files."

"And find the leak," Janek said, almost talking to himself.

"By all means."

"Her death will cause an uproar in the press. Would it be possible for her to disappear, instead?"

"I'll see what I can do," Grubb said.

"My office could receive a tip that she is missing, possibly abducted. Our investigation naturally would cover any aspect of the victim's life that might contribute to her disappearance."

"Stolen documents, for instance?"

"Perfect! We suspect that she has been involved with spies and traitors to subvert the lawful government. Perhaps they had a falling out, and she was sacrificed."

"I like it, Rolf."

"Even if your people have to kill her on the spot," Janek said, "we can still divert attention from the Wolves. A leftist group would be the best, I think."

"Correct, as always."

"You are ready to proceed?"

"Tonight," Grubb said. "First thing."

"I'll make inquiries in the meantime," Janek told him, "and see what I can learn about this leak. If she has documents, there will be hell to pay."

"I can assure you, nothing came from me," Grubb said. "I don't keep anything on paper."

That wasn't precisely true, of course, but Willem knew where every file and piece of information he possessed was stored and safely locked away. He trusted no one but himself with access to the secret files he had accumulated over some two decades of investigating, spying, eavesdropping and stealing for the government, or on his own account.

One thing that Willem Grubb had learned from the United States, and from the great J. Edgar Hoover in particular, was that possession of strategic knowledge made a man invincible. If he held adequate amounts of dirt on those with power and prestige, their strength became his strength.

It wasn't necessary to despise a man to use him. Most of those Grubb dealt with in a given day were friends and colleagues who agreed with him on every major issue, and apartheid most of all. They helped him willingly, in many cases, recognizing his devotion to the cause. But if they ever let him down, all Grubb had to do was open up his safe, retrieve some tasty data from the files and make a phone call.

Like today.

"You will be careful," Janek asked him, sounding more than slightly troubled.

"Certainly. I know exactly what I'm doing."

"Very well."

"Be sure to keep in touch, now, Rolf."

"Yes, I will."

He placed the telephone receiver gently in its cradle, smiling to himself. His appetite was coming back. In fact, he felt like he could eat a horse.

It was time that someone taught Bridget Linder to keep her nose out of other people's business.

Willem Grubb had only to select a teacher she wouldn't forget.

12

It was an honor, Jon Koenig thought, to be chosen for the latest strike. Eliminating Julius Nacala was his proudest moment to the present day, but killing blacks was one thing. Rubbing out a scheming traitor to the master race was something else entirely.

Koenig wasn't troubled in the least that he should be assigned to kill a woman. What was age or gender, in the scheme of things, when war had been declared? In mortal combat, no one was exempt from danger, least of all the ones who tried to hide behind their sex or youth to weasel out of punishment for heinous crimes.

In Koenig's view, there could be no more dastardly offense than undermining public faith in white supremacy. The so-called journalists who spouted all that leftist crap about equality were worse than kafirs, when you thought it through. They wore their white skin like a mask, to cover up a brooding hatred of their ancestors who built Johannesburg and made South Africa a power to be reckoned within Africa.

If anyone had asked Koenig to compile a list of journalistic traitors in South Africa, he would have listed Bridget Linder near the top. Her husband had been bad enough, a first-rate kafir-lover, but the woman was a hundred times more spiteful and vindictive. Koenig had a theory that her hatred for the white race stemmed in equal parts from twisted self-revulsion and a brooding sexual frustration that had plagued her since her husband's death. He didn't have to meet the woman to believe these things, much less attempt to see the world from her perspective. Koenig's mind was prone to work on leaps of faith, except where military matters were concerned, and common sense assured him that the woman had lost her mind.

It would have been a simple mission, if her death was all that Willem Grubb desired, but there was more. That afternoon, the chief had summoned Koenig to his hideaway, explaining what was needed. He'd listened carefully and didn't interrupt. He was a soldier, trained to execute the wishes of his officers, not to question the intent of this or that specific strategy.

In this case, Grubb preferred that Bridget Linder should abruptly disappear, instead of simply being killed and left for the police to find. She wasn't wanted for interrogation, so the raiders had no need of taking her alive, but Grubb instructed them to leave a minimum of clues behind. The less forensic evidence recovered from the scene, the better it would be for all concerned. If they were forced to kill her on the spot, so be it, but the corpse should be removed and efforts made to tidy up the house when they were done.

At that, it was a relatively simple job. The Linder house in Germiston had been a target of surveillance when her husband was alive, preparedness against the day when Grubb might order such a strike to kill Jan Linder. It had never come to pass—the state security police had handled matters, in the end—but preparation never really went to waste. Jon Koenig knew the layout of the grounds, the basic floor plan of the house, how many servants were employed to cook and clean on any given day.

It was amazing, when he thought about it, how such information could be found and filed away on virtually anyone you chose to mention, from the lowest kafir to the heads of state. No man or woman was immune to private scrutiny, and the collection of intelligence was only one short step from an assault.

He chose six men to join him on the raid, four veterans of the strike against Nacala and a pair who had done local work for Koenig in the past. They were his friends, these men, and die-hard patriots who wouldn't flinch from executing women, even children, in the proper cause.

They waited for the sun to set, aware that Bridget Linder often worked late at the newspaper office. A highway interception would have done the trick, as she was driving home, but Koenig had been ordered to avoid a public scene. The fewer witnesses around to speak with the police, the better Grubb would like it.

Simple.

Seven men, including Koenig, were enough to ring the house and cover all the ground-floor exits. Rushing in together, they would take their quarry by surprise, eliminate whichever servants were unfortunate enough to show themselves and make their getaway without unnecessary furor. Any killing in the house or on the grounds would mean a hasty mop-up job, but they were using silenced weapons to avoid disturbing Bridget's neighbors as they slept or watched TV.

It was a simple plan, and nearly foolproof. Koenig split his team and took two vehicles, a station wagon and a roomy van. If there were extra bodies to be hauled away, he wanted cargo space available at need. They motored into Germiston from opposite directions, minimizing the appearance of a convoy, and regrouped outside the Linder home at 10:15 p.m.

The house was dark, except for one light showing in a bedroom on the second floor. The darkness told him that the servants had to be gone, but Bridget Linder was presumably awake. As a precaution, one of Koenig's men slipped off to cut the phone line where it joined the house, in back. That still left cordless telephones, of course, but there was no such thing as finally eliminating each and every risk.

The locks were child's play. Koenig took the time to have them picked, instead of simply smashing in the door, because he hoped to take his quarry by surprise. It would be easier that way, less opportunity for the woman to defend herself with any weapons in the house, less noise for any tenants of adjacent homes to notice or report.

When Koenig stepped across the threshold, he held a sleek SIG-Sauer automatic pistol in his hand, its outline weighted and distended by a silencer. The two men on his heels were similarly armed. His four commandos entering by other routes each carried MP-5 SD-3 submachine guns, for the heavy fire support that Koenig hoped he wouldn't need.

The house was dark and silent as he started up the stairs.

IT IS IMPÓSSIBLE for white police to take Soweto by surprise. Their skin alone betrays them, even if they shed their uniforms in favor of civilian clothes. Experience has taught them that their lives are forfeit in the teeming ghetto, and they dare not go alone, or even in small groups. Soweto calls for armored vehicles, machine guns, water cannon, full-dress riot gear. The ghetto grapevine telegraphs their arrival, warning those with cause to hide, alerting others to prepare themselves with rocks and bottles, hatchets and machetes, guns and homemade gasoline bombs.

The white police have never lost a battle in Soweto yet, but neither can they seem to win the war.

The evening's raid had been designed to pick up half a dozen men, all leaders of the ANC, and bring them to Johannesburg for questioning by the security police. When Rolf Janek issued warrants for arrest of certain blacks, he wasn't required to give his reasons. Everyone involved in the procedure knew the kind of cases Janek handled, recognized his enemies as traitors to the state, and made a special effort to comply with the commander's wishes.

It was healthier that way for all concerned.

Rolf Janek knew that some of his men were questioning the old ways. If it was up to him, Janek would have purged the ranks and instituted binding loyalty oaths, but his suggestions in that line had all been disapproved, so far.

Times change, and while he waited for the wind to shift again, in favor of his homeland, Janek still did business with the same techniques that he had picked up as a rookie, almost twenty years before. When you have questions for a kafir, and he lied or stubbornly refused to answer, certain types of pressure were applied.

And Rolf Janek knew them all.

The raiding party struck at ten o'clock, a line of armored vehicles approaching from the north and entering Soweto as a single column, branching off from there to seek specific targets in the labyrinth of narrow streets. Already, ghetto residents were pouring from their homes, men shouting, women joining in that high-pitched, keening wail that at once was a protest and a warning to Soweto's wanted fugitives. A handful of the children started tossing rocks and bottles, older marksmen quickly joining in the game.

The officers relied on speed at first. They knew their final destinations, had the mug shots of their targets memorized. The drivers of their armored vehicles wouldn't concern themselves if someone—say a toddler or a pregnant woman—blundered out in front of the advancing column and was flattened like a piece of road kill by the giant tires. It was a risk of physical resistance to the power of the state, immutable as Einstein's law of relativity.

For every insult to the state's authority, there was an opposite and not-so-equal thrust against the ghetto's black inhabitants. So had it been, as long as anyone alive could recollect; so would it always be.

At least, it would as far as Rolf Janek was concerned.

He didn't join the raiding party, holding too much rank for hasty visits to Soweto after nightfall, but he monitored its progress on the radio. He knew exactly when the two fat armored cars approached Richard Modu's residence, with gunners on alert for sniper fire or flying gas bombs. He didn't know if Modu was at home, and he didn't particularly care. If he caught four or five of the intended seven songbirds, it should be enough.

In fact, Modu was at home and waiting for the raiders. When his wife suggested that he flee, he sent her out the back instead, the children clinging to her skirt. Another time, he might have joined her, but Modu had a promise to fulfill, a role to play in grand events that he couldn't control.

It would have pleased him to refuse when Bridget Linder sought his help, make some excuse and let her find another sacrificial lamb. Modu didn't fully trust the tall American, but that was Bridget's problem. He believed that something had to be done about the border raids, and soon. As the United Nations showed no inclination to respond, some other method of relief was called for.

Modu heard the raiders coming, his devoted neighbors turning out to beat on garbage cans and shout defiance, one man slipping over from next door to warn him personally. Modu smiled and sent the neighbor on his way with thanks. It didn't suit his purpose to escape, this time.

He went to meet the raiders in his yard, depriving them of an excuse to smash the door and windows. They appeared confused, behind the plastic visors on their riot helmets, looking bulky and inhuman in their flak vests, loaded sap gloves, dusty boots and rumpled khaki uniforms. Modu read a childish disappointment in their faces when he offered no resistance, falling into step behind their leader once the handcuffs were in place.

He was safe inside the armored car before his neighbors started stoning the police. Modu would have stopped them if he could, for it was never wise to taunt a jackal, but the matter was no longer in his shackled hands. Locked up inside the APC, he knew exactly what was happening outside, for he had seen it all before. The officers were forming ranks with their batons and other weapons, shouting orders to the crowd without an expectation of obedience.

The gas came next, and sometimes deadly gunfire with it. Modu smelled a whiff of gas that wormed its way around the slightly open hatch, and thought that he could still escape, if he were so inclined. His hands were cuffed in front of him, still useful, and the night would shelter him once he had run a few short yards into the darkness.

No.

He had agreed to Bridget's plan, and he would see it through. He closed his eyes and concentrated on the story he would tell, when the police had "worn him down" enough to make confession logical, and thus believable. Modu didn't listen to the screams outside that changed from taunts and jeers to sudden cries of fear and pain.

The voices of Soweto, calling out for justice.

If he played his role correctly, he thought, it just might make a difference. And, if he should fail...

Well, there would always be another chance at revolution. History revealed that all oppressive systems sowed the seeds of self-destruction over time, and the Pretoria regime had dropped its dragon's teeth on fertile ground. The crop was irrigated frequently with blood, and fertilized with murdered dreams.

Modu thought it had to be almost harvest time.

Somehow, the notion gave him strength to smile.

MACK BOLAN HAD the prowlers spotted by the time they left their vehicles out front. He watched them from a darkened upstairs window, counting heads and following the flankers as they circled wide around the house. Their movements were, if not professional, at least rehearsed and competent.

The Executioner was clad in midnight black and weighted down with military webbing. The Beretta 93-R and his Uzi submachine gun both were fitted with silencers, the Desert Eagle Magnum on his right hip ready in reserve, in case his situation called for knock-down power over stealth. He carried no grenades, but he was ready with a combat knife, if the engagement wound up going hand-to-hand.

He waited on the upstairs landing, listening to the raiders as they picked the front door's double lock, cut glass to enter through a window in the den and snapped the back door's locking mechanism with a pry bar. Overall, it was a fairly subtle penetration, nothing a distracted couch potato would have noticed from the master bedroom, with the television playing.

They would count on Bridget being in her room, perhaps in bed, because the house was dark and silent as they entered. At his back the master bedroom's door was closed, light bleeding underneath. It wouldn't cast his shape in silhouette or spoil his night vision for the coming fight.

He heard them coming up the stairs and made it three, the team that came in through the living room. The rest would be converging, checking out the rooms downstairs for any witnesses and finding none.

Bolan and his adversaries had the house all to themselves.

A glimpse beneath the streetlight was enough to tell him that these men weren't police. South African authorities might stage their raids at inconvenient hours, but they always came in uniform and flaunted their authority. The gunmen on the stairs, their comrades creeping through the other rooms below, would be White Wolves or something very similar, stone bigots, marching side by side with mercenary killers drawn to any "cause" that offered possibilities for plunder.

The warrior drifted toward the staircase, silent as a shadow in the night, his Uzi leveled from the waist. Three other shadows rose to meet him, halfway up the staircase, still oblivious to lurking Death. He could have given them a warning, made it "fair," but empty gestures served no purpose on the killing ground.

Instead he shot them where they stood, the Uzi tracking left to right and back again. A dozen parabellum manglers ripped through flesh and fabric with an ugly smacking sound, and Bolan watched his targets topple over backward, rolling down the stairs together in an awkward knot of arms and legs.

Below him, to his right, a startled curse gave Bolan the location of his next live target. Pivoting in that direction, he was squeezing off another burst when silent muzzle-flashes blossomed in the darkness. But the shots were high and wide as Bolan ducked back under cover, dodging out of range.

All four intruders were firing now, their automatic weapons chewing up the plaster walls and ceiling, gouging splinters from the banister. They had no fix on Bolan, but they weren't taking any chances. One of them was cursing angrily in Afrikaans, the others doing all their talking with their SMGs.

He had a choice of dueling with the gunners from on high, or getting down among them, with a better chance to finish it. There were inherent risks in both approaches—

namely, getting shot and killed the moment that he showed himself—and Bolan concentrated on the positives. Surprise and sheer audacity could make the difference, but the longer he allowed the fight to last, the more he jeopardized his chance of coming out with life and limb intact.

He slid up to the banister and fired a long burst from his Uzi, emptying the magazine before he rolled back out of range. Below him, four guns answered as before, and Bolan took the opportunity to spot their rough positions, laying out the deathscape in his mind.

He fed the Uzi with a backup magazine and eased the Beretta from its shoulder holster, setting the selector switch for 3-round bursts. Between the two guns, he had fifty rounds on tap before a dry-fire forced him to reload. His targets waited for him on the floor below.

The drop was fifteen feet, allowing for the waist-high banister, and the warrior had the layout pictured in his mind before he made the leap. He had been waiting in the house since sundown for the raiders to arrive, committing every stick of furniture to memory against the moment when he needed cover or his enemies went looking for a place to hide.

The Executioner landed on his feet but staggered from the impact, almost losing it. He went down on one knee to compensate, his nearest adversary pivoting to bring him under fire as Bolan suddenly lost altitude. The burst that should have chopped his head off whittled empty air instead, and the Beretta answered with a burst that punched his target over backward in a looping somersault.

One down, and three to go.

Between the Uzi and Beretta, Bolan gave them everything he had in seven seconds flat. The nearest gunner on his right gave out a little squeal of panic as the Executioner touched down in front of him, and Bolan shot him in the mouth before the squeal turned into words. The shooter's head exploded like a melon, leaving abstract patterns on the walls, but Bolan had no time to register the details as he turned to face the other two.

He came up firing, saw the muzzle-flashes of their weapons, heard the bullets sizzle past his head on either side. A ghostly hand reached out to pluck at Bolan's sleeve, another slapped against the ammo pouches on his hip, Death stooping down beside him, breathing in his ear.

And passing on.

The Reaper had no room for Bolan, this time. He was carrying a full load back to hell, his parting whisper nothing but a word of thanks for Bolan's contribution to the carnage. As the smoke cleared, the warrior counted four men stretched out on the carpet, more or less surrounding the position where he stood, his back against the wall.

Clean sweep.

He left the corpses where they were, reloaded on the move and slipped out through the back. His car was parked around the corner, half a block away, and Bolan reached it without further incident. In darkness, watching both sides of the street, he stowed his weapons in the trunk and slipped a jacket on to hide the shoulder holster.

Done.

The call could wait until he gained some distance from the charnel house. There was no urgency in summoning police, when they had other work to do—such as picking up Modu and his comrades from the ANC, interrogating them for information on the name of Bridget Linder's nonexistent source inside the government. It all came down to smoke and mirrors, offering the enemy a course to follow that would logically appeal to his inherent bigotry.

And which, with any luck at all, would lead him to his death.

13

The White Wolves kept their major urban stash of vehicles in Kensington, midway between Johannesburg and Germiston, where they could always reach a set of wheels without undue delay. The cover was a neighborhood garage, the owner and a couple of his top mechanics loyal disciples of the master race who kept the motor pool in running order, day or night.

He could have passed the target by, but Bolan had some time to kill, and it was on his way. He had the best part of an hour yet, before he was supposed to meet with Kebby Seko, and it seemed a shame to let his adversaries rest, when he could shake them up some more and keep them on the run.

It was getting late when Bolan made his drive-by, long past any reasonable hour when legitimate mechanics would be climbing under hoods to earn their daily bread. Still, lights were visible inside the office, emanating from a room somewhere in back, and moving shadows told him that he wouldn't have the pit stop to himself.

A guard, perhaps, in light of Bolan's recent strikes ... or had the motor pool been placed on stand-by for some kind of a nocturnal movement? Bolan didn't care much, either way, unless the watchdogs had him so outnumbered that the risk outweighed the possible rewards of dropping in to say hello.

And there was only one way Bolan knew of checking out those odds.

By going in.

He parked downrange, behind a service station that had shut down for the night, got out and shed the sport coat that was covering his shoulder rig. He had reloaded the Beretta and the Uzi prior to leaving Bridget's house, and they were ready now. So armed, he opened up the trunk of the sedan and lifted out an olive-drab satchel that contained six plastic charges, Semtex broken into half-pound blocks, with detonators set and ready to be armed.

The warrior reckoned it would be enough.

He walked back through the darkness to his target, boot heels crunching on the asphalt, with the satchel slung across one shoulder and the Uzi in his hands. This was no residential neighborhood; no shops were open at that hour, no pedestrians in sight.

The lot in back of the garage was fenced, but someone had neglected to secure the padlock on the gate. The Executioner passed through and closed it silently behind him, feeling better once the bulk of the garage had screened him from the street. Whatever happened next, at least he was secure from chance encounters with late-night passersby.

The back door of the workshop stood ajar, light spilling out into the yard. As Bolan closed the gap, his nostrils picked out the distinctive smell of oil and cigarette smoke, muffled voices coming to his ears. There were three men, at least, but they were speaking Afrikaans, and Bolan wasted no time trying to interpret. He had marked the occupants as members of the private army led by Willem Grubb, and that was all he had to know.

He stepped across the threshold, following the Uzi's lead. In front of him, two young men sat on folding chairs positioned so they faced a third companion, standing with his arms crossed, buttocks braced against a workbench. Bolan's entry coincided with a fourth man stepping through the door directly opposite, apparently emerging from the office.

It was number four who spotted Bolan first, his three companions and some thirty feet of open space between them. On the left, as the warrior faced his enemies, stood a Volvo station wagon with its hood up, shiny tools laid out across the fender on a rubber mat. To Bolan's right was a wall of cinder blocks festooned with tools and automotive gear hung up on shiny metal hooks.

The gunner from the office shouted something unintelligible to his friends and dropped the mug of coffee he was carrying. It hit the floor between his feet and detonated, splashing coffee and ceramic shrapnel in a ten-foot radius. By that time, Bolan's targets had begun to scatter, seeking cover, perhaps weapons.

He shot the coffee drinker first, a short burst in the chest that punched him backward, through the office doorway, out of sight in the direction he had come from.

And that left three.

The tall man standing with his backside pressed against the workbench had a balance problem. Thrusting backward with his hands, to give himself some leverage, he slipped and lost it, boot heels skidding far enough to crack his elbows painfully against the bench. He might have saved it, even then, but Bolan's Uzi stuttered out a 3-round burst that drilled into his skull.

Two down, and two remaining.

Number three had ducked behind the Volvo station wagon, momentarily concealed. His sole surviving partner was tugging at a pistol in his waistband as he sprinted for the grease pit, twenty feet away.

The Uzi helped him get there, with a burst of parabellum shockers ripping through his back and side. Momentum kept him going in an awkward, shallow dive. He hit the concrete belly-down and slithered on a spreading blood slick, finally dropping out of sight into the pit.

That left one.

The shooter popped up into view, the car between them, squeezing off two quick rounds from a semiautomatic pistol. Bolan ducked and rolled, the Uzi seeking targets underneath the Volvo, where his adversary had to show himself, unless he had discovered how to levitate.

Two shuffling feet in dirty sneakers became visible, denim ankles rising out of sight. It was enough for Bolan, as he aimed and fired a grazing burst beneath the car. At least one round struck home, generating a splash of crimson and a cry of pain before his young assailant hit the deck. The warrior had a clear shot at the gunner's shooting arm, and Bolan took it, parabellum manglers sawing through the elbow joint and leaving him disarmed in more than one respect.

The guy was slipping into shock as Bolan walked around the front end of the station wagon to kneel at his side. Whatever stimulus the pain and loss of blood provided, it was giving him hallucinations. Staring up at Bolan, he was babbling excitedly in Afrikaans.

The Executioner had nothing to lose. "Speak English," he ordered.

And the young man did as he was told. "We have to warn Herr Grubb," he said.

"I need his number," Bolan answered, "for the call."

The young man spent a moment wheezing, finally rasping a number out. The Executioner committed it to memory.

"You won't forget him?"

"Not a chance."

The gunner's eyes rolled back, and he was unconscious.

Bolan rose and checked the office, just in case, but found no one hiding there. While he was at it, the warrior checked the street and parking lot out front, in case the young Boer's pistol shots had somehow drawn an audience. A car rolled past while he was watching, but the driver didn't slow or even glance at the garage.

He backtracked through the killing room, paused long enough to plant a Semtex charge beneath the Volvo's hood and set the timer counting down to doomsday. Seven vehicles were in the lot out back, and Bolan secreted the five remaining charges among them, kneeling to fasten the Semtex blocks to gasoline tanks where he could. A van, a jeep, two pickup trucks, and three sedans—five vehicles with timers counting down, the other two positioned like the meat inside a double-decker sandwich, so the fiery detonation of their neighbors ought to do the trick for them, as well.

It was the best that he could do without more time and more equipment. Bolan let himself out through the gate and jogged back to his car, drove off and watched the charges detonate from two blocks away. It wouldn't rank as a decisive blow against the Wolves by any means, but it would keep them on their toes.

Enough.

He had a rendezvous to keep, and Bolan didn't plan on being late.

THE INTERROGATION CELL wasn't the same one where he had been questioned in the past, Modu realized, but they were similar enough in their decor and dark aroma that it hardly mattered. If you've seen one torture chamber in Johannesburg, you've seen them all.

The grilling cells were all downstairs, subbasement level, with the weight of concrete, marble and official power bearing down on those unfortunate enough to occupy the several Spartan cubicles. Each cell was furnished with a single, straight-backed wooden chair, which wasn't bolted to the floor. Apparently the jailers saw no risk of being bludgeoned with the furniture, and it was helpful if the chairs could be removed from time to time, for cleaning or refinishing.

As for the rest, a simple garden hose would do the trick, removing sweat, blood and vomit, sluicing all of it together down the drainpipe planted in the middle of the floor.

Modu sat and wondered if his jailers had a mammoth water bill these days. The foreign press had somehow come to think that things were changing in South Africa, and it was true, to some extent. Apartheid was officially defunct, the segregating signs removed from public buildings and the like, but revocation of a statute didn't change the human heart or wipe out generations of antagonism. Only time could heal those wounds, and sometimes Modu had his doubts that even that would do the job.

He knew his lines by heart. The tricky part was putting up enough resistance that the officers assigned to question him weren't suspicious. They would have his file in front of them, or fresh in mind, including the reports of his resistance to interrogation after prior arrests. An easy win might gratify the pigs, but it could also blow up in his face.

Of course, Modu thought, he was an older man these days. It had been several years since he was badly beaten, really thrashed, instead of taking one or two quick taps with a baton in public demonstrations. When they had you in the basement cells, locked up where no one else could hear you scream, the bastards took their time.

So far, in fact, Modu had been left alone. He thought an hour and a quarter had to have passed since he was picked up in Soweto. Some of that was driving time, the trip back to his present holding cell, but he had been alone for close to forty minutes. Maybe more, but it was hard for him to tell without a clock.

As if in answer to his silent thoughts, the door swung open, and a short parade of officers trooped in. Four men in wilted khaki uniforms surrounded him, while number five—their obvious superior—hung back and closed the door behind himself. It took a moment, but Modu recognized the man in charge. His name was Rolf Janek, a commander of the state security police whose death had once been ordered by the armed wing of the ANC.

Modu had a feeling that before the night was finished, he would wish that order had been carried out.

"You've been with us before, eh, Richard?" Janek's voice was low-pitched, almost cultivated, not at all the screamer from a bad B-movie.

"You have read my file."

"On more than one occasion," Janek told him. "You have labored long and hard against the lawful government."

"Against oppression."

Janek blinked, no more or less than that, and the policeman on Modu's left began the session with a solid backhand, splitting his lower lip and drawing blood. Modu clutched the chair to keep from falling. He had fallen in a room like this before, and boots were always worse than fists.

"I need some information, Richard." Janek's tone was almost chatty, a peculiar mockery of friendship. "I believe you're just the man to help me out."

"I doubt it."

"But you haven't even heard the questions, yet. Don't be so hasty."

"I was hoping I could save us all some time."

Another blink, and this time Modu caught it from the right, a stunning fist below the ribs. He doubled over, gagging on the pain, but somehow managed not to fall.

It was a challenge, staying in the chair. If he could focus on that goal, Modu thought he might survive.

"Time's not a problem, Richard. I've got all the time I need. We're not in any rush."

Modu slowly, painfully, regained his upright stature in the chair. He tried to hold the pain at arm's length from his mind, resisting the temptation to collapse.

"What is it that you wish to know?"

"You've got a friend in Germiston, I think."

"A friend?"

He braced himself for yet another blow, but Janek merely smiled. "The lady, Richard. Bridget Linder. Surely you remember her? It isn't often that you get to snuggle with a white one, I imagine."

The officers surrounding him snickered, but Modu barely noticed. He was focused on the man who called the shots. By naming Bridget Linder, Janek had confirmed the tall American's suspicion of a link between the White Wolves and the state security police.

"I've met her," Modu granted.

"There, we're making progress." Janek seemed delighted by the small admission, viewing the man's weakness as the first crack in the dam. "What else?"

"Her husband was a friend."

"Her husband's dead," Janek stated flatly. "I'm concerned about the living."

It was painful when he shrugged, but Modu kept the pain out of his face. "I don't know what you mean."

This time, when Janek blinked, two officers attacked simultaneously, one fist hammering Modu's stomach, while another slammed between his shoulder blades. He couldn't help it, then, as pain and gravity took over. In another heartbeat, he was facedown on the concrete floor.

"That's clumsy of you, Richard." Janek's tone was civil, mocking. "Next thing, you'll be blaming one of us because you fell and hurt yourself."

The boots were next, he knew it. How much longer should he wait? How much more should he suffer for the sake of an illusion?

"Please," he gasped, eyes closing tight against the shame, "no more. I'll tell you what you want to know."

HE PICKED OUT THE VAN from a distance, standing in a corner of the supermarket parking lot, but Bolan took no chances. He circled around the block and approached from the opposite direction on his second pass.

There was a chance, however slim, that Kebby Seko could have been surprised by the police when he went looking for his contact in Soweto, taken into custody and forced to spill his guts. For all he knew, the local stormtroops could have spies and snipers staking out the rendezvous right now, prepared to pounce when Seko's Yankee ally showed himself.

It was a chance that Bolan had to take.

His drive-by failed to show an ambush in the making, but he had the loaded Uzi on the empty seat beside him as he pulled into the parking lot and rolled across the blacktop toward the waiting van. He killed his headlights halfway there, once he had caught a fleeting glimpse of Seko peering at him from the space behind the driver's seat.

Pulling in beside the gray van, Bolan kept his free hand on the Uzi, checking out the shadows on the parking lot's perimeter. If anything was primed to happen, it would come within the next few moments, when he shifted from his own car to the van.

The side door on the van rolled back, and Seko motioned for the Executioner to join him. Bolan had removed the dome light from his vehicle in advance, so there was no sudden glare to make it easier for snipers when he stepped out through the driver's door. Another moment saw him in the van, the door rolled shut behind him.

"Any problems?" Bolan asked.

"None so far. I have the video equipment here."

As Seko spoke, he turned and let his right hand come to rest atop a kind of bulky metal suitcase, painted black, that sat beside him on the rear deck of the van.

"The microphone?"

"Directional and powerful enough to pick up normal conversations from a range of eighty meters, on a line of sight."

It was a decent range, for safety's sake, but Bolan still had no clear fix on the terrain he would be covering. He hoped it would be daylight, but he couldn't count on even that. Regarding distance, visibility and obstacles, the men and weapons waiting for him, Bolan didn't have a clue. Still, instinct told him that a spotter's nest beyond the eighty-meter mark would do him no damned good at all.

"I'd better check it out."

"Of course."

He scooted over toward the metal case and opened it. The camera was a good one, fitted with a telephoto lens that let him scan the lit windows of a pharmacy, some forty meters distant, reading price tags, labels and the like as if he held each item in his hand.

"Not bad."

The shotgun microphone was a distinct and separate unit, but a sturdy clip was mounted on the left side of the camera. He tried the mike for size and found it mated to the camera in a perfect fit. When it was plugged into the camera, both pieces operated from a single power source, contained in what resembled an inflated cartridge belt. He tried the belt, as well, and found that it was large enough to fit around his waist.

"Looks like we're set," Bolan said. He began to pack the gear away.

"We still don't know where Grubb is hiding," Seko stated, "or if he will agree to meet the others."

Bolan frowned. "I caught a break on that. After Bridget's place, I made a pass through Kensington and stopped off at the White Wolves' motor pool. I got Grubb's private number from a guy who didn't need it anymore."

"You killed him?"

"He has lots of company. Anyway, it turns out one of Bridget's newsies has a boyfriend on the Jo'burg telephone exchange. She whispered in his ear, and he came up with an address to fit the number. Simple."

"If, in fact, you find Grubb there."

"He'll be there," Bolan promised. "I'm just afraid his buddies might not show. If they keep playing phone tag, it will mean a lot of extra time. I'll have to track them one by one."

"You never kill police," the man from Mozambique reminded him.

"That's right. Without some decent footage or a witness under oath, my guess would be the cops should skate."

A frown suggested Kebby's lack of understanding. "Skate?"

"Go free," the Executioner explained. "We'll need an airtight case before the state will ever bring them up on charges. Even then, with a jury trial, you take your chances with the system."

"But the tape would ruin them."

"It all depends on who we catch and what they do or say on camera. A simple meeting, in and of itself, won't do the trick. Unless we turn up something solid, it's a waste of time."

"When do we start?"

"We don't," Bolan said. "It's a one-man job."

"There will be guards."

"I wouldn't be surprised. I need you working on the flip side, though, to have things ready when they take the bait."

"I should at least know where he's hiding."

Bolan named a suburb to the northwest of Johannesburg and let it go at that. He trusted Seko to a point, but when the chips were down, he knew the man had to serve his country's interest first. If that meant icing Willem Grubb, he had no doubt that Seko would attempt the hit alone, should all else fail. The danger was that Kebby's natural frustration might betray him and promote some rash behavior while the broader strategy devised by Bolan was in play.

And if that strategy fell through, well, Bridget had the head wolf's private number, address, everything a raiding party would require to do the job. She might not have the will to go that route, but it would all be out of Bolan's hands if things went wrong to that extent.

It wouldn't matter in the least, if he was dead.

But Bolan didn't plan on giving up that easily. It was defeatist thinking, and he pushed it out of mind. He'd take the battle as it came.

One bloody step at a time.

14

Rolf Janek felt relaxed as he emerged from the Johannesburg headquarters of the state security police. He hadn't slept in close to thirty hours, but fatigue wasn't a problem. Night shifts and extended tours of duty were an old routine, one of the reasons he had never married, and he knew exactly how to pace himself in order to prevent exhaustion.

It was easier, of course, when Janek felt he had accomplished something, scored a victory for some ideal or cause that he believed in. Missionary zeal could keep a soldier marching, fighting, past the limits of endurance. It was marvelous, he thought, what raw enthusiasm and a steaming cup of coffee could achieve.

Like now.

He had been working on the kafirs all night long, with two or three short respites to coordinate the information they provided under grilling. Three of them had given up surprising gems on matters unrelated to his present quest, but Janek wasted nothing, filing their reports away for future reference, items he could work with when he had more time: illicit sexual relations in the ANC, extending into middle management; a rumor of extortion practiced by a Zulu headman running contract labor from Benoni; drugs and liquor being dealt by tribes in the Transvaal.

Two others on his list were truly ignorant but tried to save themselves by fabricating ludicrous conspiracies. He let them play the game as long as it amused him, giving his interrogators a workout, but in time his patience was exhausted, and he charged them both with falsifying evidence.

They'd get six months in jail if they were lucky, and another lesson learned.

Modu was the prize, this time around, a kafir who had grown up in the radical tradition, taught by kith and kin to hate the white man's lawful government and work for its demise with everything he had. Modu had been jailed before, not once, but several times. His record showed a stiff resistance to interrogation, but the night's events proved once again that each man has a breaking point. With age, the prospect of mortality crept in to gnaw around the feet of courage, making each man face the prospect of his imminent demise.

The kafir had to have thought along those lines last night, for he had broken in something close to record time. A few light taps had done the job, and that was fine with Janek. Minimum expenditure of energy for maximum results.

Of course, he was suspicious when Modu snapped so quickly, but the man was getting on in years, his bones were turning brittle, and an older man had more to lose, somehow. On second thought, it was entirely logical that he should break down and tell them everything, providing all the details Janek needed for his next report to Willem Grubb.

He hoped that Grubb could handle it from here, but Janek knew enough of racial conflict in South Africa to realize he wasn't witnessing the end of anything. A war was coming, he could feel it. Sniff the wind that blew up from Soweto, and the stench of death would kill a vulture's appetite. No matter what the television said about a brighter day, all Janek saw when he surveyed the local scene was conflict, thinly veiled and ready to explode.

The morning sun revived him, made him blink until he slipped his mirrored glasses on. His car was waiting in its normal place, his trusted driver standing by.

"Good morning, sir."

"It is, indeed."

His driver held the door, and Janek slid into the back seat, shifting once to seat the hidden pistol just a tad more comfortably on his hip. There was a time when ranking officers of the security police had gone about their rounds unarmed, but that was ancient history. With the elimination of apartheid, Janek had observed an escalation in the sort of crime that marked a decadent society, and he would swear that most of those responsible were black.

You never knew, these days, when some fanatic from the left would try to kill you on the street. It was a travesty, but Janek never left his flat without a side arm. In the car, he kept an Uzi submachine gun and an Armsel Striker, the native semiautomatic 12-gauge shotgun, packing twelve rounds in its fat drum magazine.

If anyone accosted Janek on the highway, there would be a heavy price to pay for his impertinence.

His driver slid behind the steering wheel, and Janek told him, "Westcliff. Willem's little hideaway."

"Yes, sir."

In fact, Grubb's sanctuary was a bit outside the bounds of Westcliff proper, but he saw no point in splitting hairs. His driver knew the way, and they would be there soon.

For once, he had good news.

Modu's tale hadn't solved everything, of course, but it would make a decent start. They had the woman, now—or would, at any rate, before much longer—and her source wouldn't be far behind.

The most disturbing thing, for Janek, was the thought that someone he had trusted, someone in the ranks of the security police, would sell him out. No, it was worse than that. By selling him, and his connection to the Wolves, the traitor had betrayed a proud tradition of the master race. When white men stabbed each other in the back, it could be no surprise that kafirs were emboldened to revolt.

The craven turncoat, once he was identified, his crimes spelled out in detail, would be liable to prosecution on a charge of dereliction, leaking confidential information to civilians, possibly accepting bribes. A trial would be embarrassing, however, the defense obliged to poke and probe at matters better left to rest.

But fortunately Janek knew a better way to solve the problem. He would handle it himself, discreetly, so that nothing could be traced back to his doorstep. In a country like South Africa, a man could disappear forever in the bush—or in the back streets of Johannesburg—and no one but God and those responsible would ever know the bastard's fate. Conversely there were ways to make his death a public spectacle, a lesson to potential squealers in the ranks...and blame it on the blacks.

The latter plan appealed to Janek's sense of irony. He liked a bit of humor, even if he had to keep the punch line to himself for fear of spending life in prison if he let it slip.

The best jokes, like delicious secrets, were the ones you chuckled over in the middle of the night, when you were all alone.

ARNOLD SCHUSTER SIPPED his coffee, grimaced at the bitter taste and set the cup aside. He was about to check his watch again, the second time in a minute, but he caught himself and made an effort to relax.

No sweat.

The call from Willem Grubb that summoned him for breakfast at the safehouse also brought good news. The state police had cracked a ranking member of the ANC the previous night, and he had spilled enough to help them put their lives in order. Willem thought so, anyway, and if the information calmed him down a bit, well, that was good enough for Schuster.

He would hold off any final judgment for a while, until he heard what Janek had to say and found out what the White Wolves had in mind to put things right.

It was a bit like Humpty Dumpty, when you thought about it. Bodies everywhere, all that exposure in the press, and none of it exactly complimentary. Still, in South Africa, things had a way of working out if you were white, rich, well connected and well armed.

It was a little like the Twilight Zone, thought Schuster, and the notion almost made him smile. Almost.

Across the breakfast table, Grubb was forking scrambled eggs into his maw and chewing noisily. The man ate like a pig whose time was running out, intent on downing one last meal before he waddled to the slaughterhouse.

"You have no appetite?" Grubb asked, talking with his mouth full, staring pointedly at Schuster's loaded plate.

"I'm not a breakfast person."

"Ah. Perhaps you will enjoy the treat that Rolf brings us for dessert."

"I wish he'd get here."

They waited ten more minutes, Schuster counting money in his mind, while Grubb used chunks of fresh-baked bread to mop the leavings from his plate. They heard a car out front, and Grubb pushed back from the table, a smile of satisfaction on his face.

"You see? He's never late."

A servant came to clear the table, and they waited where they were until the houseman reappeared with Rolf Janek on his heels. The officer was decked out in a natty business suit, no hint of khaki to betray him in a social setting.

"Gentlemen." He forced a smile for Schuster and took a seat between them, facing toward the yard, the third point of a human triangle.

"Some breakfast for our guest," Grubb told the houseman.

"I've already eaten, thank you."

"Coffee, then. For three."

The houseman grunted an acknowledgment and disappeared. As Schuster twisted in his seat, attempting to find comfort in a wrought-iron chair, he spotted one of Grubb's sentries pacing off the far side of the lawn. The young man had an automatic rifle tucked beneath his arm, and he was dragging on a cigarette. He didn't seem especially alert, but Schuster told himself that they were safe. There was no danger here.

"You have some welcome news for us, I think," Grubb said.

"I do." The smile on Janek's face seemed more relaxed and natural as he addressed his longtime friend. "As you're aware, we picked up several leading members of the ANC and other left-wing groups last night."

"Mmm-hmm." The leader of the White Wolves shifted forward in his seat, his elbows resting on the table, one hand cupped inside the other, wedged beneath his chin.

"It was a gamble, even so, you understand. There are so many kafirs in the movement nowadays, the odds against locating one who has the key to any given plan are astronomical."

"Go on."

And hurry up, Schuster thought. It never failed. The boys in uniform did one thing right and spent the next six months patting themselves on the back. It was like some kind of crazy mutual admiration society, whenever two or three men got together, wearing guns.

"At any rate," Janek said, "we were lucky. One of those we bagged knew all about the setup."

"All?"

"Well, most of it. He's been a friend of Bridget Linder's since before her husband's accident." One corner of his mouth twitched slightly, like a nervous tic, and then relaxed. "He's been arrested several times for working with the ANC. A tough nut, ordinarily, but this time we got through to him."

More self-congratulation, Schuster thought. There was an interruption while the houseman brought a mug for Janek, topping off all three with steaming coffee from an ornate silver pot. The officer in charge of state security sat quietly until the servant executed his retreat.

"As you were saying..." Willem prodded.

"Yes. This kafir—"

"What's he called, again?"

"Modu. First name, Richard."

"Please continue."

"If I may. He heard about the plot directly from the Linder woman. Sadly she wasn't inclined to name her source of information, but he got the rest of it. She planned to run a series in her paper, as you said. It was supposed to stir the kafirs up, let Richard and his cronies organize a brand-new wave of demonstrations in Soweto and across the country. Meanwhile, the supposed embarrassment of links between your group and the security police was meant to break the government."

"My people missed her at the house," Grubb said. He spoke as if the words weighed several pounds apiece.

"I know." Was that a hint of satisfaction Schuster heard in Janek's voice? "I've seen the incident report. It was a very sloppy job."

"It was an ambush," Grubb protested. "They were waiting for us."

"They?"

"I don't have names," the leader of the White Wolves snapped. "You know I don't. It might have been the kafirs, or perhaps the same man who has been harassing us since night before last."

"One man, killing four of yours and taking off without a scratch?"

"I don't know, damn it! Seven of my best men dead, including Koenig. He was like a son to me."

"You'll have to see about adopting someone else," Janek replied, barely managing to keep the spiteful smile off his face.

"I want to hear about the woman, Rolf."

"Certainly. She's run away. Expecting heat, I should imagine, when the story breaks. And quite right, too."

"Run where?"

"To Mozambique," the officer replied. "Some kafirs over there are hiding her for the duration. I have full directions to the site. Of course, a border crossing by my own men is impossible."

"Of course."

"As for her files," Janek said, glancing at his wristwatch, "I believe the search-and-seizure warrants have been served by now. Suspicion of receiving stolen documents, that sort of thing. We've checked her home already. Nothing there. Perhaps we'll have good fortune at the *Chronicle*."

"And if you don't?"

"It may not matter," Janek answered, shrugging. "I left orders with my team to seize whatever seems to have the slightest bearing on the story. That includes computer disks, reporters' manuscripts and notebooks, anything at all. In the event they find the story has already gone to press or has been stored in a computer's memory somewhere, they have instructions to erase, destroy or confiscate all copies they can find."

"That might not be enough."

"It's all that I can do. Once you eliminate the woman," Janek said, "our troubles are behind us."

"I will need to know exactly where she's hiding, Rolf."

Janek nodded. "Do you have a map?"

THE PENETRATION HAD gone well, so far, from Bolan's point of view. It had been pitch-dark when he started, still three hours short of dawn, but darkness was a prowler's friend, and he could use the extra time to set himself in place.

The hideout had a Kensington address, but it was technically outside the suburb proper. The estate consisted of some fifty acres, mostly wooded, with the house set well back from the road, invisible to passing motorists. A mailbox out in front proclaimed the address, but it gave away no names.

When Bolan parked and hid his car a half-mile west, he knew that he was walking into danger, but he had no choice. He spent a moment setting up the camera, with its long-range lens and microphone attached, strapped on the power pack and slung the heavy rig across one shoulder. Traveling as light as possible, he left his Uzi in the car, but took along his side arms and a couple of grenades. With camouflage fatigues, his war paint and a combat knife, he felt prepared for almost anything.

There was no fence around the Grubb estate. It would have cost a fortune to erect one, Bolan thought, and there were always neighbors to consider. What would they think, if the quiet Mr. Grubb from Jo'burg built a wall around his grounds and started acting like the warlord of some god-forsaken jungle outpost? He was better off, all things considered, to refrain from any ostentatious show of hardware, keep his head down and allow the locals to forget that he was even there.

The warrior took his time, advancing through the woods and following his compass toward the house. He watched for snares and sensory devices on the way, as best he could in darkness, and nearly an hour had expired before he saw the house. He met no sentries on the way, but they were out there. Bolan saw a couple of them now, patrolling manicured grounds.

He spent the next three-quarters of an hour circling the house and checking out respective fields of vision. It was sixty yards, give or take, between the tree line and the broad veranda, with its deep-pit barbecue and swimming pool. He had no way of knowing where his subject would appear, if Grubb came out at all, but he was able to select a vantage point that let him watch the front and west side of the house, as well as the veranda.

The sun was burning off a layer of morning haze when Arnold Schuster drove up to the house and went inside. A flunky drove his car around in back and left it there. The Executioner was waiting, watching, when his target and the new arrival took their seats on the veranda, started sipping coffee, Grubb wolfing scrambled eggs and bacon while they talked about the night's events.

A tiny earpiece let him eavesdrop on their conversation through the shotgun mike, and with the telephoto lens, it felt as if he were seated at the breakfast table with them, an invisible participant in their discussion. Grubb was muttering about his loss at Bridget Linder's house and the flameout at the motor pool, but nothing seemed to kill his appetite. Across the table, Schuster settled for a cup of coffee, barely touching it. He answered Grubb in short, clipped phrases when a question was directed to him, clearly less than thrilled at being there.

Ten minutes later a third man joined the gathering. His face was new to Bolan, but his conversation made it plain that he was representing the security police. From what he said, it was apparent that Richard Modu had fulfilled his end of the agreement...but at what cost to himself? For all the Executioner could tell, he might be dead by now, already dumped like so much garbage on a dunghill in Soweto.

Steady. He was there to gather facts and tape the meeting for posterity. He checked out the sentries from time to time, made certain none of them had spotted him, and held the camera steady all the while.

He heard the stranger mention Mozambique and ask Grubb for a map. The houseman brought it on command, and the leader of the White Wolves spread it on the table. Schuster pinned down one corner with his coffee cup. The third man, Rolf Something, pointed out coordinates and told the others how Modu had been "forced" to give up Linder's hiding place. If he had any doubts at all about the information, they weren't conveyed to Willem Grubb.

"It should not be too difficult," Grubb said, a measure of relief apparent in his tone. "Tonight, I think."

"There's no point waiting," Schuster stated, agreeing with the man who paid his bills. "A simple in-and-out."

"Perhaps you would enjoy observing it firsthand?"

"No, thanks. The wet work's really not my strong point."

"You should strive for versatility," Grubb suggested.

"I'm plenty versatile," Schuster replied, "but you didn't hire me as a triggerman. If all you wanted was a shooter, you've been wasting cash and everybody's time."

The balding bigot shrugged and made a clucking sound. "I simply thought you might enjoy a hunting trip."

"That's mighty white of you. I'll pass."

"And I," the third man said to no one in particular, "must go about my business. You'll excuse me, Willem?"

"Certainly. Congratulations on a job well done."

"I'll be in touch with the results of our inquiry at the *Chronicle*."

"Of course."

With that, the stranger rose, shook hands with Grubb in parting and retreated through the house. His car was waiting for him when he reached the driveway, and another moment took him out of sight.

Next up was Schuster, pushing back his chair. "I might as well be on my way."

"So soon?" Grubb's disappointment was a patent sham.

"You'll keep me posted, I assume."

"Of course, dear boy."

The Executioner had seen and heard enough. He left his roost with Grubb still sitting on the patio, the houseman hovering, awaiting further orders. On his hike back through the trees, it seemed to Bolan that the final pieces were about to fall in place. The bait had been received and swallowed whole.

Now, all he had to do was reel the suckers in.

It sounded easy, when he thought about it that way, but in fact, the worst was still ahead. Grubb wouldn't send a five- or six-man team to Mozambique for Bridget Linder's head. Unless the Executioner was very much mistaken, Grubb would pull out all the stops and field his best surviving troops en masse, to guard against the possibility of any more snafus.

And he would be there to receive them, Kebby Seko at his side, without another soul to help them turn the tide.

Heavy odds didn't intimidate the Executioner. Instead he took them as a challenge, giving everything he had in the pursuit of victory.

This time around, he only hoped that everything he had would be enough.

15

Without Jon Koenig, Grubb decided it was best for him to lead the raid himself. He ordered up his last three UH-60 Black Hawk helicopters, which would give him forty-two men in the air, including three-man flight crews. That made nearly half of his surviving troops, and he had picked the very best to join him on the mission that would make or break the movement.

It was nearing nightfall by the time his troops were assembled at their Transvaal outpost, a hundred miles due north of Lydenburg. They brought their gear and weapons with them, suiting up when they arrived. Another dozen guns were posted on the camp's perimeter, to warn intruders off—or kill them, if it came to that.

Whatever happened, nothing could interfere with their mission tonight. The future of the White Wolves—and, perhaps, South Africa—was riding with them in the Black Hawk choppers as they lifted off in darkness, flying to the east.

It had been several years since Willem Grubb had fired a shot in anger at a human being, but he kept in fairly decent shape with exercise and made his way through the assault course at his private army's training center twice a year. His time hadn't been up to par last spring, but he imagined he was still a dashing figure in his jet-black helmet, uniform, and jump boots, cartridge belt and bandoliers. His MP-5 and the Beretta semiautomatic pistol on his hip were like extensions of himself. Grubb had a bit of difficulty reading tiny print these days, but he could still hunt with the best of them.

He meant to prove that point tonight.

Their journey had been mapped out at 160 miles, one way. The target was supposed to be a farm, some kafir's property where Bridget Linder went to hide while she was raising hell and printing libel in Johannesburg. She thought the border could protect her, but she was about to learn a lesson in reality.

Unfortunately it would come too late to do her any good.

Such was the price of trifling with men committed to a holy cause. Her death would be an excellent example for the leftists in South Africa, and for the world at large.

Grubb had ten soldiers with him in the leading gunship, plus a crew of three. His pilots had a map, with the coordinates supplied by Rolf Janek marked and measured for the most direct approach. It stood to reason that a kafir's ranch wouldn't have radar or advanced security devices, but the blacks were doubtless armed, and some of them might have the nerve to stand and fight before they reckoned they were hopelessly outgunned.

It saddened Willem Grubb that there would be no time for him to question the Linder woman. From the moment they invaded Mozambique, they had to be aware of passing time, make every second count. The pilots were adept at flying under radar, but mistakes were always possible. God knew they happened every day, and Grubb's luck hadn't been good the past few days. He would assume the worst, expect a military counterstrike and do his very best to leave the kafirs short of targets when they reached the battle site.

His earpiece hissed with static, and a strong voice told him when they crossed the border. Another twenty minutes air time, more or less, and they'd reach their target. Grubb felt the perspiration crawling underneath his arms like maggots wriggling on a piece of rotten meat.

For God's sake get a grip!

The losses of the past two days had shaken him. There was no point denying it. He would have been a robot, if the deaths and monetary loss had failed to touch him. Some of those who died, like Koenig, were his trusted friends. The rest had been disciples, loyal to their last extremity, and Grubb missed them all.

This night, he would avenge them in a style he knew they would approve. And in the morning, he would start picking up the pieces in South Africa. The movement had been damaged, not the least of all from media exposure, but it wasn't finished yet. As long as there was life in Willem Grubb, the White Wolves would survive.

And they would triumph in the end.

He checked the safety on his MP-5 and stared into the darkness, counting off the seconds in his mind.

THE RANCH HAD BEEN evacuated by a flying squad of soldiers shortly after noon. The house and barn were left unlocked, a single uniform on guard until the two men from South Africa arrived, at which time he withdrew and drove back to Magude. Kebby Seko and Mack Bolan were left to man the eight-room house, a spacious barn, three sheds of varied size and roughly five hundred acres by themselves.

It was a task that Seko didn't relish, but complaints weren't his style.

He wore fatigues in olive drab, a forage cap and faded webbing, with a holster on his hip. His semiauto side arm was a Spanish knockoff of the old Colt .45, but Kebby placed his real trust in the rifle that he carried. It was fairly new, an AK-74 manufactured in the former Soviet Union and sold to Mozambique as a peculiar form of "humanitarian aid." It took an expert eye to differentiate between the weapon and its venerable ancestor, the AK-47, since the major change was caliber—5.45 mm versus the original Kalashnikov's 7.62 mm. A revised muzzle break significantly reduced the weapon's recoil, and its 30-round box magazines were manufactured from distinctive light tan plastic, shaving several ounces off the total weight. The 5.45 mm bullets came with rigid cores of steel, designed to bend on impact with the softest target, making the projectiles "tumble" with destructive force in human flesh.

When they had finished scouting out the ranch, the American flipped a coin, and Seko "won" the barn as his defensive post. It seemed all right at first, with elevation in the loft, a sweeping field of fire and fairly decent cover, but the more he thought about it now, the more he started feeling claustrophobic, like a cornered rat.

How many guns would they be facing, when the White Wolves came in search of Bridget Linder? Why had Seko's government refused to help with reinforcements, when the raiders came and trampled on the soil of Mozambique? Was everyone except the American afraid of dying?

He felt that fear, himself, but Seko was prepared to die, if necessary. He had sworn an oath to help defend his country from her enemies, and he would do so, even if the blood he spilled turned out to be his own.

Belasko sounded confident, when Kebby spoke to him, but white men always sounded confident. It was a racial trait of theirs, like coveting the land and everything that walked or grew upon it for themselves. He sometimes thought the average white man, if surrounded by a hundred enemies, would first demand surrender, then be puzzled when his ultimatum was refused.

Belasko seemed to have a different way about him, though. He didn't boast of real or fabricated conquests, felt no need to dabble in one-upmanship. He had been sent to do a job, and after it was finished, he would leave.

Assuming he was still alive.

From Seko's aerie in the barn, he couldn't see Belasko in the house. He had a walkie-talkie, but the deal had been to keep it quiet, watch and wait, against the possibility that any raiding party might be scanning different frequencies to guard against a trap. Below him, parked beside a dusty tractor, was the jeep that brought them to the farm.

Their one way out, aside from body bags.

He was about to check his rifle, but he stopped himself. Repeating small precautions was a sign of insecurity, and Seko needed all the backbone he could muster at the moment, with an army winging east to cut him down.

He tried to guess their number, overestimating it deliberately to test his courage. They would fly, of course, and that meant ten or fifteen soldiers in a helicopter, at the very least.

How many helicopters?

He had no idea.

But he would soon find out.

The distant sound reached Kebby Seko's ears at 9:15 p.m. At first, he wrote it off as an illusion, several seconds passing before he realized that he wasn't imagining the noise. He faced the western skyline, watching for a light, aware that they would probably be flying dark, for reasons of security.

The engine sounds were drawing closer, getting louder. Seko wondered if Belasko heard them, in the house, but he restrained an urge to use his walkie-talkie, even for a warning. In a few more moments, as the helicopters closed the gap, their noise would be impossible to miss.

He knelt on wooden planks, the AK-74 tucked under his arm, and waited for the enemy to show himself. It was impossible for him to guess the number of approaching aircraft from the sounds that reached his ears, but time would tell. A few more moments, by the sound of it, and then...

Instinctively he double-checked his weapons, making sure the rifle and his side arm each had live rounds in the chamber, safety switched in the "off" position. Crouching in the darkness of the loft, he ran his fingers over ammunition pouches and grenades, to guarantee that he could find them in a hurry.

Done.

The rest of it depended on his skill, the number and proficiency of those arrayed against him. He had killed before, as a young soldier in the ten-year civil war that racked his country after Mozambique won independence from the Portuguese. At least two dozen dead men he was sure of, maybe others who had fallen in the heat of battle, claimed by no one in particular. The war had ended two years earlier, but Seko still recalled what he had done and seen, the way death smelled, up close and personal.

This night would be an opportunity to reacquaint himself with all that he had hoped to leave behind.

He saw the helicopters now, three of them, darker shapes against the velvet sky. He didn't open fire at once, aware that he would only give himself away by hasty action, calling down machine-gun fire or worse upon his head. They had agreed to let the raiders disembark and show themselves, providing human targets. It was risky, giving them a chance to scatter and surround the farmhouse, but he trusted Belasko's expertise.

In less than two days' time, the tall American had killed more men around Johannesburg than Seko had dispatched in five years of protracted warfare. Clearly he was doing something right.

The helicopters separated at a hundred yards from contact, flankers swinging off to left and right, the point ship coming straight ahead. It was a smart maneuver, no attempt at stealth from that point on. When sneaking was impossible, come in with all guns blazing.

And the White Wolves did exactly that.

He saw the muzzle-flash in time to save himself, leapt backward, flattening himself behind some stacked-up bales of hay. The bullets came a heartbeat later, drilling through the clapboard walls and slapping into Seko's makeshift barricade. He kept his head down, breathing dust, and waited for the gunners to complete their strafing run.

It seemed to last forever, but in fact, he estimated barely thirty seconds had elapsed before the guns fell silent. He could hear the difference in the helicopter engines as they settled, touching down outside. Another moment's hesitation, and he scuttled forward on his hands and knees to check the yard outside.

One of the helicopters sat below and thirty yards in front of him, disgorging black-clad warriors. Seko counted eleven raiders, knowing two or three would stay inside the helicopter. Three ships made a minimum of thirty soldiers on the ground, plus gunners and the flight crew of their aircraft. Call it forty men, and add another five for safety's sake.

It could be worse.

A sound of small-arms fire erupted from the south side of the house, beyond his line of sight, and that was Seko's cue to act. He brought the rifle to his shoulder, picked a moving target in the darkness and stroked the trigger lightly for a 3-round burst. The raider stumbled, went down on his face and stayed where he had fallen in the yard.

One down.

All hell broke loose at that, with half a dozen raiders firing toward the barn from different positions, dodging, seeking cover in the open no-man's-land. Instead of dueling with them, Seko chose his second target wisely, squeezing off a long burst toward the helicopter's engine block. He was rewarded with the sound of bullets striking metal.

Had he damaged it sufficiently to keep the chopper grounded? Seko had no way of answering that question as he ducked back from the open bay, a swarm of angry hornets rushing in behind him. Bullets slapped the roof and raised a torrent of accumulated dust that swirled like rising smoke inside the loft.

He palmed a frag grenade, released the safety pin and scuttled toward the open bay. Incoming bullets whistled overhead, preventing any kind of a precision pitch, but Seko did his best, unleashing a looping sidearm toss in the direction of the chopper down below. Retreating to the shelter of the hay bales, he counted off the precious seconds in his mind.

Now!

The detonation, when it came, was amplified, redoubled, vastly greater than the echo of a single hand grenade should be. Outside, a rolling ball of fire shot up beyond the peaked roof of the barn.

The helicopter!

Kebby Seko had a broad smile on his face as he went down to meet his enemies.

THE FIRST THING Bolan did, on entering the farmhouse, was prop the front door open with a heavy stone. That done, he checked the windows, making sure that each was shut and latched against the night. No prowlers would be sneaking in behind him in the midst of combat. They would have to smash the glass, and thus announce themselves. The back door was prepared for uninvited visitors by means of trip wires and a pair of frag grenades with loosened pins.

When he was done with the defensive preparations, Bolan took a straight-backed kitchen chair into the living room and sat on it, his Galil R-4 across his lap. He didn't use the sagging couch because it looked too comfortable, and he had no desire to doze off on his watch. From time to time, while he was waiting, the warrior rose and walked his beat around the house, one window to the next, examining the darkened grounds outside.

With Kebby Seko in the barn, they had the front yard covered with a decent cross fire, but the rest of it was each man for himself. Bolan could protect a portion of the barn if he had time, by firing through the kitchen window, and he knew that Seko had a clear shot at the back door of the house. Beyond that, on the south side of the house, the north and east sides of the barn, they couldn't help each other in the least.

Still, it was something, and his confidence was strong. The raiders would expect an easy hit-and-git, relying on surprise and numbers, nothing in the way of organized resistance. Above all else, they were expecting Bridget Linder.

They were in for a surprise.

He heard the helicopters coming from a distance, didn't even try to count them as he left his chair and moved to shut the door. He latched it, then stood before the nearest window, hoisting it to give himself an unobstructed field of fire across the yard.

The choppers were upon him in another moment, two birds peeling off and circling out of sight to take the buildings from behind. He left them to it for the moment, concentrating on the UH-60 that descended in the front yard, rotors beating flat the scrubby grass outside. He saw the first troops leaping from the chopper and picked a target.

A short burst sent his mark spinning, jerking through an awkward dance of death before he fell. The second man in line saw what had happened and tried to save himself but it was far too late. The 5.56 mm tumblers caught him in the chest as he was turning toward the house, and dumped him on his backside in the dust.

The yard lit up with muzzle-flashes, from the grounded chopper and the raiders scattering across the yard. Incoming rounds were punching through the walls and knocking jagged angles out of windowpanes, dismantling the furniture around him.

He spent a moment dueling with the gunner in the helicopter's open cargo bay, the big M-60 chopping abstract patterns in the farmhouse from a range of forty yards or so. His second burst from the Galil was close enough to part his adversary's hair, but Bolan had to give the shooter credit for his nerve. He hung right in there, firing at the house and covering his infantry.

The frag grenade came out of nowhere. Bolan never really saw it, but he witnessed the results. There was a flash and smoky thunderclap above the engine housing, followed instantly by smoke, a gush of flame—and then, the chopper came apart. A spark or piece of red-hot shrapnel found the fuel, ignited it, and Bolan watched the UH-60 Black Hawk shudder, buck, disintegrate. The flash was hot enough to make him flinch from forty yards away.

Two birds remained, and his plan demanded that they all be finished off, preventing a retreat by air. Delighted with their progress so far, Bolan fired a parting burst into the yard and doubled back in the direction of the bedroom.

Looking for another giant dragonfly to kill.

THE SHOCK WAVE FLATTENED Willem Grubb, and when he got up, he was spitting dirt. His helicopter was reduced to twisted, smoking rubble, hungry flames devouring the little that remained. Around him, several of his men were down, most of them unmoving where they lay. Another hardman stopped a bullet while he stood and watched, cut down by gunfire coming from the barn.

"Get in there!" he commanded, bellowing the order to his troops at large. "Root out that sniper!"

There was more than one, however. Grubb knew that much, for he was dodging bullets from the house, intent on finding cover, when the helicopter blew behind him and he wound up sprawling on his face. How many guns, he couldn't say, but there were at least two or three.

An ambush, damn it! They had flown into a trap, somehow, or else the farm was guarded on a routine basis, and the engine noise had given the sentries time to hide. Grubb had allowed for that eventuality, ordering his gunners to strafe the house and barn before the choppers landed, but it seemed he hadn't done enough. Instead of being killed or frightened off, the tenants were returning fire and scoring hits.

A helicopter had been lost, and his at that. It meant trouble on the homeward trip, since they would have to pack their dead and wounded out. The overloaded Black Hawks would be dangerously low on fuel before they reached their destination in South Africa.

He reached a corner of the house and crouched there, breathing heavily, his MP-5 clutched against his chest. So far, he hadn't fired a shot—no targets visible—but it wouldn't be long. The farm's defenders had been lucky, getting in their early licks, but they were cornered now, penned up inside the house and barn. It would take only a match or an incendiary charge to flush them out.

So much for idle thoughts. Grubb lifted a thermite canister from his web belt, yanked the pin and held the safety spoon in place as he made preparations for the pitch. Two short steps backward, and he cleared the nearest window with a burst of submachine-gun fire. The thermite can went in behind the bullets, struck the wooden floor and rolled. A moment later, it went as bright as day inside, a taste of hellfire for the living here on earth.

The house was no more sanctuary, now. Already, white-hot coals were eating through the walls and roof, the living room and nearby kitchen in flames. He felt no pity for the kafirs trapped inside, nor for the woman they were hiding.

Let them burn.

He had approached the mission hoping for a chance to face his mortal enemy, if not to question Bridget Linder, then at least to see her face. Perhaps he still might have that chance, but as he watched the bright flames spreading, Willem Grubb knew he might have to settle for a pile of ashes, after all.

Behind him, in the firelit darkness, several of his men were dueling snipers in the barn. Grubb left them to it, circling around the burning house to reach the other helicopters. Two were left, at least, and they were in position to cut off escapees from the house.

Grubb's blood was up, and he was anxious for the climax of the hunt.

16

The barn had doors at either end, both east and west, and gunners came at him from both directions. Kebby Seko had the doors barred from within, but simple wooden latch bars wouldn't hold for long against the concentrated fire of automatic weapons.

Seko had considered waiting for his adversaries in the loft, deciding it would only multiply his danger if they had him cornered on an elevated platform, where the enemy could line up underneath him and fire through the floor. Downstairs, at least, the ancient tractor, stalls and hay bales offered better cover, and the enemy would have to come at him on level ground.

He had already checked the tractor on a whim, and found its fuel tank nearly full. The motor started easily when he had tried it earlier, though it was far from quiet, the normal engine sounds augmented by the kind of clink-clank-rattle one expects from old, tired vehicles. Still, it was something and he kept the information filed away for future reference.

Seko chose a stack of hay bales as his first line of defense, and he was ready when the western doors—those closest to the burning helicopter—yielded under the combined assault of half a dozen raiders. Seko had them covered as they crossed the threshold, raking them from left to right and back again with 5.45 mm tumblers.

Three of them went down like shattered mannequins and lay unmoving on the earthen floor. A fourth was obviously hit, but staggered out of sight, around the corner of a cattle stall. Two others managed to escape unharmed and vanished back in the direction they had come from.

Seko held his ground and waited, knowing it wasn't the end. The dust had barely settled on their fallen comrades when the two survivors started sniping at him from the doorway, firing blindly, hoping for a luck score. The wounded raider, meanwhile, was producing painful grunting noises from his stall, apparently maneuvering to find an angle of attack.

Behind the man from Mozambique, a group of raiders had begun to try the eastern doors, first shoving at them, kicking with their boots, then stepping back to try a few experimental rounds of automatic fire. It would take more than that to saw a sturdy board in two, but Seko knew that he was running out of time.

The outside gunners by the west door, first. He spotted them from muzzle-flashes, calculated where they must be hunkered down between their probing bursts and lined up his sights on the left-hand target first. His weapon's 5.45 mm rounds were known for penetration—some brochures said they would pierce an engine block—and whether that was true or not, he estimated that the clapboard walls should be no challenge.

Seko found his point of reference, turned to his left a few degrees and raked the barn's wall with a burst of six or seven rounds. Was that a cry of pain outside, in the confusion of the battle?

He had no time to play a guessing game.

Hard right, and he was staring at the right-hand wall beside the door through open sights. He held the trigger down and stitched a line of holes across the dusty lumber, aiming roughly waist-high on a standing man. There was no shout of pain this time, but neither was his fire returned. Short of going out to check, it was the most he could expect.

The wounded gunner chose that moment to unleash a burst of submachine-gun fire, but it was high and wide, a clean yard over Seko's head. The African responded with a frag grenade, a looping overhand that dropped the egg behind the thin partition that concealed his enemy.

It was enough to flush the wounded gunner out, and Seko tagged him on his second step outside the stall, a burst of tumblers ripping through his chest and spinning him, a jerky rag doll dancing in the wind. The frag grenade went off two seconds later, like an exclamation point inscribed in heavy-metal thunder.

Seko made his move, reloading on the short run to the tractor, settling in the driver's seat and reaching out for the ignition key. The jeep could wait, and he hoped it would survive. The noisy motor came to life at his command, and Seko shifted out of neutral, lifting off the clutch. The tractor started forward, rolling toward the eastern doors, where unseen raiders had begun to concentrate their fire.

He was aware of shouts and shots behind him as he held the tractor on its course. A backward glance showed three men standing on the western threshold of the barn, flame spitting from their submachine guns, and he chased them with a wild burst from his own Kalashnikov.

Ten paces from the eastern doors, Seko gunned the tractor to its maximum acceleration, double-checked its course and vaulted from the driver's seat. He landed in a crouch and scuttled off to one side of the target zone, his rifle covering the bullet-riddled doors.

The tractor had velocity and weight behind it when it struck the doors, already weakened by perhaps three hundred bullets ripping through the weathered boards. There was a moment of resistance, then the tattered latch bar snapped in two, and Seko watched the tractor nose its way outside.

The raiders scattered, falling back on either side and peppering the tractor with a vicious cross fire. Seko came out on their blind side, eating dust and taking full advantage of his enemies' distraction.

Gunners on the left side, first. He counted three, all hunched together, firing at the tractor, and he killed them where they stood. Two others, on the far side of the tractor, recognized their peril and responded several beats too late. Precision bursts from the Kalashnikov dropped both men in their tracks.

Inside the barn, a raiding party was advancing on Seko's flank, and he met them with another frag grenade. He watched them scurry, pumping bullets after them and nailing one, before he dodged back out of range and ran in search of Belasko, barely noticing the blast that rocked the barn.

He still had work to do, and he was searching for an ally on the battlefield to help him get it done.

WILLEM GRUBB skirted the burning house at a respectful distance, covering the windows with his MP-5 and hoping that a target would reveal itself before the roof fell in. He would feel better, more assured, if he could catch at least a fleeting glimpse of Bridget Linder, know beyond a shadow of a doubt that she was in there, frying for her sins.

The gunfire from the house had stopped, at any rate, and that was something. The defenders, if they lived, would be too busy looking for an exit from the blazing funeral pyre to offer any real resistance.

It was perfect.

But the barn was something else again. Grubb heard sustained and heavy gunfire, most of it apparently delivered by his men against the bulky structure, automatic weapons stitching abstract patterns on the clapboard walls. Grubb didn't know how many kafirs were inside the barn, but they were catching hell.

It served them right, trying to protect a traitor from South Africa. They had no one to blame for their misfortune but themselves.

Reluctantly he broke off from the house and jogged in the direction of the barn. A number of his men were firing at the door from several feet away, as if to smash a hidden lock. As Grubb drew closer, they began to push the broad doors open, venturing inside.

What happened next sent cold chills down his spine. There was a burst of automatic rifle fire, the telltale sound of a Kalashnikov, and two of Grubb's commandos scampered back across the threshold, peeling off to crouch on either side of the open door. That still left three or four inside, but they were nowhere to be seen.

Could all of them be dead?

The firing from inside the barn had ceased, Grubb's two survivors on the door unleashing short bursts when they found the nerve. On balance, it was probably the best that they could do, and he decided it was time to call up reinforcements.

Grubb was turning toward the house to summon other soldiers, when it happened. Right before his eyes, a burst of metal-jacketed projectiles drilled the wall on one side of the door and dropped his trooper in the dust. The second man was gaping at his fallen comrade, shocked, when yet another burst ripped through the clapboard wall, on his side. He toppled forward on his face.

The leader of the White Wolves cursed and started shouting for his men to rally at the barn. It crossed his mind that he would soon be short of men, instead of helicopters, and his face flushed crimson at the thought.

The kafirs wouldn't get away with this!

A dozen men responded to his call, and Grubb sent half of them against the barn at once, the others waiting in reserve. He still heard gunfire at the far end of the barn, but there was something else, some kind of engine growling that he couldn't identify by sound.

His point men disappeared inside the barn, and half of them came back a heartbeat later, dodging bullets all the way. Grubb snarled and led his small reserve to join the fight.

Inside the barn, he hesitated for an instant, staring at the dead men scattered in his path. The engine noise that Grubb had heard was coming from a tractor, grinding toward a pair of doors directly opposite, a kafir in the driver's seat.

Grubb fired a short burst from his MP-5, the troops around him cutting loose with everything they had. Downrange, the black man swung around and aimed a rifle at them, firing it one-handed in his haste. The bullets came in close enough to make Grubb dive for cover. The man behind him never made it, dropping to his knees with both hands clasped across the crimson gusher spurting from his abdomen.

When Grubb looked up again, the eastern doors were standing open and the tractor was outside, converging streams of automatic fire dismantling the rusty vehicle. He squinted, seeing no one in the driver's seat, and then glimpsed the bastard, running in the tractor's wake, about to take Grubb's soldiers by surprise.

He shouted out a warning, but it came too late, his words lost in the racket of opposing guns. Grubb struggled to his feet, ran past a vintage jeep and stacked-up bales of hay to reach the latest killing ground. Behind him, several of his men had fallen into step.

The hand grenade came out of nowhere, arching through the darkness, touching down and rolling toward him with the wobble of its egg-shaped casing. Grubb reversed directions in a flash, and there was barely time to warn the others as he raced to save himself.

"Grenade!"

The blast struck Grubb like a giant fist between the shoulder blades, and he was airborne, gasping as he struck the hard-packed earth face downward, tasting dirt. But at least he was alive.

Grubb clasped that knowledge to him like a life preserver, crawling slowly, stiffly, toward the western exit from the barn.

It was enough. He had to reach the nearest helicopter now and call retreat, before their simple mission turned into a massacre.

THE BASEMENT to the farmhouse was accessible by opening a trapdoor in the kitchen, where a ladder offered access to the earthen chamber below. Bolan had examined the escape hatch earlier, and knew that wooden storm doors opened on the yard, against the north side of the house. He had removed the padlock with a sharp twist from a crowbar, and replaced the hasp to let it pass a cursory inspection in the dark.

The house was burning as he went back to the basement, flames spreading from the living-room inferno, covering the walls and ceiling with a network of elaborate, hungry tentacles, the whole thing merging into one great sheet of fire as Bolan let the trapdoor slam behind him.

The cellar was a dark, cool sanctuary from the fire, but it would soon become a baking oven when the floor caught fire, the walls and ceiling crumbling in on top of one another. By the time that happened, Bolan meant to be well away from ground zero.

He cut the cellar darkness with a penlight and found the storm doors, pausing long enough to listen at the panel for a sound of nearby voices or footsteps. He cracked the door one inch, enough to scan perhaps a quarter of the smoky yard outside, and when he came up empty, cautiously repeated the procedure in the opposite direction.

Still no raiders close enough to make a difference. The smoke was coming for him now, pale tendrils wriggling down between the floorboards that were Bolan's ceiling in the basement hideaway. He threw the storm doors back and scrambled into darkness, following the snout of his Galil R-4.

His enemies were concentrating on the barn, where Seko had his roost, and while the Executioner was moved to help his comrade, he had other vital work to do.

The choppers, first.

He found one grounded at the northeast corner of the house and came in on the gunner's flank, a gliding shadow in the mottled firelight from the house. The Black Hawk gunner's full attention had been focused on the barn, but something warned him of approaching danger at the final instant. Swiveling toward Bolan with his big M-60, he was still too late to save himself. A burst of 5.56 mm tumblers drilled his face and dumped him over on his back. Bolan tossed a frag grenade into the helicopter's cockpit as he passed.

Bolan kept on going without a backward glance. When the chopper detonated, he was out of range and racing toward the final gunship, grounded on the south side of the house. His angle of attack was not ideal—the flight crew saw him coming from a range of sixty yards—but the warrior had no choice.

He saw the pilot and his second in command both gaping at him, pointing, shouting at the gunner to cut him down. The gunner tried it, but he missed his chance as Bolan made a swift jog to his left and put the body of the aircraft in between them.

Bolan stroked the trigger of his automatic rifle, watching a ragged line of holes appear across the Black Hawk's windshield. He could hear the fliers shouting now, but only for a moment, then their voices were eclipsed by gushing blood.

Not so the UH-60's triggerman, waiting for the Executioner when Bolan reached the other side. There had been no time for him to unbolt the big M-60, but he had a submachine gun, leading the warrior by a yard or so with his initial burst.

The shooter was attempting to correct his aim when Bolan hosed him down, the hot Galil unloading half a magazine within a second and a half. The chopper's final crewman did a jerky little dance and toppled backward, his lifeless index finger clenched around the trigger of his subgun. It kept on firing as the guy went down, his wasted bullets ripping through the helicopter's ceiling, rattling around inside the twin T700 engines.

Contact!

Bolan didn't see the fatal spark, but he observed its grim effects at close to point-blank range. The Black Hawk literally blew its top, the massive General Electric engines detonating with a roar. Jagged pieces of the rotors sliced through the air while Bolan hit the deck. Debris rained down around him, smacking into the turf.

A moment later, he was on his feet and moving, feeling satisfied.

Whatever happened with the White Wolves now, his enemies would find themselves on foot in hostile territory, sixty-five miles from the safety of South Africa, as the buzzard flies.

He went in search of Kebby Seko, prowling through the smoke and hoping he would find the African alive.

IT WAS DIFFICULT for Willem Grubb to understand how everything had gone so totally and tragically awry. His plan had sounded foolproof, when he talked it over with his chief lieutenants. They had crossed the border many times before, typically without sustaining any casualties, and they had never left a body or a vehicle behind. This night, with the twin advantages of surprise and numbers on their side, they had lost all three helicopters, and the eighteen living members of his forty-two-man task force would be walking home.

Assuming any of them got that far.

Grubb knew the odds against them, stranded in a country owned and run by kafirs, where the military was, if not proficient, certainly well versed in killing prisoners. Each man possessed at least one weapon, with sufficient ammunition for a running fight of sorts, but they would soon be overmatched in any kind of pitched engagements with a well-armed force.

Salvation lay in speed and pure dumb luck. Unless they found some kind of working vehicles along the way, an uninterrupted march to the border would consume a minimum of fifteen hours, probably a good deal more. That gave the Mozambique patrols sufficient time to spot their trail and follow up in jeeps and trucks, perhaps an airplane.

And in the open country they were crossing, Grubb knew they would find nowhere to hide.

Their radios had gone up with the helicopters, or he could have called for trucks to meet them, even cross the border on a rescue mission. As it was, the remnant of his army in South Africa would only know that something had gone wrong when Grubb and his commandos failed to meet the deadline for their turnaround. Even then, the home team would have no idea of what had happened to their comrades, nor would they be able to initiate a search.

Grubb checked his watch. There were still at least five hours left before the sunrise put his ragged marching column on display for all the world to see. It was a stroke of luck, he thought, that they had come together near the barn, while searching for the kafir who had used the ancient tractor for his getaway, killing more than a dozen of White Wolves' best men in the process. They were scouring the darkness for him when the last two helicopters blew, and Grubb had known that it was time to leave.

He glanced back toward the east, not breaking stride, and saw that they had left the burning farmhouse well behind them now. They'd covered two miles, at least, by Grubb's best estimate, which left another fifty-six or fifty-eight to go.

Grubb swallowed a bitter curse and concentrated on putting one foot in front of the other, trudging along in front of his men. His head was throbbing painfully, and every impact of his boot heels on the ground drove spikes of agony into his temples.

On flying raids across the border, out and back, Grubb's men had never carried rations, camping gear, canteens, or any other useless items that would slow them down in combat. He had never planned on marching back from Mozambique, which meant that any food and water they required would have to be picked up along the way.

Grubb thought about his maps, all ashes in the burned-out helicopters now, and tried to recollect a lake or river somewhere on their line of march. It would be self-defeating if they swung off course to quench their thirst and wound up adding hours to their desolate journey in the process. Better to be parched and hungry than to let the kafirs catch them drinking from a stream, their asses up in the air.

At least he had the compass that his first lieutenant wore from force of habit when they went on border-hopping raids. Without it, they would have to wait for sunrise to be sure of their direction, wasting precious hours.

Even now, he half expected headlights in the distance, closing on them from the general direction of the farm. It troubled Grubb that they had been allowed to slip away so easily.

The alternate scenario, he realized, was slightly better for his team, albeit nothing to relieve their present danger. It was possible that they had wiped out the bastard kafirs or frightened them away, in the confusion of the helicopters detonating like a string of giant fireworks. Even with the kafirs on the verge of winning, perhaps they were too afraid and ignorant to take advantage of their lead.

Grubb barked an order at his men and set a faster pace. While they had darkness on their side, he meant to use it well.

Come daylight, it would be a very different game.

17

The barn was more or less intact, though pocked with bullet holes and shrapnel scars on every side. A stack of hay bales smoldered against one wall, but Bolan had no fire extinguisher, no time to hang around and douse the smoking feed. He searched for Seko's corpse among the others, hoping not to find it, visibly relieved when he discovered all the dead were Boers, dressed in midnight black, now stained with crimson from their fatal wounds.

The jeep had stopped a few stray rounds, but none of them had reached the engine or the fuel tank. Bolan palmed his copy of the jeep's ignition key and slid behind the wheel, smiling grimly as the engine caught on his first try. He steered around the scattered bodies, made his way outside and paused there, leaning on the horn for several seconds.

"Kebby? Kebby Seko!"

"Here."

The man from Mozambique jogged from the shadows, feeding his Kalashnikov a fresh magazine as he approached the jeep. Another moment put him in the shotgun seat.

"I see you had your hands full," Bolan said, nodding toward the barn that had become a charnel house.

"Their overconfidence betrayed them," Seko replied, smiling as he spoke.

"We have some mopping up to do."

"The survivors are on foot. I should have tried to stop them."

Bolan shook his head emphatically. "We had a plan. We're sticking to it."

It would be a relatively easy thing, he knew, to run the White Wolves down on open ground, but that would only force a confrontation, wherein Kebby and the Executioner would be outnumbered nine or ten to one. The plan he had in mind required more patience, but it promised to deliver the desired results, while minimizing risk of friendly casualties.

Instead of starting after Grubb and company directly, Bolan swung his jeep off to the south, accelerating over open ground, and picked out a track that would, according to his calculations, parallel the path of the retreating Wolves. The rough terrain kept Bolan's speed below the forty-mile-per-hour mark, but he was still exceeding any pace the marchers could maintain, even if they had the strength and stamina to sprint sixty miles to the border.

Bolan used his headlights freely, watching out for dips and gullies, several times required to backtrack, making up the time as best he could when flat land came his way. They rode in silence for the first half hour, broken finally when Seko cleared his throat and asked the question that was preying on his mind.

"Do you think this will finish it?"

"That all depends on what you mean," Bolan replied. "If we do it right, I'd say the White Wolves will be history. The larger problem, though..." He hesitated, finally shrugged and said, "I don't believe in miracles."

"I do," Seko told him, sounding confident. "Within my lifetime I have seen the Portuguese thrown out of Mozambique, the ruin of apartheid and the death of communism. Any one of these things would have seemed a miracle when I was born, impossible for many of my elders to conceive. Yet, they have happened. I believe in miracles."

"To me," Bolan said, "miracles have always seemed a little bit like luck. You make your own, and bad luck means you let your guard down when you should have been alert. I've seen too many good men die from careless 'accidents' and simple negligence."

"You must believe in something greater than yourself."

"I do, but I never got around to giving it a name. I don't believe that He or She or It sits down and calculates what's coming up for everyone on earth, each day, around the clock. If it's a giant chess game, and we're all just pawns, why bother with evolving brains? You don't need an imagination or incentive if you're dancing on the end of someone else's string."

The river interrupted Bolan's train of thought. Its first appearance was disguised by trees that grew along the eastern bank, but the warrior had prepared for this engagement by examining the latest and most detailed maps available, committing them to memory. He knew exactly what he wanted, and it only took another fifteen minutes to select the perfect place.

The bridge would be ideal. It spanned a narrow section of the river, widening on either side, and there was open ground directly opposite, the western tree line pushed back from the water's edge by forty yards or so. Once they had crossed and found their vantage point among the trees, he would be able to command the bridge and some two hundred yards of river, north and south.

Grubb's infantry couldn't escape a river crossing, short of following the eastern bank 150 miles north to Zimbabwe. They would cross as best they could, to reach the western shore, and if they knew the area at all, some of them had to know about the bridge.

They drove across, with timbers groaning underneath the jeep, and Bolan found a place to hide the vehicle. He took a canvas satchel from the space behind the driver's seat and shouldered it, felt Seko watching him.

"Let's go," he said. "We've still got work to do."

GRUBB SAW THE LINE of trees an hour after dawn's first light began to color the horizon at his back. Although he had been dreading sunrise, it was good to have his compass readings verified and know that they were marching in the right direction. Now, the trees he saw a mile or so in front of him stirred memories recalling times when he had studied maps before Jon Koenig led a team across the border from South Africa to Mozambique.

There *was* a river, he remembered, and it lay across their path. They had no hope of circumventing it, unless they turned the march into an epic tour, and that was bound to have disastrous results.

They had to cross it, then, but first they had to get there.

"Double-time," he shouted, hearing groans behind him as he set the jogging pace. His men were tired, some of them injured, but he had no doubt that they would do as they were told.

Their lives depended on it, after all.

Another fifteen minutes brought them to the tree line, Grubb and most of his commandos winded, trying hard to catch their breath. The good news was that they could hide among the trees, rest a bit and feel secure that they couldn't be spotted from the air, if anyone was hunting for them yet.

The bad news: they would have to find a way across the river, leave the shelter of the trees behind if they intended to get home alive.

Grubb huddled with his two lieutenants, both of whom had managed to survive the battle at the farm. One of them, Emil Kraft, had stopped a bullet in the shoulder, but he managed not to show much of the pain. The other, Hans Nilsen, had emerged unscathed from the engagement with the blacks, but his face showed signs of worry and fatigue.

"We need a way across the river," Grubb informed them. "Here it seems too deep and swift."

"There is a bridge," Kraft said. "A short march south from here, I think."

"You aren't certain?"

Kraft considered it and shook his head. "Without a map, the right coordinates, I can't be positive. The river curves above us, though," he went on, pointing to the north. "I'm sure the bridge lies south. It is the distance that concerns me."

"We must find it, all the same." Grubb phrased the statement as an order, rising from his crouch and facing south. "The trees will give us cover as we go."

Another moment had his weary soldiers back in something like a column, though their carriage would have drawn rebukes on a parade ground. Several of the men were limping, whether from the march or battle wounds Grubb didn't know or care. He had enough to think of, with the river and what lay beyond. There was no time to think of what the press would say about the soldiers he had left behind. Excuses would be called for, manufactured to fit the occasion, and most of the world would disbelieve the answers—not because they were false, but because they came from a loyal, white South African.

First, though, Grubb had to concern himself with the nineteen lives left in his care, including his own. They had to find the bridge, move on and put this cursed kafir's land behind them, once and for all.

It took them almost forty minutes, moving at a snail's pace through the trees, with Kraft out front and acting as their scout. He whistled when he spied the bridge, a single rising note that might have sounded like a bird call to a stranger in the area.

Grubb forced himself to double-time the final hundred yards and caught up with his point men near the bridge. It was constructed out of timbers, and its age was obvious, from weathered uprights to the worn and sagging horizontal boards that formed the bridge itself. Repairs wouldn't have been amiss, but Grubb had no doubt it would serve his little band of stragglers as the builders had intended, once upon a time.

He stood and scanned the tree line opposite, deciding that their enemies would certainly have manned the bridge, if they had come this far. There was a chance, at least, that no one had discovered the ungodly carnage at the farm. There might be no pursuit, as yet, but he couldn't afford to gamble on that chance.

"We cross," he told his men, and led them by example, stepping out of cover and walking cautiously across the wooden bridge. He kept his finger on the trigger of his submachine gun, felt the muscles knotting in his neck and shoulders, tension throbbing like a drum beat in his skull.

Halfway across, Grubb turned and found the others watching him. He scowled and waved them forward, letting himself relax a little when his feet touched the ground on the other side.

The western river bank was his.

He drifted toward the tree line, scanning restless shadows, ready to unleash a stream of bullets at the first clear sign of danger. Meanwhile, at his back, a dozen soldiers made the crossing unopposed.

Two more.

The last four men were in the middle of the span and walking two abreast, when it erupted from below, the shock wave of a powerful explosion slamming Grubb and several of his soldiers to their knees.

Grubb turned in time to see the shattered pieces of the bridge and four men fall back into the river, splashing into water that was churned to muddy froth by the explosion.

What, on God's green earth...

The first shot answered his question, punching through the bridge of Hans Nilsen's nose and dropping him like so much dirty laundry on the sod.

Without a target, cursing furiously, Grubb began to fire in the direction of the trees.

THE BRIDGE EXPLOSION came as no surprise to Kebby Seko. He had helped Belasko set the plastic charges, with their wireless detonators tuned to the frequency of a remote-control box the tall American wore on his belt. Seko understood the plan, to let Grubb's main force cross the bridge, then slam the door behind them, and he knew that it would happen as the last few men were crossing.

Even so, the roar of detonation made him flinch, briefly losing track of the man he had framed in the sights of his AK-74. It was a momentary lapse, and he recovered swiftly, while his enemies were staring at the ruins of the bridge in awe.

Belasko got the first shot off, his target pitching over backward, blood exploding from his shattered face. The gunshot was enough for Seko, and he squeezed the trigger of his automatic rifle, rattling off a 4-round burst that struck his chosen mark between the shoulder blades and dumped him facedown in the dirt.

The scene disintegrated into chaos, with the White Wolves running everywhere and firing toward the tree line, hoping for a lucky hit in lieu of clear-cut targets. Seko drew a bead on Willem Grubb, but as he squeezed the trigger, one of Grubb's subordinates ran into Seko's line of fire, absorbed the bullets meant for his commander, dropping in a spray of crimson, with a muted cry of pain.

Grubb saw his danger and triggered a burst that came within a foot of taking Seko down. A brief, involuntary flinch spoiled Seko's aim, and by the time he got it back, his target had evaporated.

Seko scanned the riverbank, saw Grubb escaping to the north and swung around to bring him under fire. Just then, a burst of rifle bullets clipped the branches overhead, and he was forced to pivot, squaring off against a member of the wolf pack who had spotted him.

The rifleman was close, no more than twenty yards away, but he had missed his first attempt through haste. He was about to try again, when Seko hit him with a rising burst that lifted him completely off his feet and dumped him over backward, wriggling through his death throes in the weeds.

A number of the Wolves were down and out now, others scattering to north and south along the river. Two or three had plunged into the water, seeking shelter there, returning fire as best they could across the steep lip of the riverbank.

Seko picked a running target at random and stroked the trigger. The runner lurched and stumbled, went down on his face, arms flailing into impact with the ground.

The black African palmed a frag grenade and yanked the safety pin, wound up the pitch and let it fly in the direction of three gunners who were running south along the riverbank. The lethal egg fell just behind them, but the runners were within its killing radius when it exploded, spewing deadly shrapnel high and low.

One of the three was killed on impact, dropping like a stone. His two companions suffered crippling wounds and went down screaming, writhing on the ground. A quick one-two from Seko's rifle silenced them for good and left him seeking other targets on the killing field.

He dropped the empty magazine and snapped a fresh one into the Kalashnikov, priming the weapon in one fluid motion. He scanned the field for targets and saw a pair of White Wolves crumple as Belasko cut them down.

On Seko's left, two Boers had elected not to run, crouching in their tracks and laying down a blaze of fire from submachine guns. It was bold, but foolish, and they left themselves exposed as Seko raked a burst from left to right and back again. His targets came apart like straw men underneath the rain of 5.45 mm tumblers, falling in a heap together as they died.

Three Wolves were racing to the south, along the riverbank, and Seko lost them to the trees before he had a chance to aim and fire. The rest were either dead or hiding now, no more than five or six surviving.

Seko made his choice and broke from cover, jogging in pursuit of the escaping Boers. As he ran, he glimpsed Belasko emerging from the trees, advancing toward the river's edge. The time had come for mopping up, and Seko didn't envy those White Wolves who still remained to face the tall American.

He left Belasko to it, doggedly pursuing three who got away.

BOLAN KNEW that the three Wolves in the water had to be running low on ammunition. Their wild defensive fire had grown sporadic, trailing off, and by the time he left the tree line, they were clearly hoarding any ammo they had left.

He spotted one of them, a bobbing head above the sheer lip of the riverbank, and gambled that the other two would be nearby. As he approached his target from the blind side, Bolan primed a frag grenade and held it ready in his hand.

Three bobbing heads were visible this time, instead of one. He lobbed the grenade and heard it splash on target, followed seconds later by a bloody geyser shooting skyward, mud, grass and mangled flesh mixed together by the underwater blast.

There was no more resistance on the killing field, and Bolan turned north, following the river, trailing Willem Grubb and two or three surviving stragglers who had gone in that direction. Following their path was no great challenge: one of them was wounded, laying down a blood trail, and the others took no care to camouflage their tracks. A novice Cub Scout could have tracked them in their wild flight to the north, and all that slowed Mack Bolan down was watching out for traps along the way.

He found the wounded straggler first, propped up against a tree like some pathetic rear guard, covering his comrades as they fled. The crippled Wolf saw Bolan coming, tried to raise his submachine gun, but the creeping shock and loss of blood played hell with his reaction time. He barely had his weapon off the ground, when Bolan hit him with a 3-round burst above the neck and finished it.

The next two stragglers tried to lay an ambush, but their jitters got the best of them. One fired a hasty burst the moment Bolan came in view, the bullets flying high and wide. Instinctively the Executioner went low and broke for cover, merging with the trees as two guns opened up from hiding, chopping at the earth and undergrowth.

He stalked them in a world of mottled shadows, circling around to take them on the right flank, with the river at their backs. He homed in on the short, staccato bursts they fired at nothing in particular, the nervous jitters taking over as they tried an unseen target.

Easy.

He was on top of them before they saw Death coming, his Galil R-4 locked into target acquisition, spitting 5.56 mm tumblers at a range of something under twenty feet. The nearer gunner jerked his limbs in death, keeling over in his tracks. Number two was trying to retreat when Bolan hit him with a killer burst between the shoulder blades.

And that, as far as Bolan knew, left one.

He kept on to the north, Grubb's tracks a bit less obvious without three troopers beating down the bushes in his wake, but there was still a trail for those with eyes to see. The warrior closed the gap, aware that Grubb had slowed his pace, perhaps considering the gunfire on his trail.

It might have been that gunfire, terminated by the sharp voice of a weapon that he didn't recognize, that made Grubb stop and climb the largest tree that he could find. He had a clear view of the trail and was ready with his MP-5 when Bolan came into view. But weariness and nerves conspired to spoil his aim. Grubb's bullets kicked up divots in the sod, perhaps a foot in front of Bolan, and the warrior went to ground among the trees.

It was a different proposition from his last engagement, taking out an elevated sniper. A stationary duel would be unequal, Grubb commanding high ground from his perch, and while the Executioner's Galil had vastly greater range, the forest wouldn't let him snipe his target from a hundred yards away.

His next best hope would be a frag grenade.

It was a tricky business, getting close enough to lob the deadly egg and putting it exactly where he wanted it to go, but Bolan had no other choice. He primed his next-to-last grenade and held it in his right hand, balancing the automatic rifle in his left.

The move he had in mind required coordination, speed and accuracy. Any slight mistake could get him killed, and Bolan knew that he would have no second chance to get it right.

Instead of hesitating, pondering the possibilities of failure, the warrior made his move. He came in underneath his target, taking maximum advantage of the foliage overhead for cover, holding down the R-4's trigger as he made the final dash.

He had to make a hook shot, more or less, but it wasn't his goal to put the grenade directly in Grubb's lap. The fuse would give it time to drop from there, perhaps as far as Bolan's level, and the odds against a kill from any blast below his target's feet were astronomical. Instead he had to place the egg *above* Grubb's roost, let it fall on top of him.

And he would have to do it on the run, with something like a second and a half in which to aim and make his pitch.

He came in firing, heard the answering report from Grubb's SMG, and felt the parabellum manglers whisper past his face. The toss was almost too much for his balance, but he kept his footing, held the R-4's trigger down until the magazine ran dry. Then he was past the zone of mortal danger, sliding in behind another tree downrange. A stream of bullets tried to follow him, but they were intercepted by the tree trunk, slapping into solid wood.

He didn't see the grenade describe its arch, come rushing down through leafy twigs and branches, but he heard the airburst of its detonation, followed by a scream as Grubb took flight.

The Wolfman's eyes were open, blinking rapidly, when Bolan reached his side and stood above him. Grubb was fading fast, blood seeping from at least a dozen shrapnel wounds, his legs twisted into angles they would never normally attain. He tried to focus on the face above him, but it wasn't happening.

"Who . . . are . . . you?"

"I'm your judgment," Bolan answered. "Time to pay the tab."

The self-appointed front man for the master race was gasping like a stranded fish when Bolan put a mercy round between his eyes and turned away. Sweet silence reigned in the forest as he started back along the trail of death.

"I was about to come and look for you," Seko said, visibly relieved when Bolan made their rendezvous, beside the ruin of the blasted bridge. "Is everything all right?"

"So far," the Executioner replied, "but it's not finished yet. I've still got work to do."

"Johannesburg?"

"Johannesburg."

He turned and started for the waiting jeep.

18

The guards were getting on his nerves, but Arnold Schuster didn't plan to send them packing yet. His sponsor had insisted on a five-man "escort" while the border-hopping raid was underway, and Schuster played along because there seemed to be no point in arguing.

It would have blown his plans, for instance, if he told Grubb that he didn't plan to be around when they got back from Mozambique.

There had been too much heat for Schuster's taste already, and it seemed that things were only getting worse. The border hop was one thing—Grubb's commandos did it all the time—but they were taking heavy punishment across the home front day by day, and Schuster saw no signs of an improvement.

Clearly it was time to leave.

He had already wired his operating nest egg from Johannesburg to Zurich, where the money would be waiting for him. He had enough to live on for a month or two, if he was forced to ground somewhere along the way, but Schuster saw no reason why his plans should go awry.

Ironically Grubb's honor guard might turn out to be helpful, after all. They had been ordered to accompany Schuster anywhere he went around Johannesburg, and that would logically include the airport. Getting on a flight to Switzerland was something else again, a clear departure from their standing orders. All he had to do was sell them on the notion that he had a mission to perform in Europe, sanctioned by their leader, and he didn't think that anyone would try to hold him back.

Not now.

The problem was that Grubb and his commandos should have made it back from Mozambique by midnight. It was coming up to 10:00 a.m. now, and delays of that duration only meant one thing.

Disaster.

His escorts had been acting hinky all night, and daybreak only made it worse, as if the disappearance of their friends and fearless leader was more real, somehow, in sunlight. There were five of them, and they were always fidgeting, checking and double-checking their weapons, shifting extra magazines from one pocket to another, hovering around the telephone and sometimes lifting the receiver to make sure the line was clear.

Somehow, Schuster didn't think the crew would miss him if he walked out on them now, but there was still a chance that one or more of them might think he had a part in some conspiracy against their chief. With that in mind, he thought it best to cozy them along and make his flight seem normal, part of the routine.

So far, the stupid goons were buying it. He started off by telling them that Grubb hadn't discussed the trip with the crew, because he had expected to return from Mozambique and send them home at least nine hours prior to Schuster's flight. The guards had seen enough such need-to-know behavior in the past that it made sense, but one of them suggested that the new turn of events should cancel Schuster's plans. It was a close one, that, but the ex-CIA agent won the day by asking which of them was ready to admit, when Grubb returned, that he had countermanded orders from the chief.

The rest of it was packing, getting ready, and he always traveled light. One suitcase and a carryon were all that he had ever needed, and Schuster had gotten by in many situations with a great deal less. He kept the pistol tucked inside his waistband, at the back, but he would ditch it in the car, or in a rest room at the airport, prior to checking in at flight time.

In the meantime, he felt better with the weapon close at hand.

Too many things had gone disastrously awry the past two days for Schuster to relax. He didn't know if Grubb and company were still alive or not, and that was Grubb's concern. If they were captured on the wrong side of the border, it would mean a show trial, reams of bad publicity, no end to personal embarrassment for all concerned. It would be no surprise if they were executed, and considering the state of prison life in Mozambique, a firing squad was no doubt preferable to fifty years of rat-infested cells and wormy gruel at every meal.

If Schuster had his choice, though, he would opt for freedom and a fat Swiss bank account. The sooner he left South Africa, the better. It had been amusing, while it lasted, but he craved a change of scene.

He checked his watch and found that he was due to fly in just two hours. Any moment now, it would be time to hit the road, allowing for a glut of morning traffic on the drive out to the airport, time for checking bags and passports, picking up his seat assignment in first class.

It was the only way to fly.

Schuster closed and locked his suitcase, lifted it and set it down again, deciding he would let one of the Wolves play bellboy while he had the chance. He would be on his own in Zurich, no more goon squad waiting on him hand and foot.

Too bad.

He took the briefcase with him, left the master bedroom and found one gunner sitting by the door of his apartment, two more staring out the windows at the street. A fourth had gone to fetch the car, while number five stood watch in the hallway, covering the service stairs and elevator. There was no way anyone could take them by surprise.

No way at all.

"Somebody want to get my suitcase?"

One of the Wolves, Erik, walked toward the bedroom, returning a moment later with the suitcase.

"Okay, we're out of here."

The keys were in his pocket. He would mail them to his landlord from the airport, never mind the stiff security deposit. It was all Grubb's money, anyway. The main thing was evacuating Jo'burg with a minimum of fanfare, while the White Wolves' enemies were busy elsewhere.

One of Grubb's shooters led the way, Erik next, with Schuster third in line. The first thing that he noticed was the missing outside man.

"Where's Gunter?" Erik's eyes narrowed to slits, his right hand disappearing underneath his jacket.

They called to the absent soldier as they fanned out in the corridor. One of them went to check the stairwell, stuck his head in through the door and called the slacker's name.

No answer.

The small hairs rose on Schuster's nape. He traded off the briefcase to his left hand, reaching back to grip the hidden pistol with his right. The shooter came back from the stairwell, frowned and shook his head.

The elevator chimed, distracting Schuster's escorts. The fixer shied away from it instinctively, edging toward the stairway as the door began to open. He was halfway there when Gunter staggered out, hands raised to staunch the crimson river flowing from his open throat. Another heartbeat, and his knees gave way, the soldier toppling forward on his face.

His comrades froze, and it was only for a second, but it didn't take much time for men to die. An automatic weapon cut loose from the elevator, muffled by a silencer, and Schuster saw his escorts start to dance, their bodies twitching, jerking spastically.

He shouldered through the stairwell door and hit the steps running, taking three at a time. It was some kind of ambush, and the way they butchered Gunter meant they had to have come up on his blind side, somehow, from the street.

And that left Schuster only one path of retreat.

With no clear thought on how to save himself, he started for the roof.

THE HARD PART, Bolan knew, would be surprising any guards Grubb might have left behind at Schuster's flat. It stood to reason that the soldiers would be on alert by now, unsettled by the disappearance of their leader and forty comrades on the raid in Mozambique. There had been nothing on the news about their fate, so far, and Seko had promised to buy Bolan some lead time. But there was only so much that one man could do in diverting the press.

The doorman at the swank apartment house made no attempt to question Bolan, who was decked out in a stylish business suit, with an attaché case in hand. In place of standard paperwork, though, the case contained an Uzi submachine gun with a folding stock and custom silencer attached. Spare magazines were slotted into clips inside the briefcase lid.

The warrior waited for the elevator, checking out the lobby in the process, spotting no one who would bother giving him a second glance. When the elevator car arrived, he stepped inside and punched the tenth floor's button, then got out before the doors hissed shut. Nobody watched as he ducked into the service stairwell and began to climb.

On eight, he ditched the briefcase, slipped extra Uzi magazines into the pockets of his suit coat and flicked off the submachine gun's safety with his thumb. He took the last two flights in something close to total silence, half expecting sentries on the staircase, breathing easier when no one barred his way.

A small decal to Bolan's side instructed him to KEEP DOOR LOCKED, but someone had forgotten to, or maybe the lock had been deliberately unfastened out of spite. In either case, he cracked the door just wide enough to scan the hallway, picking out the guard stationed at the door of Arnold Schuster's flat.

It was an easy shot from where he stood concealed, but that would mean at least some minimal commotion in the hallway, critical exposure as he ran to drag the body out of sight. His plan depended on the target to reveal himself, and it could fall apart in nothing flat if Schuster and his watchdogs holed up in the posh apartment, under siege.

Which meant that it was time for him to improvise.

He doubled back to eight, picked up the briefcase and tucked the Uzi out of sight. Emerging from the stairwell, Bolan moved to stand before the elevator, punched the button labeled with an arrow pointing up and waited for the car.

Two minutes were wasted, standing there, and Bolan felt a restless, antsy feeling creeping over him. He pictured Schuster and the others bailing while he was one floor down, a shooter summoning the elevator even now.

Or would they take the stairs?

He shook the feeling off and concentrated on his plan, if such it could be called. He had to draw the gunner off from Schuster's door and get him in the elevator, silence him before he had a chance to call for help.

It came down to a gamble, and he knew that he would have to take the chance.

The elevator came, and the warrior stepped inside, punching the button for nine. With seconds to spare, he set down the briefcase and drew a clasp knife from his pocket, opening the four-inch blade. The knife fit easily into his sleeve, the smooth brass pommel cupped in Bolan's palm.

On nine, the elevator door slid open and a bell chimed overhead, announcing his arrival. Bolan pressed the button labeled HOLD and took a step outside the car, a calculated look of worry on his face. He seemed relieved to spot the gunner standing in the hallway and beckoned to him urgently.

"Please help," he called. "She just collapsed. I don't know what..."

The gunner frowned, distrustful, glancing backward at the door of Schuster's flat before he grudgingly approached the elevator car. He craned his neck to peer inside, but Bolan blocked his view of the imaginary fainting victim, bending toward a hidden corner of the car.

He felt the gunner close enough to touch, behind him, and he made his move. A simple pivot, whipping backward with his elbow, driving hard between the gunner's eyes. The stunning impact drove his adversary back against the far wall of the car, and Bolan just had time to punch another button that would close the elevator door. Another jab, at the button labeled STOP, and they were frozen where they stood.

He half expected an alarm, but there was nothing audible, and Bolan hoped there would be none downstairs to put repairmen in the line of fire. The thought was barely formed, when his companion in the elevator shook himself and made a grab for hardware hidden underneath his jacket.

Bolan closed the gap between them with two quick strides, and hit the man with a snap kick to the chest, immediately followed with a hard right hand below the rib cage. It was relatively simple, then, to reach inside his coat, slip the automatic pistol from its holster and toss it aside.

A quick slash across the sentry's throat all but guaranteed his demise. But it was amazing, the strength that lingered in a man as good as dead. As Bolan turned to retrieve the Uzi, the gunner lunged at him. He missed by a yard, and slapped one bloody hand against the elevator's control pane, smearing the brass plate with crimson. In the process, he released the door, and it whisked open to reveal three startled men.

They stood outside the door of Schuster's flat, and Bolan glimpsed the former CIA agent drifting toward the stairwell, on his right.

Escaping.

Bolan's late assailant staggered from the elevator car and instantly collapsed. His three companions were recovering from their surprise, two of them reaching underneath their coats for guns, when the warrior opened fire. They never really had a chance against the Uzi, parabellum manglers ripping flesh and fabric as he tracked from left to right, then brought it back again to finish off the job.

There was no sign of Arnold Schuster as Bolan stepped into the hallway, but the door was gently closing on the service stairs. Without a second's hesitation, Bolan started after his intended quarry, pausing briefly on the landing, listening.

The ringing sound of footsteps came from overhead.

His man was headed for the roof.

He kept a firm grip on the Uzi as he started up the stairs in Schuster's wake.

THE FORMER SPOOK from Langley didn't have a clue where he was going, but he knew he had to get away. Grubb's men were being massacred downstairs—in fact, unless he missed his guess, they were already dead—and Schuster's intuition told him he was the intended target of the raid. If he was wrong, it made no difference, since the faceless enemy had left damn few survivors in the past two days.

Six flights, and he was breathing heavily before he reached the roof. There was no latch on his side of the door, but Schuster set the inner lock, for what it would be worth. A few brief seconds, fumbling with the knob, but he was desperate for time.

It was his second visit to the roof of the apartment house, his first occurring on the very afternoon he signed his lease. He made a practice of examining his quarters in advance, mind-mapping exits, angles of attack. The present digs had pleased and disappointed Schuster all at once, because the building loomed three floors above its neighbors on the east and west.

The good news was that it would be a chore for anyone to scale that man-made cliff, break in above his floor, and thus assault him by surprise.

The bad news: if he wanted to escape from where he stood, it would require a ladder or a parachute.

He looked for cover, instantly dismissing the flimsy television aerials, and settled on the bulky air conditioners, where he would have a fair view of the access floor. He checked his pistol to make sure there was a live round in the chamber, cocked it and assumed his place behind the squat compressor housing, on his knees.

It took another moment, but he saw the problem with his chosen sniper's nest. The access door would open *toward* him, blocking Schuster's view of any new arrivals on the roof until they stepped out and revealed themselves. His slugs would penetrate the door, of course, but that suggested other problems. What if he wasn't pursued at all? Suppose the next man through that door turned out to be another tenant or the house custodian? Suppose it was a cop, for God's sake, and he dropped the hammer on a badge!

No, he would have to wait and see . . . but as it happened, Fate didn't intend to keep him waiting long.

He heard the doorknob rattle, then a click that spoke to Schuster of a latching mechanism disengaged. The door began to open outward, and he had his automatic lined up in a firm two-handed grip.

He waited, feeling sweat that wriggled down inside his collar like a nest of maggots.

He wasn't expecting anyone especially, but if a passerby had asked him who he least expected to encounter on that roof, there was a good chance Schuster would have named Jack Armstrong, his informant from the shooting incident at La Parisienne.

And Schuster would have been dead wrong.

He recognized the stalker at a glance and saw the Uzi in his hand, put two and two together in a rush and came up with an answer that appealed to his ingrained paranoia.

Someone in the Company had finally decided it was time for him to die.

The sudden rage came out of nowhere, and his first shot missed the target by a clear twelve inches, punching through the access door. He tried again, but Armstrong wasn't standing still for target practice. Schuster saw the Uzi swing in his direction, and he ducked before the first short burst of parabellum rounds rattled on the air compressor's housing.

Schuster lost his moving target in the time it took for him to duck and roll, pop up a few yards to his left and try again. He caught a glimpse of Armstrong, flitting like a shadow, dropping out of sight behind a canvas-shrouded ventilator duct.

It was a standoff, and the police would soon be rolling in to save the day. Unless . . .

He had another inspiration and reckoned he had nothing much to lose.

"Yo, Armstrong. Can you hear me?"

"Loud and clear," the deep, familiar voice replied.

"I'd like to work this out."

"No can do."

"That's hard to swallow. Hell, I never knew a Langley man who wasn't just a little short of cash."

"Does that include yourself?" the hunter asked.

"Damn right, until I finally wised up. What say I give you half of what I'm carrying, and you tell Langley that you couldn't find me. Let me have a head start, anyway. It makes the game more sporting."

"Just one problem," Bolan told him.

"Oh? What's that?"

"I wasn't sent from Langley."

What? For just an instant, Schuster thought his mind was shutting down, but he recovered with the smooth reflexes of a pro.

"You want to tell me what that means?"

"The party's over, Arnold. Time for you to pay the tab."

"Who sent you, damn it!"

"What's the difference?"

"We can make a deal!"

"No deals. It's judgment day."

"Is this about that problem in Kuwait?"

"It's all about you, Arnold. Let's say you just ran out of borrowed time."

Okay. If he couldn't negotiate, then he would have to fight his way out of the trap, and that meant flanking Armstrong, flushing him from cover, putting him away.

Or, he could jump.

Three stories down to the adjoining roof, and what was that? Some thirty-five or forty feet? At Benning, where the Company had sent him for his airborne training years earlier, he had been taught to tuck and roll. Hell, if he had the time to dangle by his hands, it should be less than thirty feet.

The grim alternative was to charge the hunter across a roof that offered nothing in the way of cover, precious little hope for coming out of any grandstand play alive. At least, if he was jumping, there would be a chance.

Go for it!

Schuster came up firing, keeping Bolan's head down, dodging toward the nearest parapet. He tossed the brief-case out in front of him and watched it drop from sight. If he survived the jump, it would be waiting for him down be-low.

He didn't hear the Uzi stutter, but he saw the bullets strike in front of him, a line of instant divots marching right across his path. The ex-spook veered off course and broke in the direction of the street, winging a wild shot over his shoul-der as he ran.

No good.

Another heartbeat brought him to the edge, and there was nowhere else to go. Between three floors and twelve lay all the difference in the world, and Benning's jump school never taught him how to make that kind of drop success-fully without a parachute.

He turned to face the man who held his life suspended from a trigger finger with a three-pound pull. The Uzi's blind, cyclopic eye stared back, daring him to try his luck.

"Okay," he said, "you win."

"I never thought about it that way," Bolan said.

"It's just a job, I guess."

"Not quite."

"You like it?"

"No."

"What, then?"

"It's necessary."

Schuster blinked, and thereby lost his staring contest with the Uzi. He had one chance in the world, if you could call it that, and he didn't like the odds at all.

"I guess that's it, then," Schuster said, speaking to him-self as much as to his adversary.

"Pretty much."

Schuster brought up the automatic, surprised that he could even handle it, but the Uzi got there first. He saw a puff of flame, and a mighty fist punched him in the chest.

He felt himself begin to topple over backward, twisting as
he fell, and saw the street below him, the pedestrians like
insects at the wrong end of a microscope.

He thought he might be screaming, but he wasn't sure.

It was a miracle, he thought.

He didn't even have to flap his arms to fly.

EPILOGUE

The sun was setting on a new day in Johannesburg, as Bolan sat and sipped his coffee underneath a massive shade tree. Facing him across the ornate table, Bridget Linder seemed at ease with her surroundings, perfectly relaxed. Despite his battered face and bandaged ribs, Richard Modu also seemed at peace. If he was brooding over the events of his last night in jail, it didn't show.

"It's working, then," Bolan said, setting down his cup.

"You sound surprised." The smile on Bridget's face was almost playful.

"Not surprised," he replied. "Relieved."

The late edition of the *Chronicle* was spread between them on the tabletop. Its headline trumpeted the firing and arrest of Rolf Janek, formerly an officer of the security police. He had been charged with dereliction of his duty and malfeasance, on the basis of a certain video recording, given to the prosecutor's office by a member of the newspaper's reporting staff. The source of the cassette was still unknown, but it depicted Janek meeting with a pair of cronies to discuss illegal border crossings into Mozambique . . . and other things. The state's solicitor told newsmen that a list of "other charges"—up to and including murder—might be waiting in the wings.

As for the friends of Janek who were captured on the videocassette, unfortunately both of them were dead. Willem Grubb had been identified as one of forty-odd "adventurers" dispatched by troops in Mozambique, while executing an illicit trespass on that valued neighbor of South Africa. The other, an American of shady origins named

Arnold Schuster, had been shot and/or ejected from the roof of his apartment building in Johannesburg. Four known associates of Willem Grubb were also killed in the same incident, a circumstance that prompted the police to pick up all surviving members of the White Wolves they could find. Authorities were grilling them around the clock, and prosecution hadn't been ruled out.

"I used my best reporter on the videocassette. It was the safest way."

"Your call," Bolan said.

Turning to Modu, he inquired, "Did you have any trouble getting out of jail?"

"It took some time, but delays are normal. When the news came through on Janek, things began to happen rather quickly."

"And you're all right now?"

"I will be. This is nothing that my people have not suffered and survived before."

"At least the White Wolves should be out of action for a while," Bolan said.

"If the state's solicitor fulfills his obligation to the people," Bridget said. "I can assure you, we'll be watching him along the way."

"I had a feeling that you might. Your husband's case?"

"It's been reopened. Naturally there are no guarantees."

"But it's a start," the Executioner replied.

"It is a start." She smiled at that. "And what of you?"

"I'm finished here," he said. "Tonight, I catch the redeye flight to Amsterdam, and home from there."

"Where's home?"

He hesitated, finally said, "I'll let you know when I find out."

"We cannot thank you properly for all you've done," Modu told him. "And still, it saddens me that there was so much violence."

"Maybe next time we can try it in a perfect world. I'm game, if you are."

"To a perfect world, then."

Modu raised his cup, the others likewise, china kissing with a soft clink in the dusk. It wouldn't hurt, Bolan thought, drinking to a perfect world. It never hurt to dream.

"Will you be coming back?" Bridget asked.

"That depends. I wouldn't count on anything immediate." As if there should be more, he added, "I get around."

"I can imagine."

Bolan made a point of glancing at his watch. "And speaking of departures, here I go. I've still got packing left to do before I hit the road."

In fact, his single bag was packed and waiting in his car, the military hardware suitably disposed of where he calculated it would do no harm. The warrior hated long goodbyes, with their attendant questions and the promises that no one ever really meant to keep.

"I'll walk you to your car," Bridget said, rising as she spoke.

"God speed." Modu covered Bolan's hand with both of his and shook it twice before he sat back in his chair. "I hope we meet again."

"I wouldn't mind myself."

He walked with Bridget to his waiting rental car, a stroll through dappled shadows, with a cool breeze whispering among the trees.

"We bought this place the year before my husband died," she said. "I love it here, but there are still so many memories."

"There always will be," Bolan told her.

"You're an expert?"

"Getting there."

They reached his car and stood there, in the last rays of the setting sun. The lady asked, "Who are you, really?"

"You don't want to know."

"I wouldn't ask if that was true."

"The name's disposable," Bolan said. "One's as good as any other. What you see is what you get."

"I see a man who cares enough to risk his life for other human beings."

"I'm just taking out the garbage. Savings souls is some-one else's job."

"You're no evangelist, I grant you that. But you're no mercenary, either."

"No."

"I think you're a believer."

Bolan smiled. "In what?"

"Mankind. I think you look around at all the pain and suffering and can't help pitching in. It's what you do, be-cause that's who you are."

"I get involved because I can," he told her. "Some don't have the skills or the experience."

"And most don't have the heart," she said. "Deny it if you will, but I'm convinced you're something special, even if I never learn your given name."

"Will you be safe?" he asked. "With the investigation going on, I mean?"

"The truth is, I feel safer than I have in years. I still have enemies, of course, and plenty of them still wear badges, but at least we've made a start at taking out the garbage, as you say. You will be careful?"

"It's my middle name."

"Goodbye, then. And farewell."

She stood on tiptoes, brushed his lips with hers and quickly turned away. He stood and watched her disappear among the trees, dusk closing in to draw the shadows out and run them all together, merging into night.

And he was moving on.

The Executioner had places to go and people to meet. A few of them might be relieved to see him coming; others wouldn't live to formulate opinions on the subject, either way.

His war was everywhere, and any respite from the fight-ing was a short-term bivouac, no more, no less.

He hoped that he had made a difference in Johannes-burg, but only time would tell, and time had a peculiar way of doubling back upon itself. A wise man wrote that those who failed to learn from history were destined to repeat it. He forgot to mention that they sometimes had no choice.

The same insistent issues kept resurfacing in every land and every generation, time and time again. Good versus Evil. Right and Wrong. The Civilizers versus Savage Man.

So would it ever be, until a generation yet unborn created that utopian ideal: a perfect world.

If Bolan saw it in his lifetime, that would truly be a miracle. But he wasn't about to hold his breath.

He put the rental car in gear and started back toward town, the airport, Amsterdam and Stony Man. Another battlefield, and new enemies to measure and defeat.

So it had always been in Bolan's life. So would it always be.

War without end.

Amen.

DON PENDLETON'S THE EXECUTIONER ®

NEW COVER
COMING IN
JANUARY 1995

The Mack Bolan team will be coming your way with new eye-catching cover graphics.

We're bringing you an exciting new cover design, but Gold Eagle is still committed to bringing you action adventure heroes who confront danger head-on. We are dedicated to action adventure at its best—now in a bright, new package!

Don't miss the new look of THE EXECUTIONER— available in January 1995.

In the quest for great adventure, watch for the new Executioner cover from Gold Eagle books.

TAKE 'EM FREE
4 action-packed novels plus a mystery bonus
NO RISK
NO OBLIGATION TO BUY

**Blazing a perilous trail through the
heart of darkness**

JAMES AXLER
DEATH LANDS.

Road Wars

A cryptic message sends Ryan Cawdor and the Armorer on an
odyssey to the Pacific Northwest, away from their band of warrior
survivalists. As the endless miles come between them, the odds for
survival are not in their favor.

In the Deathlands, fate and chance are clashing with
frightening force.

Asian warmongers draw the U.S. into a Pacific showdown

STONY MAN™ 13
WARHEAD

Tactical nuclear weapons have been hijacked in Russia, and the clues point to their being in the possession of a group of North Koreans, Cambodians and Vietnamese, all allied with Chinese hard-liners to solidify Communist rule in Southeast Asia. The warheads are powerful enough to decimate the population of a large city, or destroy an entire port or airport facility, and are dangerous tools of extortion.

When the warheads are traced to one of the largest military installations in Southeast Asia, Stony Man Farm puts together a recovery mission.

A diabolical psycho puts CURE in the family way in

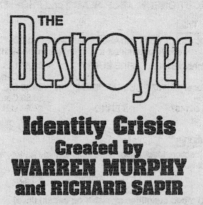

THE Destroyer

Identity Crisis
Created by
WARREN MURPHY
and RICHARD SAPIR

Could Dr. Harold Smith be Remo Williams's biological father? Or is this "family ties" freak-out the brainstorm of one of CURE's archenemies? And is it enough to destroy the secret crime-fighting organization forever?

Don't miss IDENTITY CRISIS, the next installment of THE DESTROYER.

Look for it this November, wherever Gold Eagle books are sold.

**Don't miss out on the action in these titles featuring
THE EXECUTIONER®, ABLE TEAM® and PHOENIX FORCE®!**

The Terror Trilogy

Features Mack Bolan, along with ABLE TEAM and PHOENIX FORCE, as they
battle neo-Nazis and Arab terrorists to prevent war in the Middle East.

The Executioner #61186	FIRE BURST	$3.50 U.S.	☐
		$3.99 Can.	☐
The Executioner #61187	CLEANSING FLAME	$3.50 U.S.	☐
		$3.99 Can.	☐
SuperBolan #61437	INFERNO	$4.99 U.S.	☐
		$5.50 Can.	☐

The Executioner®

With nonstop action, Mack Bolan represents ultimate justice, within or
beyond the law.

#61182	LETHAL AGENT	$3.50	☐
#61183	CLEAN SWEEP	$3.50	☐

(limited quantities available on certain titles)

TOTAL AMOUNT	$
POSTAGE & HANDLING	$
($1.00 for one book, 50¢ for each additional)	
APPLICABLE TAXES*	$_____
TOTAL PAYABLE	$_____

(check or money order—please do not send cash)

To order, complete this form and send it, along with a check or money order for
the total above, payable to Gold Eagle Books, to: **In the U.S.:** 3010 Walden Avenue,
P.O. Box 9077, Buffalo, NY 14269-9077; **In Canada:** P.O. Box 636, Fort Erie, Ontario,
L2A 5X3.

Name:_____

Address:_____ City:_____

State/Prov.:_____ Zip/Postal Code: _____

*New York residents remit applicable sales taxes.
 Canadian residents remit applicable GST and provincial taxes.

GEBACK7